An American Outrage

Also by G. K. Wuori

Nude in Tub: Stories of Quillifarkeag, Maine

An American Outrage

A NOVEL OF QUILLIFARKEAG, MAINE

BY G. K. Wuori

ALGONQUIN BOOKS
OF CHAPEL HILL
2000

Published by
ALGONQUIN BOOKS OF CHAPEL HILL
Post Office Box 2225
Chapel Hill, North Carolina 27515-2225

a division of
Workman Publishing
708 Broadway
New York, New York 10003

This is a work of fiction. While, as in all fiction, the literary perceptions and insights are based on experience, all names, characters, places, and incidents are either products of the author's imagination or are used fictitiously. No reference to any real person is intended or should be inferred.

Library of Congress Cataloging-in-Publication Data
Wuori, G. K.
    An American outrage : a novel of Quillifarkeag, Maine / by G. K. Wuori.
    p. cm.
    ISBN 1-56512-292-5
    1. City and town life—Fiction. 2. Police corruption—Fiction.
    3. Eccentrics and eccentricities—Fiction. 4. Maine—Fiction. I. Title.
PS3573.U57 A83 2000
813'.54—dc21   00-056586

10 9 8 7 6 5 4 3 2 1
First Edition

For . . .

  Althea

  Ardeana

  Bonnie

  Claire

Grateful acknowledgment is
made to the *Maine Sunday Telegram*
for permission to use copyrighted
material; to Wester Wuori and
Jennifer DeWall Wuori for
invaluable research assistance;
to Noah Lukeman of Lukeman
Literary Management Ltd. for
unwavering support and
encouragement; and to my editor,
Shannon Ravenel, whose faith
and patience made all the difference
in the world.

I am but mad north-north-west.

When the wind is southerly,

I know a hawk from a handsaw.

—WILLIAM SHAKESPEARE, *Hamlet*

Act II, Scene 2

An American Outrage

QUILLIFARKEAG, MAINE
(History)

Newcomers find it in questionable taste, while for Quilli natives of a certain age, it brings back childhood thrills. The myth of the '50s as a time of innocence is cherished, but that monument on the north side of town, high on a hill, recalls how quickly and how readily innocence would have been exchanged for guilt had the time been right.

It is an old Nike missile, kept washed and waxed to an alabaster gleam by certain veterans groups. Those same groups, on Memorial Day, see to it that flowers are delivered there, that taps is played, that a gun salute is fired off to the west, and that Mayor Hobadopp makes a speech. The former teacher enjoys the occasion, though his speech is the same one every year.

The missile is on a mount but it has not been casually set. Two professors from the small branch of the state university in Quilli have seen to it that, taking speed and thrust and all the necessary variables into account, it would land, if fired, directly on the Old North Church in Boston. ONE IF BY LAND . . . *is printed on a plaque near the missile, below which are the names of Quilli war dead.*

The original plan called for the missile to be aimed at Washington, D.C., but certain deliberative types were persuasive that Massachusetts was the greater threat.

1

NIGHT FALLS UP HERE to the haunting call of unseen loons on the lakes and ponds that are everywhere in this part of northern Maine. It is a lonely sound, as though nature had worked hard to define sadness and had come close in the unforgettable cry of that bird. Nearby, the careworn homes of St. Antoine de Plupart bear human witness to that sadness. This is a rough town of good people who are not strangers to desperation, though it is safe to say that the events of last night will test their fortitude.

Some miles from here is the home of one Ellen DeLay, a reclusive woman in her forties, about whom, so it is said, there were always stories — tales of a sort that led people to question her sanity, or just tales of a woman who'd had enough of life in its conventional sense, who opted out and took to the woods.

Last night, this Ellen DeLay was shot and killed by four police officers who stormed her small house. Early police reports have it that she, herself, fired a weapon at some fishermen who were near her home. As the officers, responding to a complaint from the fishermen, approached her house they were met with gunfire. Nearly two hundred rounds of ammunition were expended in the gun battle. . . .

Corky Crépiter
Maine Public Radio
August 13, 1994

It is easy to make fun of small towns and I have done so myself. Perhaps it's because we find our human follies more manageable on a smaller scale. Perhaps, indeed, it is because these urban miniatures are simply funnier. I once wrote to a friend in New York that it's the job of society to pull sensibility, constructive behavior, and even upright posture out of at least a few promising souls in any given group. That society often fails is what keeps people telling stories, and I guess the ridicule begins there.

Quillifarkeag (Quilli) has its basic streets and roads, its basic services. Its institutions consist of a few churches and schools, a branch of the state university, a modest hospital, and a good-sized potato-processing plant whose french fries you *have* eaten.

Beyond the basics, the only things worth noting in Quilli are the people themselves: worthy, unworthy; large-minded or small-talking; cribbage players, mechanics, farmers, hustlers, young academics, cripples; the pious, the unrepentant, the unrelenting. Good folks in service to metabolism, but they are neither more nor less goofy than those in the big cities. Walk up the steps of the New York Public Library, as I did once when I was in the army, and while you're being mesmerized by the grandeur of stored knowledge, you're not about to notice the sane or insane or meaningful or totally ludicrous behaviors going on in the offices and apartment buildings at your back and sides. There isn't an attention span broad enough for all that, nor is there time.

Walk up the steps of the Quilli library, though, and the first thing that might happen is you'll smell fiddleheads cooking upstairs and you'll think, *Isn't that weird?* Personally, I hate fiddleheads. They are to me what slugs would be if slugs were vegetables.

The building itself is a communal construct: white, clapboard, double-hung windows, a porch and four gables. What else can you focus on but the fiddleheads cooking upstairs, or that our librarian is blind, a menacing misanthrope whose spirit never left the Vietnam that blinded him. He's a good librarian, though, and that matters in a small town.

Quilli is built on two rivers and sits between two smaller towns: Quiktupac, well to the north; and St. Antoine de Plupart, forty miles west. One of the rivers is the Quilli Stream, an insipid thing that rises to true majesty in carrying off the winter melt, then turns to simple mud for most of the summer. The other river, the Pappadapsikeag, cuts around the Quilli area like a drunken bee as it makes its way to the St. John. The Pappa (as we call it) is said to contain buried stashes of British gold. Even at its beginnings, long after the grand Algonquin natives overpopulated themselves into second-tier units, this part of the country was thought to be a good place to hide, whether treasure or people. No one's ever found any British gold, but once a year Don's Grocery has a Gold Pound Sale where they offer some great bargains. I'm not sure the British unit of money was even the pound back when some troops supposedly carted a general's retirement fund up the river, but mercantilism thrives only on success, not truth.

About me, a few things ought to be said, although the following account is not about me. That I am short, white-haired, middle-aged (a personal definition), divorced (for now), opinionated (thus: wordy, talky), educated, healthy, a newspaper reader, a book reader, and a little chubby are all tags that friends might hang on me if the question was, Who is Splotenbrun Doll? That I am missing the middle finger of my left hand might suggest an answer to the question, What does he do? Carpenter is the best answer, cabinetmaker, tradesman. More obliquely—problem-solver; it's what carpenters do.

Completing that public self then is the nickname: Splotchy. People feel comfortable calling me that, though the truth is I have no idea where it came from or when it was first laid on me. Sometimes names just happen.

There is another quality, however, another tag that is now properly mine, and as I write it here for the first time the door will open into this narrative, the beginnings of purpose will be seen: I am the father of a killer.

There are many ways that could be written, but I wanted to put it down sharp and nasty the first time, to take myself out to an edge to see if there was any way back. Could I, in other words, redeem my child, my daughter? Could I somehow find in the truth a way to say, *You did the right thing, child?*

Such is the ultimate in parental forgiveness, but my daughter, Wilma, is no child. She's a woman in her forties who, quite frankly, is fully capable of redeeming herself, though in this matter of Ellen DeLay and Cary Andersen and the strange things that have come out of St. Antoine de Plupart these past five or six years—Wilma has grown strangely silent.

That's unusual because Wilma is not a silent woman. She is wordy, God knows. She was born talking from a talking mother, and, if you recall my "tags" from above, that is my vice, too. I have often joked with friends that her mother and I didn't give her genes, we gave her words. She knows them all, too, and she is sometimes rough with her language, very rough.

Still, she came up to me one day when I was working an easy job and she said, flat-out, "I have a problem, Pop."

"What's your problem?" I said.

"I want you to tell my story," she said. "It's getting away from me; it's getting away from everyone, and there are some things that shouldn't be forgotten—not ever."

"Why me, dear? Surely, there must be—"

"Parts, Pop. It's all parts—big ones, little ones, scattered ones. You can put them together. There needs to be a wholeness to it. There really does."

"I'm not exactly the town historian, Wilma."

"But you know everyone, Pop. You've built half the houses in the area, and there isn't anyone who won't talk to you. I don't know that you need a credential to be the historian around here. Maybe you just need to know the story."

Since the first subheading under the heading *Parenthood* is always *Manipulation,* there was never any doubt what my answer would be.

So the carpenter slips out from the joists with sawdust on his beard and becomes the teller, the sentinel of history. It's a large task at a time in my life when I would have thought all my major purposes had been accomplished—or at least written off as silly or unattainable.

Certainly, my purpose has not been found within marriage. My daughter's mother, Grenada, and I have been married and divorced from each other three times, and we may even be headed toward a fourth union. Grenada is a headstrong woman with a zest for sass (her description of me, I believe, is similar), but neither of us has ever loved another, nor will we. It just seems, though, that once each decade we both start thinking *forever?*, and a black cloud of panic descends upon us. Permanence, we decide, is not a desirable condition, "not an American condition," Grenada said once, and so we'll split, our union trumped on a geopolitical plane.

Nor did I ever, to be honest, find much purpose in my work, at least not in that lofty sense where the romance of the trades clashes with dirt, sweat, and the constant entanglement with spiders and mice. (There are no rats in northern Maine.) I once thought that things of the mind had little worth compared with things done with the hands. I'm still not sure about the mind, but my hands have gotten pretty beat up over the years. At least the hands heal.

But it has been a life of good work and things accomplished. It has taught me that nearly everything is malleable and that nearly everything can be changed. It has also taught me that there's hardly ever any good reason behind the things that people actually do.

Very well. I will embrace this new purpose then and put 1990–1996 into a package small enough to be held with horror or embraced with wisdom. If there's a nice part to all of this, or at least a part that accords well with my own nature, it's that it's all about people, nothing more—lives that tried to be good and didn't make it.

There's Joe DeLay, a man whose work is similar to my own, and who has struggled to find words for the way in which fate pulled him out of modest comfort and threw him into expensive duress. Joe, however, is so laid-back that his shouts tend to be whispers and his screams merely conversational. I know for a fact, however, that there have been screams.

There are the boys, too—catalytic fools, I've wanted to say; kinder than calling them the Three Stooges—Maine's culture flipped over onto its French Acadian side: Liam, Igor, and Pierre. They entered this thing as young men on a lark, and emerged mature and ready to settle down. Two of their three wives even became pregnant within a year of Igor's being shot. Someone once said that tragedy makes parents of us all. Seems true.

The law enforcement community was surprisingly forthcoming. I got so much truth from them I became confused, people like Anna Pancake and Valerie Dooble and Debbie St. H pushing me off into quiet places like Bud's Bar or (once) Czyczk's Lingerie, and nearly exhausting themselves as they would see to it that I knew every last scrap and shred of detail of what happened that one night—as they saw it. The police around here are like the police everywhere. Sometimes they lose sight of who the enemy is and the politicians won't tell them. Wisdom gets you no votes.

Poison Gorelick and I get along, though he's an easy man to dislike. You didn't hear the expression in the early nineties, but today we'd say he has an attitude. The easy shot is to say it comes from his being about as big as your thumb, but the truth is he had to scramble out of a childhood that contained both gross poverty and nasty injustice and he never found much good in any of it. They say that struggle enriches, that a hard chase ennobles. Maybe so. Sometimes it just wears you out.

Poison, however, was also Wilma's first boyfriend, so I have known him a long time. They have been other, more adult, things over the years, but the height they have risen to—for as much as there has been love and all of that; sex and its gyrations, naturally enough; even anger and long periods of resentment—has been the height, the altitude, the Olympian vastness—of friendship. Even today you can see them walking down the street together and it's a touching sight. There's Poison at maybe five feet with good shoes on, and there's Wilma, six-two the last time I measured her (years ago). She'll be hanging on Poison's every word and Poison has a lot of words, and Poison will be holding her hand as though he's about to guide her to only the finest places.

My former wife (Grenada) once said that Poison and Wilma never married because they found friendship first and love second and love couldn't survive the competition. A fair assessment, and one that goes a long way toward explaining, too, what happened with Wilma and Ellen DeLay and Cary Andersen. These latter two women, by the way, I did not speak to as I put this strange thing together.

They are both dead.

2

NOT LONG AGO, on a Saturday night, I met Joe and Poison and Wilma in Bud's Bar on Main Street in Quilli. I am comfortable with all of them, and since I haven't lived at home since my last divorce, it is always a joy to see Wilma. Sometimes I wonder if I've ever said that to her, then I tell myself I need to do it. That might be another reason why I agreed to be both sleuth and sage for her—guilt works.

Bud's Bar is long and thin, a dark haven of neon secrecy where a shelf not far from the ceiling runs the whole perimeter of the place and holds the stuffed remains of foxes, skunks, raccoons, deer, moose, bears, hawks, and eagles. Lower down and in the back, the head of a doe marks the ladies' room, the head of a buck the men's. Even so, Bud's is not an uncomfortable place for a woman to be. Much of that is owing to the nearly constant presence of Michelle Monelle, Bud's ex-wife, who runs her taxi company—Michelle's Taxi Company—from the last booth in the rear, a phone installed right on the table by her thoughtful ex. In exchange for her business site, she helps Bud out. Cleaning, some food prep, she'll do that. She's a terrific bouncer, too, even though Bud's crowd doesn't need that service quite so much anymore.

It is smoky in Bud's Bar, smoky because in this part of northern Maine the smoking laws are thought to be stupid and so they are ignored. Complaints might be directed to Bud, but it is Bud's Bar and Bud—Orville Crépiter—is six-eight and weighs three hundred and fifty pounds. Bud, someone once said, is litigation from which there is no appeal. Nevertheless, he is an affable man and an easy friend. Sometimes he sings as he works and there is a true show in that. He has the gestures, the moves, even the facial expressions of a professional singer, though his voice sounds like a wood rasp being drawn across some PVC piping. What you admire, though, is that he just does it.

As I walked in that night Wilma came over and hugged me and said right away, "You look good, Pop, a little pink to the cheek. All that brain work must be doing you good."

"Not started," I said. "That's the hard part. Thanks for the compliment anyway."

"Just do the ending," she said, "and go back from there."

"The ending I know, honey. The world knows the ending. With all the stuff I got, though, there's a thousand beginnings. Buy me a beer. I'm a little short."

Poison, whose full name is Fendamius Gorelick, though he is never called that, was sitting atop a bar stool that Bud calls the "trainer." A cushioned box, four inches high, has been permanently fastened to the stool and the stool, as everyone knows, is permanently reserved for Poison.

I hadn't seen Poison since Wilma was arrested early in the summer. He said, "Splotchy," and shook my hand. There were tears in his eyes. Joe, to my left, said nothing, but he patted my shoulder lightly with his open hand. It was a man's bit of delicacy and I appreciated it.

• • •

Wilma, as I think I said, is a big woman—tall, leggy, commanding—who would do absolutely anything for Poison. He has suffered injuries in her service during these recent events, and though his healing is well underway much stiffness remains. Wilma treats him with great tenderness and respect. Her arm, her strength, is there in the helping, though she makes it appear that he has sat himself effortlessly. It's the way Wilma is and I'm nearly always proud of her.

On the bar in front of Poison are two pictures, one an actual photograph and the other a newspaper photo.

"That's you, Joe," Poison says, pointing to the photograph.

My mind has been filled lately with Wilma this and Wilma that, Wilma the murderer or maybe not; Wilma the daughter, plainly a knockout (Poison's words), clearly winning battles many other women her age pay good money just to fight.

And suddenly here is Joe, pivotal in all of this though I'd hardly given him a thought, a good man and a good-looking man: his hair bushy white, his mustache perched, as Wilma said one time, like two pigeons on his lip, a dignified, well-weighted man with not much fat below the heart, a man, I'd heard it said, you'd not only borrow money from but toward whom you'd feel good paying it back.

Joe is so quiet it's easy to think of him as inconsequential, yet here he is, both next to me and in the photo in front of Poison.

The picture was taken by a high school girl, a student of photography, who'd "discovered" Joe, shirtless, in her mother's bathroom, replacing the wax seal under the toilet. Joe has a business called—I've always liked this—*Things That Need to Be Done.*

An appointment must have been made, for in the picture Joe is standing in a spruce clearing out in the woods. He is not a young man, certainly, not a high school boy, and he is centered in the photo artlessly. He appears to be on the edge of a cold drop, nothing *there* in his immediacy beyond space and gravity. Quilli is in the distance, the spire of the Methodist church vaguely visible. That spire dates the photo, too, since it was not long ago that the Methodist church was burned down by two drunken boys who'd run out of things to do. A woman was killed in the fire.

Joe is naked, his back to the camera. He has his arms up so that, with his shoulders, they form a squarish U, his shoulder muscles knotted down his back and his buttocks clenched, the clenching continuing down thighs that seem caricatures of meaty teardrops. His calves are big, so his socks are probably always bunched around his ankles, and his feet appear sprouted from the ground. It was a daring photo for a young girl to take.

"My God," says Joe as he looks at the photo.

"Nice butt," Poison says.

Wilma, noticing a small bump on Joe's spine in the picture, points to it and says, "Back trouble, Joe?"

"Not then," Joe says.

Joe is not embarrassed by the photo and that does not surprise me. Joe is one of those men who think that anything happening in the world, big or small, is exactly what it should be and thus worthy of neither regret nor too much praise. The bad side of this attitude is that calamities, nasty bosses, bad times, and stupid deaths are all seen as having a place, as being acceptable. My own view is that we have to say no to certain things at certain times, to tell them that they do not belong, that we have no room for them.

I would not argue the point with Joe, because his outlook gives him peace. But it's the peace of accommodation and it used to irritate his wife a great deal.

If I am, with the eternally nascent Joe, beginning to get an idea of where to go with all of this, it is Poison who slams the point home as he holds up the other picture. That photo is less clear, the newsprint beginning to yellow. It is of a woman not yet old with dark hair, long dark hair, curly. Wilma says the proper expression is "big hair." That sounds fine.

The woman is smiling and wearing a sheepskin coat. There is a large knife in her hand, its blade slightly curved. On the table in front of her is a large, dark mass, identifiable in the caption as a dead bear with a broken leg. The caption says further that the woman will skin and dress out upward of twenty dead bears in a year, along with countless deer, the occasional moose, and a scattering of foxes, raccoons, even skunks.

The woman in the picture is Ellen DeLay, Joe's wife. Her smile is beguiling and clashes with what I think I know of things. Field dresser, hunter's butcher, deer skinner—there were many names for what she did, but few names for why she did it. A good woman leaves a good man to spend the rest of her life up to her elbows in animal guts?

It made good copy for the newspaper. Her work fulfilled a need for any city boy or city girl who'd just blown the innards of some animal outward and didn't know what to do next. But it didn't make sense—not to me, not to anyone. Sometimes I think you can be judged as much by the questions people raise about you as by any answers those questions might yield.

Why did she do it? puts her right out there, on the edge, a town girl with a good marriage, a girl who that same paper — the *Maine Sunday Telegram* — also described as "a registered Maine guide, a plumber, electrician, carpenter, cook, boat handler, naturalist, pianist, seamstress, hunter, and patriot."

Because she was nuts, is the easy answer you get around here. I find that answer crass, maybe insensitive. A small town, though, while it might tolerate your living a lifetime on the near edge of being weird, won't necessarily defend you with a treatise.

3

SO QUILLI, LIKE ANY TOWN, never cutting with a fine knife when a dull one will do, said Ellen went nuts. To be fair, Quilli intends no disrespect when that term is used. It's a common expression in town, but, more than that, it's the only term that accurately describes what happened to her.

Certainly, the niche pathologies won't do it. Before any of the big things happened she had no behavior disorders. She was not paranoid; she was not schizophrenic; she was not depressed. She told Wilma one time that she was a "revolutionary without complaint," and there's something in that you can get your teeth into—even if it's not an answer. But when someone just stands up and says—not to anyone; rather, to the entirety of the cosmos—*Well that's enough of that,* what else can you say? "Nuts" works.

Personally, I confess a fondness for a time when a tortured psyche was thought tenanted by the devil or a delegated assistant. You were still a candidate for treatment, but also prayer; that is, there was something those who loved you could do that felt meaningful.

Today, we simply find you lacking something ending in an -ic, -ac, or -zine. Somehow, your mate's complaining to a doctor about your dosages is not the same as having a whole congregation approach hysteria seeking the righteous cleansing of your troubled spirit.

Joe told me once that Ellen, a Canadian child, was born in the Maritimes east of Maine, while he was raised in Indiana—a wild place, Ellen always said, though she'd never been there, a tough alley on the streets of the American west. Early on, she called him cowboy, although that irritated Joe. "Indiana's not what you think," he'd say.

"I don't think anything about Indiana," she'd answer, which led him the one time to tell her, in his cryptic manner, in his American manner, as she said, indirect, veiled, truth never by the pound when an ounce would do, that even wandering wasn't always enough to establish rootlessness.

"I have made homes for myself in my head when necessary," he told her.

"What I mean, cowboy," Ellen went on, "is that you have about you a sense of place, an orientation toward the sun, and a knowledge of where to look for things when there's danger."

Joe said his mind sometimes did flips when Ellen talked like that.

They met in Quilli, according to Joe, on Main Street. She was walking north and Joe was walking south.

"I said hello," Ellen said one time. "Don't you remember that?"

"Why did you do that?" Joe asked.

"I had to. You looked precious."

"Oh. Did I say anything?"

"You said hello."

"Precious?"

"Uh-huh."

"Hm."

• • •

"Joe is security," Ellen told Wilma. "Joe is patience, a feeling, I think, that if he ever fell off the edge of the earth he'd bounce right back and say, 'What's for lunch?'"

Joe and Ellen were married for twenty-six years. Ellen kept house, mostly, and Joe ran Things That Need to Be Done. She ironed the sheets for their bed and she ironed Joe's underwear. She ironed his socks, his knit hats, even his baseball caps.

There has always been something in Quilli about women and ironing. Perhaps in a rough place it's simply a matter of smoothing out those things that can be smoothed. One time, in our first marriage, I found Grenada ironing a canvas I used to cover a kindling bin. Young as I was, I knew enough not to tell her it wasn't necessary.

"I learned how to iron when I was six," Ellen told Wilma, "and I ironed everything—my dad's long underwear, his mittens, my ma's bras, bath towels, dishcloths for the sink. There must have been in my family a horror for the crease."

On weekends Ellen washed Joe's truck, the "pick-meup," as she called it, and vacuumed the cab. She would get in back then and organize the big plastic toolbox that she sometimes called "Joe's toolhouse"—four feet wide, three feet high, its length spanned the width of the truck bed. Sometimes she would empty it out and clean and degrease and polish everything, all the wrenches and power tools and hammers; she'd recoil rope, sort nails and screws, and bundle up scraps of wood left over from jobs. Twice a year she'd take the stiff and sticky and wrinkled overalls and wash them outside in a washtub set on top of a wood fire.

The toolbox emptied, she would climb inside with soap and water and pine oil and, if the wind was good, ammonia, and wash it all down. Ellen understood a lot about tools, having both rewired and reroofed their house one year (a rare year) when Joe was super busy.

"A clean workplace," she told Joe. "It keeps quality in front of your mind."

Joe said that was a high idea, a thing he appreciated, but later, as he told me, he saw in it—because of the one incident, nearly tragic—the roots of all the bad things that happened, and sometimes he wondered if he could have prevented them by just telling her that the tools were the most basic parts of his work and that it was part of his work to maintain them and not a part of her work, which was to provide a comfortable, snug, and cozy house.

Ellen, Joe said, would have argued the point—"I think I know my duties, Joe," and argued it again: "Do not presume to tell me what to do"—because there was no end of work, no end of effort that had to be put into a marriage. It wasn't a lark, not a game. If the marital union was good, you lived; if not, you died. Ellen believed that for a long time.

There was something else, too, a small thing. She'd married a foreign man, this Joe DeLay, years before when she was still Canadian, and to Joe she was still a foreign woman, American by study and vow or not, and whether a moment's decision demanded pork chops or donuts, or a purchase deferred in the choice of which bill to pay when things were tight, there was always a cultural leak to be watched, and the job belonged to whoever had the bucket.

No, Joe said, this whole thing didn't happen because Ellen was Canadian. She was French, too, as nearly everyone in Quilli is, and it didn't happen because she was French, either.

"Your heritage only gets you genes," he told me. "It doesn't

get you off the hook." Joe *will* have Ellen bear her share of re-
sponsibility for what happened, but, like a man trying to catch
butterflies on a windy day, he keeps seeing things he can't quite
nail down.

What happened, what changed everything and quickly
overturned love and even habit, came about on a normal day.
I have to guess here, but I would say it was maybe early summer of '90, some four years before she would be killed.

Joe got a call one Sunday afternoon from L'mit D'Oro. His
sump pump had stopped working and his cellar was flooded.
Could Joe do anything? L'mit was afraid even to wade to the
breaker box "since there is a good chance I could electricize
myself, not being a very fat man and all."

L'mit could not afford to have his furnace flooded and
ruined. He asked Joe to hurry and even said, as men will do
with each other from time to time in this part of the country,
"pretty please?" Still, even hurrying, Joe feared that L'mit, in
wanting to appear busy, not wanting Joe to think him a total
electrical fool, might mess things up. There was damage, Joe
said, and that was a problem. But runaway earnestness could
also damage the problem, and that was worse. L'mit might,
Joe worried, send his wife, who is fat, on over to pop the
breaker box. Joe was relieved when he saw that L'mit had had
her make a big pot of coffee instead.

With several wood potato crates L'mit and Joe quickly built
a bridge over to the breaker box and Joe turned off the power.
L'mit was lavish in his praise over the simplicity of Joe's idea
and too hard on himself, Joe thought, for not having come up
with the solution on his own.

L'mit already had the new pump and even his own tools

laid out for Joe—"I'd been meaning to put the dang thing in, you know?"—so installing the pump only took a half hour. Within a half hour beyond that, L'mit's cellar returned to the normal damp that tended to leave a haze of mildew over everything. People around Quilli often joke that if the New England ground in these parts can't hold water worth a damn, most people's cellars sure can.

During all of this—Joe's methodical survey of the problem, the quick repair, some easy talk with L'mit and his wife—Ellen had been inside the big plastic toolbox on the truck.

"I just burned ass leaving the house," Joe told me. He was unaware Ellen was deep inside the toolbox on her knees, scraping dirt with a putty knife. As the lid slammed shut and the latches caught she knew it right away, though she didn't know, as she later told Wilma, this would start a chain of change that would change her life and nearly everything she did.

She began to think Joe was trying to kill her that day, Joe her husband, Joe with his slow ways and his deep acceptance of everything and his roadkill mustache and the big, nearly giant, hands that she was always talking about, that she said she could feel on her back constantly, and honestly think there was nothing in the world that could harm her. She thought she was mostly Joe's everything and loved even the thought of loving Joe, except that when he tried to kill her, or she thought he tried to kill her, which in the end was the same thing, a whole storm of things seemed to crash right up there near her left ear, and she didn't think she could manage a normal conversation after that. She had suffered an amputation, she told Wilma, but of what she didn't know.

"She changed," Wilma told me, "something swift, not the way we usually change. I saw it happening—physically. A blankness would come into her eyes and she'd begin trembling like she was cold. Then it would stop, and she'd smile at me and say, 'Just gotta watch those damn husbands every *minute*.'"

Ellen knew the box was sturdy, which was why she was in it, the plastic three-quarters of an inch thick. Her first thought had been, *Oh, fart,* as the lid clunked down and she felt the pickmeup begin a quick, bumpy progress down the Quilli streets. She would, she told Wilma, have to pick just the right moment for pounding or yelling, or at least hope that wherever Joe was going and whatever he was doing he would need a tool, which he would find all over the bed of the truck since that was where she always put them prior to cleaning the toolbox, and maybe she'd be able to sense him picking through them for what he needed, or sense that sly wonder that would hit him about how Ellen didn't usually leave his things like this, had never left his things like this—her work for Joe just as tidy as her work in her own house—and maybe, she thought, in the middle of Joe's developmental methodology, she might extricate herself with little more than a gentle scratching against the box or a coy, "Yoo hoo?"

"It should have been funny," Wilma told me. "That's what it should have been."

4

ELLEN WAS IN the box for three days.

That's an easy sentence to write, but the fact is that if she'd emerged from that experience a raving lunatic we would have muttered, "Understandable," and hoped that Joe could figure out what needed to be done. It would have been a sad accident talked about by ladies who gather together, by men after a third, maybe a fourth, beer.

That she was neither raving nor loony does not, however, mean that something didn't happen, something deep within where the things we talk about only occasionally nudge those places we dare not go.

She told Wilma that after several hours she became angry, stunningly angry. She began to think this was how a lot of men liked their women: packaged and available, out of the way, recyclable—a special tool for a special problem.

"I began to feel like one of those veal calves pulled soft and milky white from some dark pen. I was being tenderized, weakened. Perhaps there was a code somewhere I had missed—a permissible thing a man occasionally does to his wife. Novel—not every man has a big tool chest—but hardly unique. I've seen more than one man come into Bud's Bar downtown with wife in tow. As he sits there and drinks and eats pig's feet and Bud's burgers, she'll be in a booth with a glass of water. She'll sit and for a while she might be pissed, but after a longer while she's not anything—she's not a will, she's not an anger, she's just a large cell wearing clothes.

"But don't make this a woman's issue, Wilma. It was just a Joe issue and an Ellen issue. I thought at first that if Joe simply wanted me to change—a man aims that remote at you, Wilma, you'd better move, babe—why hadn't he just asked? We'd always talked. Always. Joe's never been a babbler, but I've never known him not to listen to me or not to offer a comment when I've wanted one. For a long time I ran through all these points of our talking, all the bedtime chats, the talks at mealtimes, the joking anywhere and everywhere. No secrets, hon. Maybe we should have had some but we didn't. I was left there with the psychopathology of a starving retina making twinkles and rings of light in the blackness, and could only ask, *Why, Joe? Why would you do this?*"

"It didn't occur to her that it was a simple accident?" I asked Wilma. "That's what anybody would have thought."

"After eight hours, ten, twenty?" she said.

"Yes?"

"She thought he was trying to kill her."

"Oh, Jesus," I said, profundity eluding me at that moment.

"Husbands don't kill wives?"

"Of course they do, but—"

"Just not here?"

"I'm not arguing, Wilma."

"I know, Pop."

• • •

She felt, she said, like some upcountry chick tossed down a well because she forgot to chop fresh kindling. While sliding around in her own pee and being covered with sweat and hungry enough that she started feeling around with her fingers to see if there might be some old candy bar or cookie scrap she'd failed to catch when she'd cleaned the box, she'd grown furious that this was such a coward's way to do something like this, just let her starve, fade away, maybe nudge the truck over one of the cliffs down into the Pappa or the St. John. Happened all the time, didn't it? Hard thoughts but, worse, Joe knew her so little? It hadn't occurred to him that they could both drag their latent resentments out to some buggy slough on the Allagash and together they could dig one good, deep hole and, in the time-honored tradition of marriages everywhere, just have at it with muscle and bone, the loser getting the ditch and no more argument? Her Joe?

Hard thoughts in a time of increasing panic, hard enough because she just didn't know why Joe would want to do this to her, their marriage functional, not bad; productive, but never a notion, sweet or silly, that the whole thing might just be wrong. All twenty-six years of it? Seething, she tried to think if there might be some sweetie on the side, but the thought had no staying power. Not Joe, she would have known it.

Was it kids? That decision they'd made so long ago and stuck with through a mountain of pills and IUDs and condoms and on and off abstinences to give her chemistry a break? She could still see his face the day he'd said, "I'm not a father, not the type."

He'd meant that, and she'd loved his honesty even as she

said, not at all trying to steal his integrity, "I can't imagine myself with kids, Joe."

Joe said then, unusually philosophical for him, "You
shouldn't do things if you can't see yourself doing them."

Honesty, a word right out of their wedding vows—had she
missed something?

He served her breakfast in bed every Sunday, she
told Wilma, a grand thing, she always told Joe, but he just said
he liked to do it. He washed her hair for her every night, too,
and sometimes when she was way, way down he could sense
it and, without saying anything, he'd take her downtown for
coffee or dinner or a movie. This was Joe the fiend? A man
filled with regrets and thwarted desires, consumed by revenge,
a monster? Could it just be that you could never, really, know
someone at all? Not at all?

Her fury, thus, by the time Joe finally found her, was un-
abated.

"Ellen stank," Joe said, "like sweat gone bad on
a sick person. I said nothing to her but watched her carefully.
She went into the house and ate and drank and went to
the bathroom. Twice she walked back out to the truck,
looked at it, said nothing, and went back inside. I listened
while she played the piano for a few minutes, then there was
silence."

He expected to find her in the shower but she didn't do that.
Instead, she went outside to the small barn where she got Joe's
ax and a bow saw and his sledge hammer and went over to the
old outhouse.

"We'd gotten that thing years ago from Quitno Blêd shortly

after he'd had plumbing installed in his house. You worked on that, didn't you, Splotchy?"

"Believe so," I said. "I took some walls out and built some pipe chases. It's a small house."

"Ellen was excited about that old privy," Joe continued. "She said such things grew in resale, even antique value."

"People would buy shadows these days," I said, "if they could find some way to haul them home."

" 'Necessary delicacies,' was how she put it, Splotch. 'I can't imagine a bed-and-breakfast down on the coast that wouldn't want one of these tucked into the shade in a deep yard.' "

Board by board, Ellen cracked, smashed, axed, sawed, and pounded the little building into splinters. She raked it all into a pile and then began adding to the pile: a fifteen-year collection of *National Geographic* that she took directly from the shelves in the living room; box after box of kitchen goods—cookers, steamers, heaters, poppers, pantry-ware; canned and boxed food that was years and years old and food that had been bought at Don's Grocery only a week before; newspapers; old and raggedy towels; bundled collections of paid and unpaid bills; paperback books that seemed in her frenzy not library but litter, and finally the coffeemaker, toaster, microwave, and the kitchen radio they'd gotten with a paid subscription to *TV Guide*.

"She didn't take the TV," said Joe, then he really choked up when he added, "She said to me, 'When you've finally killed me, honey, you'll want to watch it on the news.' "

Then she set fire to the whole pile.

• • •

Joe had been careless, we both agreed, of course he had been that. And like any fool anywhere, he'd searched hard for the thing he loved most in the world, not realizing she was within arm's reach nearly all the time.

But he didn't search long, and I come up as puzzled with Joe on this as I am with Ellen. There are few worse things you can say to somebody than to tell them they've overreacted to some wrong. Certainly Ellen was *ready* to believe that this supposedly successful and long-term marriage was rife with the seeds of spousal carnage—whether it was or not. If it was, then that first slamming of the box lid down over her must have sounded like the warden opening the door to death row and saying, "Ellen, it's time."

If it was not—well, that's a moot point. She believed he was out to get her, and beliefs manufacture more facts in a day than science has throughout this past millennium.

But Joe, a strong man, quiet; physically muscular; intuitive, thoughtful, never an easy con; a gentleman by our definitions up here—Joe who'd bite a bear on the ass if you told him it was necessary to get a job done, he collapsed in his own way about as fast as Ellen had in hers.

Two hundred miles he said he put on his truck beginning that Monday morning. He ran out to St. A de P and on up to Quiktupac—where Ellen had done some tutoring with Mic Mac kids—then hit every logging road he could scrape, bounce, or bull his way onto, his tools (and Ellen!) bouncing around just behind him.

By noon, though, he was done.

"She'd left me," he said. "I believed that truly. I ran into Cary Andersen in Quilli and she said she'd been all over the place that very morning because someone was having a great time putting skunks in mailboxes, but she'd seen no one walking or hitchhiking, had not seen anything of Ellen but she'd most definitely keep her eyes open."

"You both believed the worst of each other, didn't you, Joe?" I said.

"I believed she had left me. Yes, sir."

"No real reason for it, but you believed it."

"Sometimes it's the lies that hold a marriage together, Splotchy," Joe said. "Until one of them don't work no more."

"Which lie was that, Joe?"

"Right in front of you, Splotch."

"Okay."

"That we loved each other."

5

ELLEN HAD THINGS in her life and a bit of work. Joe had things in his life and a bit of work. They got by, comfort not lavish—bought at a discount—but there still. They got by (the standard in Quilli).

A man I once knew had an entire plan for his life. He was a young man, though I always called him Old Tom. Certainty, I think, can bring on aging quicker than anything. Old Tom's plan, though, was actually written down, the final goal on the last page, a page he would not let me see.

You could not, he would say, proceed randomly through life. There need to be touchstones of accomplishment, even scars where you'd sunk your teeth into your own life and said things will be this way—not that way.

He was impressive and competitive, a man it was uncomfortable to be against. Only in his late twenties when I knew him, he wore three-piece suits and smoked a pipe because it was an image and, back then, image was everything.

Then his wife found his plan one day, and it's hard to know what irritated her more, that she was Section III (or some such) with a heading of "First Wife," or that there was an actual Section VII with the heading "Second Wife."

The next time I saw him Section VII was in effect.

Old Tom and his plan would not have made it in a place like Quilli. He would not have been understood, nor would he have understood the ways in which people like Joe and Ellen put their lives together. Ellen did some substitute teaching and some tutoring over in New Brunswick. Now and then one of the schools would need an aide for a child with odd needs and she'd do that for as long as she could stand it. She'd tend bar, too, down at Bud's if Bud was sick, and if things were tight she'd work the potato harvest in late summer and early fall. That was hard work, and Joe would massage her sore muscles every night, but Ellen was patient, not only with the work but with time itself: sunrise into noon, noon into evening, then mid-August was early October and it was all over.

Time, then, to help Joe put the plow on the truck. He had Things That Need to Be Done, of course, but self-sufficiency is a high virtue in Quilli so Joe's customers tended to be mostly old, alone, or just lonely. He had eight driveways to plow when the snows came and that was good money, cash money. By the time he and Ellen put the plow on Joe would already have cut thirty or forty cords of wood over the spring and summer. At the time all this was happening firewood was around ninety dollars a cord cut and stacked, so a good summer more or less took care of the year's house payment, which was $349.75 a month.

Beginning in early December, Joe and Ellen also ran a small Christmas tree lot across the street from the state university. Though Joe never calculated things closely enough to know if they made any money at it, the Christmas tree lot was a hoot, either he or Ellen wearing the big, pillowed-up Santa Claus suit and the beard that flowed down nearly to the knees. They had fun with that and children loved the DeLays, loved it especially when Ellen would go "ho-ho-ho" in her shaky tenor squeak. She told Wilma that some years she and Joe wouldn't even decorate at home, not because they were feeling sour on Christmas, but because for nearly a month they were living with hot cider and Christmas cookies and people who managed, if only for a few minutes, to leave all the badnesses elsewhere while they selected a tree and one of Ellen's wreaths.

No plan to any of it, no Section V or XII or subsections D or 6.3. It was survival only—no time clocks, no meetings— the few constants in a day more than enough: the brewing of coffee; the sound of a knife buttering toast. *Morning, hon.* The one time I put it that way, however, Joe quickly added, "with quality, Splotchy. Survival with quality."

As I look at what happened following the toolbox incident, I often wonder if lives that are put together on the outside with little more than need and circumstance controlling things might also be put together on the inside in the same way.

Joe's account has Ellen squarely cool, a little angry, though as he goes on with it Ellen becomes like a ball of twine, not simply unraveling until there's nothing left, but turning in on itself, twisting, tangling, becoming knotted and, eventually, unuseable.

"I thought you knew I was in there," she told Joe. "I sat in the heat and the dark and lost track of time except when it got goddamn hot. I assumed that was day, probably noon. Why in the hell can't Joe park in the shade? Everybody parks in the shade. It's easier on the paint and not so warm when you need to go somewhere."

"You thought I knew you were in there?" Joe said. Ellen had slept two nights already on the floor of the barn and her eyes looked tired, Joe thought, her hair straggly and greasy and particled with things.

"That you were going to leave me to die and rot," she said, "that it was an opportunity—some things you just don't know about your husband."

"Or your wife," Joe said.

"Your wife?"

"I thought you'd gone, that you'd left me."

"Why would I go? Where would I go?"

"It's what I thought—that you'd run out, run off, run away. Your happiness hasn't been very high lately. I could see that. I hear you sometimes at night when you cry, and you drink a lot—you do. You don't turn to me so I can't say anything, but I'm not blind. People leave."

"People kill, too, Joe, and it's always the ones nobody thought would do it, kind people who haven't been thanked enough, calm ones, shy ones. Did you look for me?"

"I looked. Sure, I looked. I even talked to Cary and she said she'd keep her eyes open."

"You talked to Cary? So it's all over town, then?"

"Everything's all over town, Ellen. I think the only things to worry about are the things that aren't all over town. You thought I was trying to kill you? You really thought that?"

"I thought what I needed to think, Joe."

The next morning Ellen emptied the freezer of all meat and threw everything away. Outside, the pile from her earlier catharsis was still smoldering, but Joe said nothing. He kept adding up the dollars she was tossing out, but he told himself it was cheaper than a doctor if it helped.

He thought at first this was some kind of shock she was

working through. His eyes started to fill and his throat choked up whenever he thought about the killing business, but if that was what she'd thought, then that was what she'd thought. He decided this was one of those things that happens in a marriage, a painful thing, that you look back upon as having existed for a time until you moved away from it. You were richer then, but there was sadness, too. Struggles overcome sometimes left good things behind, things earned with quiet pain.

Joe hoped that whatever had given rise to Ellen's ugly thinking didn't have more ugliness behind it.

"I decided later, though, that 'ugly' didn't even begin to cover it, what happened."

Increasingly, when Ellen made meals, she served food cold, often raw: thinly sliced vegetables, bread, cold cereal, canned soups (Joe, saying nothing, would put his bowl of soup in the new microwave), eggs, more bread, ice cream. Beer and ice cream became one of her favorites, and she began keeping the television on while they ate, always tuned to the news channel. Joe noticed, too, that when she used the bathroom just off the kitchen she kept the door open, her head turned toward the television. There had been a modesty before that no longer seemed important to her. Joe didn't mind. Regardless of who thought what about what, the thing had still been just a nasty accident, something about which recovery was simply an issue. You thought about it. You talked about it. You got through it. That was how the world worked.

For a time Joe even thought she'd finally gotten past it all. She stopped talking about it and she didn't destroy anything else. She began to make love again, too, and Joe seemed to think there might be something new there as well, maybe a nuttiness or a different energy, maybe it was that change in modesty now adding something to the bedroom. One time, though, she was on top of him, both of them just short of deliverance (as he put it), and he looked at her, something he always did, and he saw her lips moving, nothing sexy or goofy but moving with words behind them, and he whispered, "What are you saying?" and she said, without any explanation, "I'm praying."

"Joe?" I said.
"Yes?"
"That's really awful. I mean, just horrible, a horrible thing."
"Really, Splotch? I'm not sure what I thought."

One morning, Ellen stood in the kitchen with Joe there and pulled her hair back over her ears and wrapped it in a tight bun, severe. Joe didn't like it because it made her look mean, and that was the last thing in the world you could ever have said about Ellen. A listener, he said, she was that—a nice cushion that other lives could drop their breakable parts on without fear. People used to talk to her and she would touch them, a hand on the shoulder for this one, just the touch of a forefinger on a wrist for that one, small things—silent alliances. Joe didn't like Ellen mean.

She kept her hair up, and each morning she would smooth over or cut off any flyaways and add another layer of hairspray. She repeated this day after day until her head looked smooth and shiny. Joe told her he thought it would ding if he bounced a spoon off it.

Another day, she didn't dress at all except for the silk robe

Joe had bought for her in Freeport, an anniversary present some years before.

Ellen, that day, said only, "Clothes hurt."

Joe thought she might be coming down with something and wondered if there might not be a beneficial side to that—a good fever, some honest aches.

"I think I just wanted to *see* some recovery," he told me.

She'd worn nothing but the robe, though, for three weeks straight. She bathed, he noticed, if he was not working and was home, three times a day, maybe more, always careful not to wet her hair.

All of this affected Joe, surprisingly, in a sexy way.

"Was it her struggle, Splotchy? That she was alone out there, really alone, fighting nasty enemies?"

His woman, he would say, prepped and tough, her cheeks pink with the blood of pursuit. Her eyes would narrow and she'd nail him to the wall with stares.

She made him increasingly nervous, however, more nervous than he'd ever been in his life, and the nerves seemed never to go away. Embarrassed, but desperate to go after this truth he was sure was out there, he told me he started masturbating, sometimes in his truck, sometimes in hidden places out on a job. Ellen's troubles, he'd think, and then he'd feel his breath shortening up and tightness in his crotch.

One evening, the worst, he recalled, she sat at the table after supper, a six-pack right there and the newspaper in front of her. Saying nothing, which was beginning to seem sadly normal to Joe, she rubbed a small dollop of margarine onto each nipple, the nipples shining and growing fat, growing in Joe's mind until he finally found himself actually gulping and short of breath, barely able to excuse himself as he got up from the table and went out to the barn and without even a shred of fantasy sent a hundred million of his troops out onto the dirt floor.

"It's just her," he said quietly to himself, the barn, as usual, the silent witness of his smaller deeds. "Nothing personal."

Joe threw himself into his work, though there was not much of it. He doubled his time on the simplest jobs. Getting paid by the job and not the hour, the decision was his. He would clean gutters and use a detergent, hand sand the bark wounds on trees where he'd removed dead limbs. For the old widows and their endless needs for sink washers and the changing of high lightbulbs, he would plunge pipes unasked and move heavy tables and couches to vacuum carpet sections that had been untouched for years. For most people, none of this was noteworthy. Joe's way had always been a thorough one, methodical to the point of near-paralysis, yet never less than perfect. In a place like Quilli, it would have been impolite to notice that someone was trying to go beyond perfection.

He was tolerant and patient, he told himself, the way it was expected that, as Ellen's husband, he would be. She was out there, she was somewhere. She was working, trying to find a way out or a way in, trying to best something, to crush it, defeat it, destroy it. Joe thought he had good reason for some tough pride in his wife.

He also thought Ellen was losing the battle.

6

"**IN THE MIDDLE** of understanding things," Joe said, "you sometimes wish you just didn't have to do it."

Let it be, is what we really want to say. *Let it go now.* Joe didn't hold back, and his frankness was giving me an Ellen I'm not sure even Wilma had seen before. A cold northern place is no stranger to tragedy, and you quickly learn to see this spot of ground in front of you is not so much a grave holding someone you love, but a nice spot of land where flowers grow beautifully in a short season.

Grenada called me one night a few weeks ago, and without even asking me if I was eating well (her usual question), she said, "I hear you're doing a history of the town."

"You heard that?" I said.

"I did, sir."

"Maybe a history of Wilma," I said. "Something she asked me to do. The town will have to take care of itself."

"You think that's smart, Splotch?"

"I think it's what Wilma wants, hon, and I'm trying to help her out."

"Might be better just to let it all slide. That's what I think."

"I know you do."

Joe wasn't all that far from Grenada's point when he continued, "Maybe we just need a little more faith that there are some things that can't be understood and the world will still go on."

"The Reverend Joe DeLay," I kidded him.

"Splotchy—if I scratch my head anymore about this I'm gonna be bald."

Joe knew, at the time, that the incident in the truck box wasn't the whole reason behind what was happening to Ellen, though he knew her reaction was more than he originally thought it would be. An hour or two, that would have been one thing, a laughable bit of carelessness, and maybe to say it had been three days was still getting lodged in his mind as just hours, something he needed to shift around on. He wanted to feel like Ellen had felt, but she had said so little about it he didn't know where to begin.

He knew what he'd felt. He said he'd never forget that Tuesday night when he'd been worrying and worrying about where she'd gone and if she was all right—had she taken some money, some good clothes, food?—and in the middle of all that he'd finally decided to go out and put his tools away since they'd been rattling around in the truck bed since Sunday.

Nor would he forget how "my heart about slapped my mouth shut with joy when she lifted her head up as I opened the box and she said, 'Did you chicken out?'

" 'Chicken out?' I said, not even thinking what either of us meant by that."

"The first accusation?" I said.

"I suppose. Mostly, I just said, 'Holy smokes,' and helped her from the box. She was weak and a little dizzy. I asked her if she wanted to take a run over to Ponus Hospital.

" 'Looking like this?' was all she said."

• • •

One day, when Ellen seemed particularly bad and had cut herself peeling an onion for onion sandwiches, and then had just stood there letting the blood drip all over herself, directing it onto her knees and her thigh and foot and even her nose, Joe finally said, "If you think it will help, why don't you put me in there, in the toolbox? Keep me there for as long as it takes and then we can talk about it."

"Oh, Joe," she said.

"I will go in there, really."

"But you would know I wasn't trying to kill you," she said.

"You thought that?" Joe said. "You really did? You keep saying that and I keep waiting for you to mean something else but it's not coming through, is it?"

Joe said he looked at the tablecloth with blood all over it, Ellen's blood, and the words that came to mind had less to do with meaning and felt more like a line thrown out to someone falling from an unknown place.

"I love you, Ellen," Joe finally said.

"Do you, Joe?"

"I need to say it?"

"Maybe you shouldn't. Maybe you just feel you have to because there's nothing else to say, like 'Let me go, Ellen.' "

"Jesus, honey."

" 'I want to be alone, Ellen.' Doesn't that sound even a little right? Could that be what you really, really want, Joe? Is there some life you want to live that I don't even know about?"

"I think so," Joe said, his voice a whisper. There didn't seem to be any way to talk where they were both going in the same direction.

For a moment, he said, she brightened up. She pulled her

robe together and came over to where Joe was sitting at the kitchen table, a paper towel finally wrapped around her cut finger.

"What is it?" she asked.

"The one where you're happy," he told her. "That almost strange one from what feels like long ago, where you tell me you want to walk downtown to buy a card for someone, to get a cup of coffee at the diner and to do that with me, or you ask me for just a little money and we both try to see where it should come from, or at night when we've got the TV on and you tell me, 'Joe, would you mind brushing my hair?'"

They both almost laughed at that, he said, because only the day before Joe had said something about brushing her hair but he'd said the way it is now he'd probably have to use a belt sander to do it.

He and I were sitting just then in Ponus Park, a wind down from the Gaspé pushing the hawks and grosbeaks into motionless flight. The park is built around a small lake and Quilli keeps it up pretty well. It sits atop a hill and in the warmer months it's a refuge: quiet, a good place to talk or nap or just to sit and imagine your life being other than what it is. In the winter, however, the walker, the dreamer, the snowshoer— stays out of there. The park is an intersection for at least three major snowmobile trails and those sixty-mile-an-hour torpedoes will blast through there at any time of day or night. The Quilli council will do nothing about that, since even at high speeds the tourist money still flies off the sleds and it's good money.

The Quilli council did pass an ordinance one time, though, governing the raising of livestock in town. Like most laws in places like this, it was a silly bunch of words, and enforcement was limited to specific complaints with the complainer usually ending up wrapped in a shroud of guilt. A few chickens, as anyone knows, can finance a family's Christmas as well as any credit card, or a couple of pigs can fund the surgery for a cancerous spot needing to vacate a high cheekbone. Livestock do poorly this far north anyway, so there is little chance of anyone's husbandry getting out of control.

Which made it not usual, but not rare, the night Ellen heard the sheep on their street and began to change things forever, began to dismantle a long and good marriage because, as she told Wilma, "it wasn't enough." That was it.

"Wasn't enough of what?" Joe asked me when I repeated what Wilma had said.

We both decided that it was something that had more meaning for a woman than a man. Most men tend to feel they are natural failures at handling almost any wants, their own or others.

A bleating, it was, the one part of a sheep it's hard to like. Infrequent, perhaps; it was a sound similar to the shrieks and squawks heard all the time in the woods west of Joe and Ellen's house, a woods that marked the end of Quilli and the beginning of a tax district where few people lived. In the other direction, Quilli slept, its comfortable capes and frame homes dark; low homes mostly, snug to the ground for warmth, two-story homes with steep gables for the shedding of a hundred (at least) inches of snow each winter. Quilli, before Ellen awoke, was the lone sentinel guarding against the darkness to the west.

The sheep's cries woke her, and she went out the bedroom

window onto the roof of the front porch, where she sat, her legs drawn up, her chin resting on her knees. Restlessness, even insomnia, was increasingly the norm, the porch roof not a bad place to work on it. More than once Joe had found Ellen asleep out there. If it was dawn, he'd go out and wake her up and help her inside. If it was earlier than that, he'd put a blanket on her and leave her be.

Ellen heard the truck, Wilma said, a slicing meatiness to the exhaust, an engine working hard. A logging truck? That would be the best guess, but the worst part, according to Ellen, was that she could hear, but not see, the sheep close by, and she could hear, but not see, the truck not at all close yet, and she knew the way you know you're sick even though you're feeling just fine that something was going to happen.

"I just knew," she wrote to Wilma much later, "that for as much as both that sheep and that truck had a blazing infinity of points in space and time from which to choose—they had chosen a flawed infinity. That seems to be the story of most victims, isn't it? They make choices. They lead themselves by the hand. They blow it big, babe."

The sheep, hardly more than a shadow, flew up against the dark sky—the truck passing beneath it while it was still airborne—and landed in the ditch in front of Ellen's house. Ellen went back through the window and into the bedroom. She slipped out of her robe and put one of Joe's undershirts on.

Downstairs, she turned no lights on and went out the back door, not the front. Silent and stealthy, she remembered Joe's undershirt was black and she thought that a fortuitous thing. It was important to be unseen.

She walked slowly along the wilderness side of the house, certain the trucker had driven on, but not wanting it to be otherwise. This whole flurry of moments seemed extremely special, not something to be shared.

She walked into the ditch in front of the house. The sheep, she could hear, was not dead, not yet. Ellen touched it with her foot and heard a milky wheeze, a sigh. "Poor thing, Wilma. She'd done her job well—the victim's job, all that work: site selection, environmental impact, an assured namelessness. Lots of choices, though it's a bigger choice than most as to who is with you when you die." Ellen knelt and lifted the sheep's head up onto her lap. It was snorting blood and now and then vomited a splotch onto her legs. The blood ran over her thighs and hips and even down into her crotch. She thought she was kneeling in mud, too, but it didn't matter.

The sheep died with the heavy last gasp of an aerobic athlete.

Ellen got the wheelbarrow from the barn. The sheep was no lamb, but many dogs were bigger. In the barn, she put it on top of one of Joe's workbenches and turned on an overhead light. The light had a brown and red Molson shade and looked like a big glass baking dish.

" 'Catastrophe again, Ellen?' Joe would say. He'd look sad saying it, too, Wilma, and his sadness is beginning to wear me out. I could see him calling a friend, and Joe and the friend would stand together in the yard and talk and look at me— dear Ellen; poor Ellen—circles under my eyes, lines on my face. They would chew things over in a mumbled colloquy, a little throwing of hips, an adjustment of respective crotches.

Joe would clear his throat and blow his nose, the friend would look away. In the end, they would conclude: 'She's upset.'"

Joe had many friends though in truth he never brought them home. "We have fun," he'd told Ellen once, "chance we labor together. But that's it."

Chance we labor together. Oh, Joe.

7

WILMA AND I were taking her boy, Bylaws, down to the Hunellia Faulk Ponus Medical Center in Quilli one day. He'd been running an on-and-off fever and Wilma's van wasn't running at all so I said, sure, I'd pick them up. The child was between us in my truck, sitting in one of those carry-chairs that's about the size of a Yugo.

"That sheep," I said. "There's something I don't understand about what happened that night with the sheep."

"Only one thing?" Wilma said.

"I like to narrow things down, sweetheart. One thing in my hands, one problem, work it out—then move on."

She lit a cigarette and opened the window a crack. It was still early fall but we were in a white woods, a crusty frost and a light fog giving us all a pastel moment. The sun would change things soon.

"It was dying," I said.

"She couldn't leave it. Why was that unusual? A lot of people would have done the same."

"Or called the night cop," I said.

"Think of the whole, Pop," Wilma said, "not the part."

I'd been in Joe's shop before, maybe one half of the small barn behind their house given over to the dross of a professional whose professions were evidenced by equipment, not degrees. There were tins of parts, and cans of screws, nuts, bolts, nails, washers; a whole marketplace of wood pieces and metal pieces; sheet metal; piping; chunks of fiberglass, wall-board, asbestos sheets; the assorted parts of a man ready for work yet unconcerned about order. His tools were all around, things Ellen could feel comfortable near because they were his, though she also felt comfortable enough to use them whenever she needed to. She knew how men felt about their tools, but she also knew there was only one unbreakable rule: If you use it, put it back.

Some things were clean and some were not. Rope sat about in piles and coils, as did chain of varying lengths and thick-nesses; wire, twine, cable, duct tape, glue, paints and thinners, drop cloths—all of it a collection of things used, yet useable again. Joe had no romance with fine hammers, fine saws, ex-pensive power tools, either.

"Never use anything you can't afford to break," he told me once.

It's easy to fill your life with rules when your life is building things. There's a comfort to it, though it tends to make those in the trades crusty, a little too conservative. That might not be all that bad.

"Joe was so predictable," Wilma began, "and their life so predictable—not bad, Pop, just predictable—that it began to seem silly to her to waste so much time living it. Can you see that? It sounds so prosaic, but it was really desper-ately radical. Those things she did, you know—throwing things out, eating food raw, meat especially, not bathing for way too long—grenades, Pop, that's all. There was a war go-ing on."

"Ellen and Joe?"

"It wasn't Joe—"

"So—"

"—nor was it anyone else."

"It was life," Ellen said to Wilma, "right there in front of me in manageable form. Life now absent but not long gone yet. She looked peaceful and sweet in her death, her injuries not visible. There was some blood around her mouth that I wiped away with one of Joe's rags, and there were some thistles in her wool that I pulled out or cut out with one of Joe's utility knives.

"At one point I went inside and got a comb and brush (I left muddy footprints on the kitchen floor; that seemed appropriate) and came back to her and unsnarled and untangled her rough spots. Flecks of things, mud chunks, bugs, began littering the bench, and she seemed to be getting whiter and whiter. I stepped away from the bench a few feet, then a few more. I stepped in and out of the stalls and the storeroom but that radiance never quit, her glow on me like something from a clouded moon.

"Did I hear voices, Wilma? Legions of sheep corpses calling to me, all the many secrets of purpose ready to be laid out in front of me? I wish, Wilma. But it was Joe's shop and there are no voices in Joe's shop.

"Something of purposes—maybe. I came out of the shadows and picked her up and sat on the floor with her, not a bad thing for the living to do with the dead. She was heavy enough but not that heavy, and I began to sense within her an explanation, an *apologia*, a 'why' for wool and not scales or bristles or thorny armaments; a hoof and not toes that needed painting and an occasional suck. It seemed to me that a foot gave you the earth in a way that hoof or claw did not—feeling, divine and omnipresent feeling: a searing macadam, snow past rain and into numbness, a grand and predawn stubbing. We create—we hominids—the hoof through shoes and boots and in doing so we sever a connection. Too bad.

"There was use, too, usefulness. We shave her and use her hair to make fine clothing. We use her in nursery rhymes. Alas, we'll even eat her—the mint jelly industry depending on it.

"Maybe what I was after, Wilma, was mourning. Something had been lost and I needed lamentations. I needed to return to a time when a woman could pound rocks against her face and rip out her hair and pour ashes on herself so that I could scream to the world, 'You give so little and you take so much! Here, you bastards, you missed a few things!'"

"Pop?" Wilma said.

"Yes?"

"What had she lost?"

"Can you tell me?"

"I don't know. I really don't. Something big, though. If it was only in her head, something deep in her heart—Jesus, this all sounds so odd—it was still big, and she was really alone with it."

Wilma was looking at me as she talked and I drove. In one hand she had a wet washcloth that she kept dabbing on Bylaws's cheeks and forehead. The child kept giggling, not knowing he was sick, grabbing the washcloth from time to time and sucking on it.

"She told you all of that?" I asked.

"She told me some of it. Later, she was writing pretty regularly. Joe said some things, too."

"Joe did?"

We were at the clinic door to the hospital. Wilma asked if
I was coming in but I said I wanted to stay in the truck and
jot a few things down. Mostly, I was worried about the boy
and just wanted the news (good or bad) without the institu-
tional trappings. Particularly did I not want to be in the ex-
amining room trying to figure out if every thump, twink, or
probe was good of its kind or was prefacing something dire.
Wilma has had abortions—never something hidden from either Grenada or me—and Bylaws came from an abortion
that turned into a delivery, almost three years ago now. Feisty
kid, he would not be denied. I just thought it was better to let
Wilma do the mothering. Quite frankly, she's not yet very
good at it.

Wilma said Joe found Ellen the next morning without
knowing she needed to be found. He concluded later that
she'd needed it pretty bad.

He woke early, a red dawn pinking up the bedroom. Ellen
was not next to him but that was not unusual. Sometimes she
spent the night in the spare bedroom, "and sometimes, Pop,
she even slept on the roof of the porch."

I told her Joe had told me that.

She drank beer there, in bed or on the roof, and forgave Joe
for sins she would not reveal. Joe went along with all of it. He
wanted only to be there in case the beatings (as he thought of
them) she gave herself became needlessly cruel.

One night he found her in the kitchen at bedtime and she
said she did not think she'd go to bed at all. She preferred, she
said, "to be the sentry in the kitchen, Joe. You'll know you're
safe."

"I didn't know I was at risk," he said. He'd come down

with the alarm clock in his hand to check it against the clock on the stove.

"Look around you. You could be dead in a second, a bullet from an angry man—"

"Ellen," Joe interrupted, "no one's angry at me."

"I'll finish?—aiming at his wife. A bad shot clear across town, a walloping sadness. Should that happen, I'll be the witness. That's very important."

"You can come to bed," he said.

"It used to be that men beat their wives, an expected thing. That was bad, but now they kill them. Times change."

"Ellen? Will you come with me?"

"I think not. There is much in need of watching. Would you check the windows, though? I think it's going to rain."

There had been many nights like that, Joe told me.

Ellen's back was to Joe as he entered the barn. She was sitting on the floor, legs in front of her and bent slightly at the knee, her buttocks bare. She moved—a sway, a tremble—and she seemed to be singing something.

Joe thought the barn smelled: iron, copper, a thickness in the air. Her hair looked red, the rising sun splashing through the dusty window, and there was a bulk of something between her legs. Joe could only think, feeling well-rested and weary at the same time, *What's it going to be now?*

More and more it seemed like Ellen's thoughts, more extreme than anything Joe could imagine, were dropping down right into life, dropping whole in ways they shouldn't, like when you thought things about someone and then said them and quickly realized that a key glue in civilization was realizing the difference between thought and speech. Forget it, and you could have people taking shots at your tires.

Things had been thrown from the workbench and the shop was a mess, would need a day. He had lots of those. He wondered if Ellen did, if maybe he wasn't worrying about her in the right way. These things she did, Joe knew no one like her. He remembered long ago vowing presence and fidelity, the only things, he thought, two people ever really had to give to one another. If her need was an audience, that was all right. He didn't think she wanted applause.

"Ellen?" he whispered. Joe thought for a minute he should go back inside and get dressed. He was only wearing flip-flops and the old robe where Ellen had embroidered above the pocket, *Ellen's Man*.

Certification enough, he decided.

QUILLIFARKEAG, MAINE
(Male Bonding)

"So after she beat you up, Poison, what was you thinking?"
Bud was making one of his famous shredded beef cheese-
burgers for Poison. Just beneath the cheese he placed a dollop
of peanut butter the size of a nickel. It is his secret ingredient.
"I was thinking I didn't like her, Bud," Poison said.
"She whomped you good, didn't she?"
"She caused me pain."
"No doubt," Bud said.
Poison held his right arm up then, a slight bend between
wrist and elbow, and said, "She caused me crookedness."
"That won't go away," Bud said.
"No, sir."
"A good job," Bud said. "That's what it was."
"I have always been a fan of excellence," said Poison.

8

JOE AND I HAD gone down to Bud's for shredded beef burgers (most people call them "shrugs") and some beer. Joe needs to get out, and I like to think I'm one more weapon in his arsenal against that reclusive urge that can lurk in anyone, that tendency to lock the doors and turn out the lights and whisper, whether anyone's there or not, *just go away.*

Bud and Michelle could see that the talk between Joe and me was serious so they worked a bit to keep the bar folk in a settled condition. Bud's is not a wild place anymore, but it can be raucous. Higher-end people tend to go to Le Père's where they have plants and chicken wings. Bud gets those who would find a chicken wing something handy to throw.

That's manageable, whereas Poison Gorelick and Pistelle Philomene often are not. Poison hates Pissy (he says) and Pissy loves Poison, so the sparring is constant except for those times when Pissy is crying, which is often and she's a noisy weeper. She cries, I think, she weeps because Poison's a good catch. As dependable as a husband, occasionally grumpy, he's a woman's man and lonely women take to that—as has one in particular, Miss Spicy Pelletier: college graduate, motel maid, and motel manager down at Pizzle's Inn. Poison and Spicy are close and everyone knows it, including Pissy. So she weeps because things in the world are often not very fair. Maybe that's why we all spend a lot of time at Bud's.

Pissy's talented, though—a union carpenter (I am not), brassy, intuitive; maybe forty-five though she looks much younger; a skilled roofer, too, who, like most of us in the trades, has less than twenty digits. Pissy lost a toe on the roof of a three-story house when she stepped into a steel trap someone had set to keep raccoons out of the chimney. She was young then and used to work in sandals. Pissy wears steel-toed boots now and nearly always, as she will proudly show, pantyhose underneath.

In the barn that morning, Joe finally went up to Ellen and knelt down behind her.

"I had a need of holding her," he said. He ran his hands over her legs, under her thighs; her hair was sticky as he pressed into it. He worked down to her neck and tasted her, her skin hot to his tongue, then he pressed against her back. She brought her legs in, shifting onto her knees. Joe thought she tasted terrible.

She tasted like bad sweat and old feed and she needed him. Joe could not bring himself to ask anymore why she did these things. It was not something you could fairly do. People were as they were and they were on their own, every call a tough one.

He thought of houses he'd worked on, solid structures resting on foundations carved out of granite. Things fit, yet still they breathed, shifted slightly. On a sunny day a beam might be pounded with nails and bound with boards, a shadow built in. You created darkness that way and it was forever. Families came to be above that darkness. They prospered and they knew sorrow, were cranky and stupid and sometimes funny and sometimes made bad decisions and no one ever thought about the darkness that had been built right into the house, into the family. You could become mysterious about it if you wanted to, posit curses, ghostly remains. If you fell through the cracks of the family, as everyone did from time to time, you knew darkness, a rich black as real as the sky. Yet the darkness was as much a part of the fundament of life as any multipaned bay window framed with plants and exploding with flowers and luxurious joy on a summer day.

"Ellen pressed against me, even reached back and slapped me on the butt. I thought for a second if we just didn't look at each other she could stand me, maybe imagine I was someone else if that's what she was doing, but for once it seemed important that we just be bodies, nothing else, just two more things happening early in the morning and no one had to wonder if there was a secret meaning to it, to anything."

He held her tight, he said, and could feel the thing in front of her, something furry that looked like a sheep, maybe a dog. He brought his hands underneath her shirt and her breasts were heavy, hanging down, some belly flesh hanging down, too, and he remembered one time when he'd been on top of her and had raised up some to let her breathe and he'd looked down and seen his own belly hanging there and what he later called his forty-watt tits and he'd straight out said to Ellen, "How long have I been looking like this?"

Joe's mind wasn't strictly on sex, or not on the breath dances and wind kisses, the garter belts or painted nails or the damning and confusing pleasure smelling like the crisp wind of a blizzard, the man above or below the woman on top or the bottom, reading some afternoon body poem with substance to it and toes dug into a mattress, with all of it being a shared wetness, the holy water of spit and intimate business. Words, then, could be as good as a blow job depending on who's talking but here, now, early in the morning with neither of them (Joe assumed) breakfasted, and he so far with only one cup of coffee in him, he thought of Ellen as standing in the middle of an awful storm, lightning bolts elevating this personal suffering up into something to be shared and talked about. Bare-knuckle thoughts, he told himself, things you'd want to put aside before they hurt you.

Still, Joe couldn't imagine loving someone more than he loved Ellen at that moment. He kept saying it and saying it even though he knew she was so far away that by the time his letters got to her the postage would have been changed, so, feeling more desperate than he'd ever felt in his life, this loss beginning to assume shape now, to have a face with even a few moats and trenches of character—

"We had intercourse, Splotchy."

—he looked around at the bewildering darkness that was his world and his work now and felt Ellen moving on him, saw her head rock from side to side, heard her voice, too, a delicate whisper of songs made up, of tunes fabricated from the sheer rawness of nerve rippling through both of them even as the sunlight shot through a window and fell onto them like an old honey brew still thick at a hundred and eighty proof. The warmth felt good to Joe, neither of them naked but neither of them clothed much, either. He was sweating by then, but it was a cold sweat, a sex sweat evaporating in its own breeze, and not at all like this sunny warmth that connected them to the coming day.

"It was amusing," he said, "my mind both taking its pleasure with this glorious woman as well as thinking the lawn needed to be mowed and some shingles needed replacing on the front porch roof, and there were groceries to be bought down at Don's. And while a part of me was going *Oh, well, my goodness, my oh my,* I remembered the oil needed to be changed on the truck, too, and Ellen had said she'd do that, though I had mixed feelings about it, was even considering trading the truck, and I think Ellen had said she wanted to take all of the downstairs curtains down and wash and iron them, and she'd said, too, the night before, that she wanted to make a good lunch for me today, something fine, even cooked, and it all just seemed like I was once again where I was supposed to be and things were good, Splotch. Everything was good. Ellen was good. I was good. The whole damn thing was good."

All of which, he later decided, would be remembered under the rubric *Last Things.*

When Joe was done behind her Ellen asked him to leave and he thought he understood that, how sometimes you felt so used up you had to be absolutely alone just to see if anything was left. He understood that, felt for a second like he understood everything, and for as much as there wasn't anything on the earth he wouldn't do for Ellen, he also would not leave her—not this time. He stood and pulled the robe back around himself and decided he would make this, on the instant, without any thought or his craftsman's deliberation, one of those dark moments of light love that goes on between two people who've known all the light and dark they would ever need to know—and he said, his big ruddy face flushed with a sweet exertion: "That was fun."

• • •

Ellen stood then, Joe's big T-shirt covering most of her thighs. She looked at him and ran her hands through her hair, then looked down at the sheep at her feet. Joe was able, finally, to see clearly what it was, and it didn't seem odd anymore that Ellen, his wife, would be here like this, silent and, as he could see, goosebumps on her arms. Nor did it seem odd that she wouldn't ask his help as she bent to pick the sheep up and put it in the wheelbarrow. It was all Ellen, too, this new Ellen, who couldn't find a way to say she wanted out of all of this that they'd built together—when she laid a shovel gently next to the sheep and began to maneuver the wheelbarrow toward the door and the woods to the west and a soft spot somewhere on the ground, so that when Joe said, "It was, Ellen," and Ellen said, "I'm leaving you, Joe. Today," his first thought was of a poor Ellen dressed in only a T-shirt heading west with a dead sheep and a wheelbarrow and it all seemed like a funny thing to do, almost a hilarious thing though his laughter had already been swallowed so many times he felt a huge burp coming on. But then Ellen said it was time to take this poor dead thing and do with it the most absolutely appropriate thing and Joe finally said, "Of course."

After she came back—Joe noticed right away she'd stopped somewhere to pick a big bunch of flowers that were lying in the wheelbarrow—they just watched each other as the hours went by until Ellen finally got up and took a shower and put on a good dress, then put a few things together in a small box and walked out the door.

From that day on Joe heard about her more than he saw her—little rumors, small truths. He, himself, became sloppy in his work, which people understood, and he no longer ate very well.

9

"THAT REALLY WAS HER," Joe said as we butted down our smokes and finished our beers. "We had our way with each other and then she left."

It was late and I wanted to get back to my room above Czyczk's Lingerie. Joe, too, his eyes, his hands—a nervousness; maybe the sly haunting of someone who feels he's said too much and knows it can never be enough.

"I have to tell you something, Splotch," Joe said.

"You've been doing fine so far, Joe."

"About Ellen—about when she left? When she left for real?"

"Okay."

"I went out—" He stopped for a moment then, something coming but not easily. I thought his eyes looked a little teary.

"That night, Splotch—I went out to the truck. I had to do it."

I smiled then and said, "You checked the toolbox?"

"I did, sir. Damned if I didn't."

As we left, I looked up and nodded at Poison. He was sitting on the shelf up there with the stuffed animals. Pissy will do that to him, put him up there maybe two or three times a year. She just lifts him up like he was a small beam about to buttress something arched and beautiful. He had a look of goofy disgust on his face, but I had the funny thought that if you could bottle Pissy's love there wouldn't be a sober man in America.

By 3 A.M. I was back on the street, sleep becoming more and more a fool's errand. With my little recorder in a bag and about three hours of Wilma on tape, I walked out to the Bangor and Wulustuk Railroad tracks. There's an overpass over the highway there, and it's an elevated spot on the south side of town. Quilli, with its lighted Main Street and the widely scattered lights on the side streets, seemed tidy, maybe manageable. The downtown is low because of the two rivers, so everything that leaves that area does so uphill. A needly glow from the lighted spire of the UCC church was north and a little east of where I was, and a sodium pinkness east of that marked the parking lot of the Hunellia Faulk Ponus Memorial Hospital.

In another context I could go on and on about Hunellia Faulk Ponus, whose home up on Ouelette Street is the closest thing Quilli will ever have to a mansion, a seventeen-room Victorian with twelve gables—a roof you don't mind seeing someone else get the job to redo. At the age of seventy Hunellia Faulk Ponus began throwing her dead husband's money at every major problem that surfaced in Quilli, provided—if it was relevant—that only *her* name be attached to the project. We have, thus, Hunellia Faulk Ponus Pond, Hunellia Faulk Ponus Park, Hunellia Faulk Ponus Medical Center (and Memorial Hospital), Hunellia Faulk Ponus Historical Society Museum, Hunellia Faulk Ponus Elementary, and quite honestly, a lot of gratitude. When asked discreetly, the first time, if she wanted her husband, Carolina's, name on the new elementary school along with hers, she said only, "Don't think so. I hardly knew the man."

Her greatest pride, however, came in founding the Parental Guidance Clinic, our euphemistically monickered abortion place. "No more lonely drives down to Bangor," she said. "Our girls can have their crisis moments right here at home."

A different cadre took bitter joy in Hunellia's suicide, going so far as to have a bumper sticker made up that read, GUILT WILL OUT. All Hunellia was guilty of, however, was breast cancer, and her last public words were, "I'm too old to be this sick."

There's nearly always a train parked for the night on the tracks near the overpass. That night was no exception. I climbed the front steps of the first of two diesel engines and waved as Jelly Wruhreure, the Quilli night-shift cop, passed below me on the highway. Jelly's used to seeing me out and about at all hours, and I even kidded her once that if she'd get me a radio we'd automatically double the night shift.

"We don't have a dispatcher, Splotchy," she said. "All you could talk to is me."

She seemed a little put down so I said, "Nothing wrong there."

"What happened to Ellen," Wilma said as the first tape began, "is that she ran away—a journey of the heart, though, not distance. She got a room in a widow's house up in St. A de P and stayed there for some weeks. It wasn't easy. Her room was an old pantry near the back door, and it had a toilet and a sink right in it—the jail cell comparison was not lost on Ellen—and the old woman would not let Ellen into the rest of the house, forbade it, in fact; she'd even painted two white stripes on the floor leading from the back door to Ellen's room. It was childish, but Ellen said that at the time the idea of clear boundaries to things wasn't all that bad. Ellen snooped, of course, if the old woman was taking a nap or if she went out somewhere, and she said the place was unbelieveably filthy, 'crusted unto stench, Willy,' was how she put it.

"Still, it was a temporary time where everything was temporary. She thought she had some dreams but she couldn't remember what they were and she wanted to find them again.

" 'I lost them in some average prosperity,' she said. She worked hard, Pop, not to slam Joe in any of this, although Joe (she knew this) was being pretty well slammed by the town. Joe had let his wife go. He'd made a crazy person out of her. Someone said she was living down on the St. John in a cave, and someone else said she'd nearly ruined Joe—had the man no brains?—running up a tower of credit card debts.

"Eventually, I brought Ellen money from Joe, every penny of savings that they had and it was not a small amount. She would only take half, though, but the half she kept sparked hours and hours of conversation between us. She thought maybe she'd learn how to do hair, or possibly she could take a course somewhere in massage therapy. A store came to mind, several stores—children's clothes; a pet boutique; a sporting goods store for girls only; maybe a music store with piano lessons—until we both began to realize she wasn't going anywhere with any of that because it's hard to do business without people, and, having just given up the most important person in her life, she wasn't about to start, as she put it, 'survival dealings with the periphery people.' "

Ultimately, of course, that's exactly what happened. Exhausted, Wilma told me, by speculations that went nowhere, they drifted apart for a time. Wilma, like Joe, kept hearing things and disregarded nearly everything she heard: the DeLay woman (no longer in a cave) was living with a fifteen-year-old boy; the DeLay woman was a drunk selling herself to the Mic Macs; the DeLay woman was dead. The latter story surfaced about once a week, the circumstances always different.

The truth was a little more straightforward, though it had an odd twist. The odd part is that the old lady in St. A de P caught Ellen taking a drink of water from her kitchen sink one time and threw her out of the house. Ellen said it was just habit from her days in her own house. The sink in her room was working fine.

Ellen found herself standing in the rain in that wretched little town and looking across the street at St. A de P's two businesses—a bar and a real estate office—and without a moment's hesitation she walked into the real estate office of Vendrum Ponus and said, "Get me out of this."

Vendrum Ponus did that, offering up an old mining exploration camp of less than an acre for $5,500—exactly what she'd taken from Joe. There were buildings on it, Vendrum Ponus said, none of them in very good shape: a house, a couple of sheds, an outhouse. There was a stream, though she thought the property did have a well, and there was a phone wire and an electric wire.

"A hunting camp?" Vendrum said. "You hunt?"

"I hunt," Ellen said, "but for now it's just a living camp."

Vendrum Ponus told me that Ellen said she didn't even want to see the place, that she wanted possession immediately.

"Freaky-eyed lady," she said, "soaked to the bone and her

hair flattened all over her face. You have to understand, in a place like St. A de P, you turn down no deals. If she'd wanted to go up country and gnaw on birch bark I would have given her some salt and pepper and a deed. However—"

"She'd been through a lot," I said.

"—when we drew up the contract and she'd signed it, and I said I'd take care of the closing and she could have the keys right now because no one's lived up there for years, she started crying and then she smiled at me, an amazingly warm and totally happy smile. Peace, I think. It seemed like peace, and I felt good about my job."

Wilma's final words on that first tape were harsh, but she said it was gettting annoying how Ellen was trying to do nothing more than make a new life for herself and every damn deed, gesture, mood, or bit of posturing was being analyzed right on down to spit and indignity: "A boutique would not have made it, no children's store or pet shop, and you would have had to *sentence* half the women in the county if that's where they'd have had to go to get their hair done. The land was ugly, wondrously ugly the way bears like ugly land, and it was ugly the way second-growth pine is always uglier than the old hardwood forests, and the deer thought it was grand-ugly how they could just disappear into saplings of short black pine and weeds sometimes taller than the young trees. Ugly land is good hunting land, and Ellen's new place was surrounded by land so ugly the early pioneers who left it could write back home about the beauty of vast ranges of nothingness on the Great Plains. Ellen's place—she knew this because she and Joe had been hunting for over twenty years— was the Times Square, the Ginza, the Michigan Avenue of hunting lands, so she taught herself how to gut and skin and butcher and package anything that could be shot and killed and brought to her and she made money at it—just this woman alone, finding her way.

"She made a lot of money at it."

QUILLIFARKEAG, MAINE
(Crime)

Ten Finn got into trouble in that matter of growing vegetables that could be smoked. (Ten never entered into that debate over whether what he grew was truly a vegetable or actually a fruit.) Apparently, a skunk pranced on through Ten's barn where Ten was working — storing some of his crop — a skunk on the run from Ten's black-and-tan, and to avoid a smelly collision Ten leaped upward, grabbed on to some old conduit, and completed a fairly poor circuit; enough, however, so that Ten's thoughts couldn't reach his hands and he'd hung there for six hours until some Quilli boys, needing smoking vegetables, found him. Without even a nod about what reason folks might wonder they had for being out there, those two generous boys got him uncharged and down and he was all right, though hungry, and uninjured beyond losing feeling in both arms on a permanent basis.

The doctors told him feeling might come back but it never did. After that, Ten always wore red ribbon bracelets on both wrists to remind himself that he had to feel with his mind in the matter of those two extremities.

10

PISSY LOST A TOE in the trades and I lost the middle finger of my left hand. Wilma says to stay away from toes and fingers, but as I begin to shape what must have happened next to Ellen, I am stuck for a minute, an image, maybe a cartoon, of incomplete bodies and incomplete lives floating in front of me —parts for the workman, maybe? Perfection lying all around, needing only to be assembled? It seems a symbolic moment, but as I look at my notes—

A sheet-metal cutter—not my usual tool—performed the severance early one morning in a kitchen I was re-modeling. Both witness and cause were present in the visiting aunt of my customer, which aunt had two-and-a-half breasts, or two good breasts and an adjunct, as I also thought of it—a condition, I have since found out, not necessarily rare. Anyway, she walked into the kitchen at the wrong instant covered with some heat and linger-ing pink and that was it. She had just showered.

I remembered that modest protrusion not because it was unusual, but because I squirted finger blood all over it, said breast (actually, all three of them) diverting my craftsman's finger just enough to modify the old rule, which I still live by, measure twice, cut forever.

The aunt, as I recall, was cool, not at all addled. She wiped the blood off herself with a paint rag and dressed

enough to take me down to the hospital. I refused that
trip as a point of honor.

—I am torn about taking Wilma's advice. A point of honor?
What in the hell did I mean by that? It (the finger, Ellen, Pissy's
toe) is all expendable?

Still, for the moment, the nether extremities have been introduced, and while I can look back at my own fingery fate
and laugh about it, I am shaken a bit as I sit on the big diesel
locomotive and listen to Wilma's first words on the next tape:
"It was a goddamn finger, Pop, and Ellen never knew about it.
She knew everything else about that day, though she was
drunk when she told me, drunk on the phone, and it was late
and we were both tired, although she had the luxury of fading
away while I had to summon the energy to go over there because she needed me, needed someone and I was it. But she
never knew about the finger."

Ellen guessed there were a million ticks on the moose.
It was a good guess. A million, she knew, was always sufficient
for quantifying many.

The moose was lying on its side, a tough position for an animal with a four-foot rack, a good old boy mossy and tattered,
a serene self-impalement. Of its head, only the end of its snout
was touching the ground.

An exemplary partnership, Ellen said to Wilma—bad news
on a beautiful day—August 12, 1994—the woods leaking
leaves and filling up with cool air, prefall inklings of things to
come. She wondered how long the moose had been lying
there.

She lay down on the ground next to the moose, a parallel

companion, one hand on one great hoof. The moose could see nothing through the blood swill, the ticks, that covered its eyes.

"Big dumb deer," Ellen said to the moose. "You remind me of Joe."

She hadn't thought of Joe in a long time. "I'm sure you think this all makes sense. It's the way things are so don't try to change them. I don't know. Look at you. You're a mess."

Ellen's walk, rifle in hand, had been meant for leisure, not work. She was wearing a dress and sandals, a light sweater. Her hair was snarling and tangling in the light breeze; when she worked, she kept it tucked up under a baseball cap with a Maine Potato Growers logo on the front.

Side by side with the moose, Ellen could feel the fever-heat coming from the animal. Her rifle was over against a rock, the safety on. Joe had given her the gun as a Christmas present one year, a Winchester .30-06; she'd given him a chainsaw. That had been a good money year.

A froth was coming from the nose of the moose, a bubbly pink signal that things were getting very serious.

"Insufficient drainage," Ellen said. She recoiled from the hot wash of moose breath, blood in the exhale, a gurgle.

"Is it bad enough yet?" She told Wilma there were few questions of greater importance. "Would death be better than anything at all?"

Tick was on top of tick was on top of tick. Even in a time of plenty there was struggle. The unfed were feeding off the fed, robbers in line at an ATM. In the end, the last would get the goods—handled by many—and the first would be convicted, punished. It was an old story.

• • •

For a few minutes more she talked to the moose. She patted its hoof while it blew blood, and she talked about being a father moose and a grandfather moose, and about being old and responsible for a whole population, many of which were chased and savaged by stray dogs. A few of the boys got their racks caught in trees, too, skull and bones dangling weirdly off the ground for decades. Mistakes tended to be public and enduring in the woods. You didn't get to be this age without seeing it all, though, and that was worth at least a moment's conversation with a stranger. There was so little civility in the food chain.

Ellen shot the moose.

She shot it in the chest and the bullet exited the anus. The steel tip was clean and intact and took little flesh with it. The bullet pierced the heart and nicked a piece off the liver but otherwise its velocity remained unchecked.

There was more to the brief life of that bullet that Ellen never knew, its biography determined by ballistics and misfortune, and easily reconstructed by hindsight. It traveled straight and far over the ground even as the ground dropped away for a hill, gully, ditch, or ravine, missed everything that could have been in its path, all the twigs, saplings, stumps, and emerging conifers in the new-growth woods far from reasonable people, what Ellen often called in talk with Wilma "scrub gloom," an atmosphere not shown in the symphonic commercials of International Paper or Georgia-Pacific or Boise Cascade because gloom and high shadow could not be replanted. Ellen said she felt sometimes like the sexton in a new church entrusted with the mysteries of high oak and busted maple, the only one who remembered the echoing forests of another time, the ontological emptiness of big purposes and big dreams.

The bullet stopped after a long journey. It stopped at the first joint of a pinky finger of one man in a group of three, drinkers all, the hand of the pinky finger holding a can of beer.

Ellen was on her feet by then. She brushed the dust and twig dross from her dress, the moose in front of her no longer some teddy moose of wan pity, but a real job. Her house was a good half-mile away and she had no car, no truck for hauling. She had told Wilma once that vehicles were for traveling and she had no intention of going anywhere now that she had a place of her own.

Wilma had said "bullshit" as Ellen continued to argue emissions and waste and fuel resources, saying "bullshit" again and again until Ellen finally relented.

"Everything I had went into this place. It was enough, but not enough for a car."

"So much for nobility."

"Could you help me get groceries in town once in a while?"

"What Ellen called her 'modular poverty,'" Wilma said, "her 'shag and shit hut; hell, honey, hovel, shanty, shack,' with the cutting patio and the cutting shed, a woodshed, too, filled with bones, and something of a garage, even a log, board, stone, and tin-covered walkway to the outhouse way out back (no such luxury for the outhouse in front, off the parking area, though it was bigger, reserved mostly for the use of her customers), all of her property a linkage, a chain of cautious craft, all of it unplanned, and yet, as she said in her sincere way, a smile of contentment not at all contrived, with clusters of dark gray and black curly and truly long hair flying all over her face on a windy day, streamers of an almost celebratory wisp, and her deep brown eyes, modular in their own way, sometimes appearing independently focused, a flustered pink flush usually on her cheeks and nose, neither Mary Kay completely nor a total alcoholic wash (though rumor had it, Pop, that the dark nickel of addiction had been slipped in her slot, the handle pulled) . . . what she called all of that was 'peaceable maintenance—a soft hovering between life and death, as if in a nap, only better. I've made it all myself, and that might be important.' "

She would say things like that to Wilma, the only person she ever saw, except Joe, who was not business, talk about her things because things, now, were important to Ellen, the whole boxed and unboxed, trashy mess of possession that spilled all about her links and modules and inbuildings and outbuildings and jammed her quarter-acre sitting at the end of, though the only thing on, a long public road, an old logging road that even the kids at St. Bleufard's High School had learned was not a place to take a case of beer and an unsophisticated pair of libidi. You could, they said, end up spelled, hexed, gravity no longer meaningful. That woman, they said, spoke a private language the translation of which was just too awful to think about.

Kids.

Overall, that road was not thought to be a good place to go on a dare, even a drunken dare, all of that something of a sur-

prise to Ellen, who had only left her husband, who had not—
as far as she knew—gone awry.

"Did I, Wilma?"

"If you did, you're not now," Wilma would say, toughly
ambiguous. How *did* you judge the sanity of a friend?

"But they're saying those things? A lot of people are talking
about me like that?"

"A few."

"Only a few?"

"Quite a few."

But the whole shit-and-shag conglomerate was still,
Ellen would say, a quantum jolt over, ahead, and beyond what
she had had with Joe in Quilli, Joe who had tried to kill her
once though she was no longer quite sure of that, ahead of
anything in that life notwithstanding running water, an indoor
toilet, satellite dish, computer, microwave, programmable oil-
heated hot water furnace, light switches, bedspread with
flounces, respectability, regular hours, hand and body lotion,
and, "at my age, an ass like an ache, Joe would say, framed in
pantyhose and skinny niblets of underwear, skin plucked and
plumped like a marketable chicken, my rough spots chemi-
cally smoothed until I was slick as a church speaker seeking
funds."

One day, unintentionally, Wilma backed Ellen into a corner,
the conversation sliding like a car on a slick road right into
Why did you do it? Why did you leave Joe? Ellen, trapped—
Wilma uncomfortable—finally said:

"Somehow, Wilma, all that goodness was not enough. I was
a revolutionary without complaint, so the only thing I could
do was give it up, give it all up—that was the imperative and

there was no bargaining—including Joe, the real Joe, the real and true and straightforward Joe, to release him into a swarm of divorcées and untimely widows and the generally under-married knowing in full faith and, Jesus, my own heartbreak, that I was everything to him, all the average happinesses you could ever want; Joe who would say, *Ellen? Ellen's loony? Ellen's goofy? Ellen's nuts? Hell, she's my girl,* which is exactly what he would say because he's the kind of man who will not see badness, who will not *allow* the world to be anything less than perfect, so that it will only be on his deathbed, after a long and busy life, that his forehead will wrinkle and his eyes will squint, and it won't matter if I'm dead or alive by then be-cause it's just a thought, a nagging grunt that's been pestering him for years but he was always too busy to work it out, where he says to himself or whomever, a nurse, an old friend, some teenage aide to the elderly, where he says in a moment of high grandeur for him, his exact words, bite, spite, spit, and liquor all wrapped into a summary package: "I believe she re-ally kicked the dinkus out of me."

It was only later Wilma realized that Ellen hadn't an-swered her question, not at all.

11

ELLEN'S BULLET STOPPED at the first joint of a pinky finger of one man in a group of three. The beer in the man's hand was unscathed by the bullet and fell to the ground with an aluminic clunk.

Much of what happened next ultimately became public information. Corky Crépiter from Maine Public Radio actually drove up to Quilli. She had something of a "scoop" as they put it—her source unknown to anyone around here. For a long time it was assumed she'd gotten her information from her uncle Orville (Bud, of course, of Bud's Bar). That would turn out not to be true.

There were others from the news outlets, but if there was a media frenzy it was a quick frenzy. Maybe some of the media types were put off by the way so many Quillies break into the old French when they get excited. I like to think that, to think that they found us all a bunch of buffoonish goons who can barely handle English rather than to think they just didn't find what happened to Ellen important, newsworthy.

As I go through some quotes from the various records, some of it may sound stilted, awkward. It was difficult pulling a good translation out of the reports of the incident that were given in French. Wilma's school French was helpful, but as she becomes a player in all of this her usefulness lessens. The level of openness varied, too. Some people grew fond of the smell of fame, others found in it a stench.

The three men—Igor, Liam, and Pierre—were not hunters. They were friends who had driven out of Quillifarkeag to drink in the woods near Hunellia Faulk Ponus Pond not far from St. A de P. They were all under forty and had packed sandwiches and sleeping bags for when it was time to roll down and buzz for a while. They had bought their beer— three cases—at Bud's Bar in Quilli, but when Bud suggested they stay at the bar and drink and he'd even throw in a free ride home from Michelle's Taxi Company, Pierre, the oldest one, said, "Mr. Bud, now and then a man has to drink in the open, before his God."

Bud laughed and said, "Be careful, boys. That's nasty land up there. You don't want to find yourselves before your God before your time."

Igor, Liam, and Pierre had traditional wives who disapproved of nearly everything they did. These were the young wives of young men and the tradition of disapproval was a part of growing up.

Their mothers had berated their own men, had called them uncertain and hard to trust. The men, on their part, had scoffed. Their work was wretched. They knew how the sassy slap of a pine buck could push a lower jaw out through the brain and change a morning into eternity without a call for lunch. They knew the body could do anything, could answer any demand. They also knew it wore out in ways marked by no coming back. Work was abysmal, a fit punishment for the corruption of the soul.

The young wives, with their young men, called them immature and unfocused. They said they were good for a paycheck while their bodies held out, and then became just furniture after that. Unlike their fathers, however, the younger wives' men were finding less and less body-breaking work to do. They tended to live longer unmaimed, and tended, too, toward more of a gentle disgruntlement with life and its times than toward the pissed-off rage of their fathers. More and more, as they got older, they were confused over not being as bad as their wives said they were. Their wives shared this confusion.

Igor looked down at his finger. The hand shook, hard, and blood drops flew off of it.

"It has just went away," he said, to no one in particular.

One of them, Liam or Pierre, said, "What has?"

"My pinky part."

"The hell?"

Scenes of accidents become scenes in retrospect. Times and sequences were already important, although none of the young men knew that as Igor spoke, his voice wobbly.

"The end of this part. See?" He held his shaking hand up and then sat down on the ground. Hard. Nearly falling over.

Liam said, "Friend?"

"Are you about to lose anything else?" Pierre asked. He was smiling, the wound not his, unaware that it was anything more serious than a bug bite. "Checked your dick?"

Innocence was over all of them and they felt that, but body pieces, as Igor later said, didn't just fall off unless you lived near a landfill or worked for a bad company.

"This is," Liam said, "a heartbreaking wound. You can live without the finger piece, but less of you is going home than came here."

"I heard a shot," Pierre said, late with his information and finally serious. He could see that Igor was whiter in his face than he'd ever seen in any man.

Igor said, in a shaky voice, "A shot of what?"

"What?" Pierre was used to having only his wife question his words.

Liam said, "He's less than sensible for the moment, Pete. Leave him to be."

"A shot of gun," Pierre said. "That's what I heard."

"No." Liam thought they should do something for Igor.

"No, what? Yes, sir. I heard what I heard."

"Then you think this man has been shot?" asked Liam, a whole world of possibilities scrambling around in his mind: newspapers, television, long explanations (some having to do with an absence from work), courtroom appearances, bandages, and the smell of hospital alcohol.

"You think some critter just leaped out of the ground and bit the titty off his pinky?" Pierre countered.

"I have no thoughts," Liam answered. "I'm using yours and I don't like them."

"Maybe we should not stand here?" Pierre said.

Liam took a hankie, clean and ironed—his wife still ironed his hankies, his shorts, too, but, as he later said, his shorts were not available for presurgical dressings—and wrapped the wound. He tied it with some gray electrical tape he had in his coat pocket.

"Igor?" Liam asked.

"I am all right," Igor said.

"You've never been all right, friend."

"I am now."

"Then I don't recommend the cure." Liam put two aspirin in Igor's mouth and handed him a can of beer.

"You always carry aspirin around?" Igor asked.

"We came here to drink, didn't we?"

"Makes sense."

Pierre had moved away from the other two, a thought in his mind of investigation. He looked up the hill from which the bullet—he thought—must have come. The pond was to his back and nearly a mile across. It was unlikely anything could have come all that way to hurt Igor.

It was unlikely, too, he thought, that anything could have come down that hill without a hard mind and an acute aim behind it, something going right after the tiniest part of Igor's parts.

Odd, Pierre decided. Sharply odd.

Igor was a friendly, even gregarious person. He was foolish sometimes, Pierre told me, as good-looking men can be, but Pierre didn't think anyone would want to shoot him except maybe his wife, and then only on principle.

Pierre began to think they should hide. This was an angering thing, but you never knew who might be in the woods these days. Tourists were all over the place, not all of them looking for beauty, not all of them innocent, either, of smuggling powders and smokeables across the border from New Brunswick or Nova Scotia. There were people, too, who just wanted to hear what it sounded like when a bullet hit a body, while others—technicians, Pierre thought—saw guns as equipment, tools, something to be used. If a gun wasn't going to be used, why invent it? Why buy it? The police, he knew, might laugh at that and speak only of prevention, but how could you know you were preventing anything unless you actually pulled back the hammer and *prevented* once in a while?

Still, fighting back was always an issue. Nothing in you wanted that. Fear kept telling you this was a normal day and that courage was for another time. Something else, though, a harsher thing: you gave in, or you did not. It didn't matter if you didn't know, really, what had happened, if Igor had truly been shot in his hand pinky, if someone was still up there in the humps and shallows, aiming a gun at you—or not. The fear, too, might be baseless, silly, but if the legs said run, the heart said no—you cannot do that.

Pierre's cheeks flushed pink, the unpink sections as white as Igor's face. They had no weapons, only beer.

Shadows were beginning and confusion was working its way among the resting men. Igor's wound had subsided from a crisis to a situation. Someone had raised the question of finding the pinky part so that it could be surgically glued. This devil, another said, left no trash behind. But all of them were technological enough to check the scraps in the shoreline rubble anyway. Medicine increasingly said no to fewer and fewer people so it had been worth a look.

"I heard once," Liam said, "of a guy who chopped a thumb off in a trap. He put it in a plastic bag and peed on it and they got it back just fine."

Pierre noticed Igor had peed, but it hadn't been into any plastic bag. The man did not look good, and Pierre felt ashamed over the unkind thought about Igor's wife shooting him. He hoped he wouldn't have to tell her something terrible before this was all over. Could a man die from a pinky wound?

"Okay?" Pierre said.

"I just wanted to say that," Liam answered.

"So you have."

Liam finally said: "Does anyone not live far from here?" He looked at neither Pierre nor Igor, said it to the darkening woods.

"Joe's old lady," Pierre said. "Used to be. I think she still is."

"Who?" Igor asked. He seemed weak but relaxed.

"Joe DeLay. He put me a roof on my house."

"He lives here?"

"Ellen."

"Which is?" Liam asked.

"A woman, maybe his wife, but I think she busted up on Joe. I don't know. They say she has light ways, too, but I don't know what's true."

"Light ways?"

"Who knows?"

Pierre said later he wasn't sure they needed help, and help was so often much worse than whatever needed helping. Besides, if they needed help they could just leave. There had been no more bullets. There had been no sign that puffs and zips of gunshot bullets would follow their getting into the truck and getting the hell out of there. They could do that. They could do anything. But running out—he didn't know. Sometimes bravery just meant sitting down on a rock and having a beer.

Ellen DeLay, though—Pierre said his first thoughts came down to her pretty quickly. There had been so many stories about her and Joe, difficult gossip you didn't even want to listen to—the way it was when a marriage went up a tree. But this Ellen was not a stupid person, so he'd heard. She was working out here, doing something, and Pierre thought maybe it wasn't far from where they were just then. She might be trapping, there was still good money in that. He was pretty sure she could dress something out for you, too. She might even be damn good at it, he thought he'd heard: no one faster, neater, or tighter in ripping down and folding out a bear; a good cutter in deer season—fancy packages you'd swear came from Don's Grocery down in Quilli.

Rumors, the leading edge of truth. Everyone talked and was talked about. In shaky times, especially, the talk got weird, even though it was the tales of aberrance, harsher and harsher, that held things together. Better to be thought a crazed and craven individual than not to be thought about at all, because that's when people got tense and worried, sent the wardens out or the social workers and then you had law in your life and that was never a good thing. Better to be a nut verified, he finally decided, than a normal person under suspicion.

Pierre thought they should drink a little more before this all got out of hand. He thought maybe they should drink a lot.

12

BY THE TIME I GOT to the third tape and the end of the phone call between Ellen and Wilma, the engineer had boarded the train and was beginning to get the big diesels going. As she climbed the berm and saw me sitting on the train, she came over and offered me a cup of coffee from her Thermos. Melissa Fantapper is the daughter of Maheska Fantapper, owner of Le Père's, Quilli's snobby gin mill. Melissa used to play basketball with Wilma and didn't seem concerned that I was camped out on the front porch of her train. Quilli has a lot of places where you can be alone, but it would be untoward to question someone's choice of a place that comforted him.

"Karen and I will be leaving as soon as she gets here," she said. "She's a late sleeper, though. Don't know how she does it."

In other words, relax, Splotchy. Enjoy your coffee.

Ellen felt no joy of chase this time, Wilma said. The moose had done itself in; she had only registered the final score. The end of any killing, however, was complicated. She walked home for some burlap bags and her log skidder, then came back and, cutting quickly and well, emptied the innards of the moose into the bags. The moose, whole, was too heavy. She needed to spread the weight around. The skidder that she'd made from birch saplings and three wheels from an ATV would hold anything, but that didn't mean she could pull it. The moose, dead, was a thousand pounds.

She carried the bags of entrails home and put them in the freezer to be tended to later. The head—another cut that was swift and clean—was a harder carry, a more intimate struggle, arms around the neck or through the rack. An odd, yet not unknown, sensation arose in the carrying, too.

A migration of ticks was taking place. She thought alcohol—vodka, perhaps—drunk neat, might be a deterrent, but after the head and neck were home there would be no more of this close carrying. She stopped for a moment on the small hill overlooking her house, put the head down on the ground, and slapped at her dress. A dusting of the ticks fell off. Already, though, she could see tick butts on her arms and legs. They were digging in, permanence a special hope.

By late afternoon she was sitting next to the stream as naked, she told Wilma, as bread dough, a bottle of vodka on one side of her, a jar of kerosene on the other. With a cotton swab she dabbed a drop of kerosene on a tick butt, then eased it out with a tweezers. Occasionally, she would ignite the drop with her cigarette lighter. She took care to puff the flame out quickly as the bug wiggled out frantically. The vodka made precision in the deticking possible, Ellen's movements smooth.

She was thinking of Joe. A long time had passed and she still couldn't imagine living without him, yet she had been doing just that. There had been nothing legal, litigious: no separation, no parsimonious squabbling over property, no divorce. She supposed he was seeing other women; was having dinners of his favorite casseroles; his laundry done; sex, too, on a well-made bed, Joe nothing if not polite. Pissy Philomene came to mind. She was their age, a carpenter, maybe more muscular than Joe might prefer, but Ellen imagined the woman would throw an energetic fuck. *I'll just take my tool belt off here and wash the grout from my hands.*

Or Michelle Monelle, the cabdriver—Bud Crépiter's ex. She would outweigh Joe, big as Joe was at six-two, but she had that same manner as Joe: open to the world, trusting. And she had tits. God love the man who'd love you for your teeth. Joe joked with Ellen once about how she, Ellen, was a fine size, good collarbones—as if he were measuring her for a porch swing—a fine angle. With his carpenter's level he'd shown her breasts to be plumb with the earth—a good sign. They'd been young, very young. Sex had been easier back then; being sexual had not. She'd thought it funny how those things reversed themselves as you got older.

Joe had contacted a lawyer only because there was a business now, Ellen's business, and he'd wanted clarity on matters of liability and indebtedness.

A good business, yes—the taking apart of life and repackaging it: the skinning and gutting and cutting, some tanning, though not too much since she wasn't at all good at it, and no taxidermy. The last thing she wanted to do was to pretend that anything that was dead wasn't dead.

The money was good—astoundingly good—but she bartered, too, because that was what poor ladies did, and her customers needed to see a poor lady out in the woods. They wanted wood fires and outhouses and that foxy line of dirt-sweat draining down into cleavage and she gave them that. It was what they expected, so naturally such a woman had to be helped out. Someone had wired her buildings up to the Quilli Township code, another had given her a safe woodstove and chimney, and someone else had dug a new well. Early on in all of this—1991 and 1992—when Joe visited, she could see him nosing out these benchmarks. He'd approved, though he'd said nothing. There was, then, a new tautness to his words, a sadness, that revealed a worry that something more was being traded than skillfully cut venison. But there, too, he would not comment. A wife had a right to privacy.

"I got out the letter today, Wilma." Wilma says on the tape Ellen's sentences were starting to slur so badly they sounded like one word.

The letter, though. Ellen had never gotten over Joe's letter. Its pages were wrinkled and spotted with whatever happened to be near where she laid it down after reading it, blood and gravy most often.

"On this last afternoon of her life," Wilma says, "remember it, Pop, August 12, 1994—" There's a catch in her voice as she says it, the details never failing to wound. "Ellen said the letter was dotted with ticks and a splotch or two of mud."

Ellen had been struck as much by the profundity of Joe's having written it as by anything he'd said, though he'd said a lot and all of it was sweet and moody, the sort of thing two people who'd found communion in silence after many years would say if they were really forced to say it. *Here's the inside,* Joe seemed to say. *Here it is. Take a look.*

Then there was the labor of it, the care with which he must have shopped his brain for the words. The letter was dated July 11, 1992, and postmarked July 27—typical for Joe, Ellen said, since it would have taken him a long time to write and he would have let it sit around for a while to make sure it fit the natural order of things—and had come about because of a smart-ass remark, something she'd said when he'd visited one time, "at least a year, maybe two years," she told Wilma, after she'd crossed a rainy street in St. A de P and found destiny at the desk of Vendrum Ponus—"time enough, Wilma, that we shouldn't have been still hurting each other, but I think I hurt him. I really do."

She'd been on the cutting patio with an old black bear laid out in front of her when she'd said it to Joe, the smart-ass remark, a joke in a way, and she was dressed in hardly anything and feeling vulnerable with him around, dressed half-naked because the animal juices could fly, and she was more readily washable than anything she might put on except the vinyl rain outfit. That would have been too hot that day and much too bright in its gaudy yellow for Joe's mood.

And he had been moody, a certain bitterness clashing with a certain generosity, a feeling of waste, he said. He kept telling her he didn't care for the radio being on and could she turn it off and she hadn't, this woman with both a college degree and bear bile on nipples Joe had once sucked, and an air of contentment about her that made him miss the electric bitterness he'd always felt a need to tend gently.

"When a man says he misses your pain," she told Wilma, "he's missing a lot more than that."

Several times that day and on other days he'd asked Ellen to tell him what was wrong, what he had done, so that he could undo it and she could join him back in Quilli and all the sensible things could start again.

"With me?" Ellen said to Wilma. Wilma stops there for a long time, the tape running.

A tune came on the radio that took them both back years and years, to a smaller town and, maybe, smaller lives;

cars anyone could fix and only one channel on television; no zip codes or credit cards or scares about anything other than DDT; a Cold War nobody ever honestly believed would become a hot war; a time when even nostalgia meant nothing more than a toothless sweetness from some grandparent who lived no more than two doors and one street away. Nostalgia was worse than cancer when you were over forty, Ellen said, so when that special tune came on she asked Joe, asked his mood or whatever part of him was still with her as they both listened to the song, "Want to dance with a bloody woman, Joe?" and he thought, she knew, she meant she was having her period, since Joe could look right at her and deny that his wife was covered with bear blood in a minimally habitable shack, wearing only a towel around her waist, because Ellen knew Joe just couldn't look at anything anywhere and think to himself, *Isn't this unusual?* because nothing in Joe's life was, could be, unusual, not even me, Ellen thought again and again.

"Dance with you?" Joe asked.

"It's an old song. Remember how we used to dance all the time, down at Bud's?"

"When it wasn't Bud's?"

"Right."

"The Shake Me Break Me?"

"Yup."

"Friday nights," Joe said.

"More faithful than churchgoers."

"I believe we were."

"A quarter for the jukebox, wasn't it? Three songs for a quarter?"

"I was a good dancer, wasn't I?"

"Yes you were, Joe."

"But you, Ellen."

"Yes?"

"You were hot."

"Joe!"

"That's what everyone said."

"I only danced with you."

"I know that."

"Hot?"

"Wild woman. 'You got yourself a wild woman,' someone would say to me when I was in taking a leak."

"It all meant something, too, Joe."

"What did?"

"The music, our music. It was like every song just dug right in and said here, do this, or here, be that."

"Did it work?" Joe asked.

"What?"

"Did you do it or be it?"

"I think I did, Joe."

"Took a long time, didn't it?"

"Yes, it did."

Joe said, sure, he would dance with her again, he would do anything for her, anything at all, which was how Ellen's unfortunate—"smart-ass," she repeated—comment came about, the joke she made that would lead poor Joe to that precipice of articulation that forced such a long letter out of him.

Joe took Ellen into his arms and they danced, the motivating song having given way by then to a commercial, a jingle, his love seeming no less of something just because it was being hammered out on the sweet anvil of toothpaste sales. Ellen said to Joe, a cool niceness about her because she knew how awkward he felt: "It's all right."

Joe said then to his own wife of more than two decades something he had never said to her before, "I am attracted to you, Ellen."

Ellen felt the towel around her waist slip to the floor. She didn't mind because Joe was actually dancing with her, about as loose as a piece of oak paneling but dancing anyway. She thought it gracious, too, charming in Joe's bumpy way, how, even though they were alone in a small clearcut, alone in the back of a private dwelling, no people anywhere, not at all, her own house with small rugs, and shades on the lamps but no order at all, he, Joe, remembered it was still a business and that she just then was a naked businesswoman, so he pulled the wrinkled hankie from his pocket and held it across her backside even as she said, the smart-ass comment, her innocent joke, "I bet you say that to all the girls, Joe."

She told Wilma Joe just gently released her, then turned around and left.

"She never saw him again," Wilma said, ending the tape just as Melissa cranks out a massive thwack on the diesel's horn.

13

THOSE BOYS—LIAM, IGOR, AND PIERRE—were not hard to talk to. They met me at Bud's several times, and one day we even took a drive out to Ponus Pond near St. A de P. They all thought it was strange how the events of that day and night—now over two years in the past—just would not fade away.

All they asked of me was that I not let their wives know that we'd had these meetings, that we'd talked.

It was Pierre, they all agreed, who finally began to get things moving that afternoon. He said he didn't know if there was such a thing as group shock, but he said it began to seem as though they'd been standing around with their toes up their noses long enough for Igor to grow several new hand pinkies.

His first thought, he said, was that they should find out if this Ellen had shot Igor to his hand pinky. Truly, if it had been her, then other thoughts wouldn't be necessary.

Liam didn't think it was a good idea.

"There would be apologies," Pierre said. "She could offer to pay for treatment."

"What treatment?" Liam asked.

"This brave friend has knocked on the door of death but someone said, 'We're on break.' There is still infection to consider, though, and I'm sure a stitch or two to be taken. This is some money these days."

Liam, growing impatient, finally said, "We'll report this to the legal authorities. Why would we do anything else?"

Igor looked up at Liam then and said "Because my wife will think me stupid."

Pierre laughed. "I have heard her talk. 'Stupid' would be an improvement."

"Asshole," Igor said. "I would think, instead, of some heroic deed I did. It cost me a knuckle but there was gratitude in it."

"Gratitude?"

"For what I did," said Igor.

"What did you do?" asked Pierre.

"A great deed."

"Oh."

There seemed no other course, Liam and Pierre finally agreed. Igor was still trying to come up with a story, something better than having a beer can shot out of his hand and taking a nose-picker with it.

Liam called Cary Andersen, provost in Quilli Township, on the phone in his pocket. I guess that call piqued someone's interest down at the *Bangor Daily News* because they put together one of those shaded boxes in the paper that shows how things got going that afternoon.

Cary told Liam she'd transfer him to the sheriff, who transferred him to the warden service since the story sounded like a hunting accident, although Cary, a few minutes later, decided she might as well take a look, since there was no crime in Quilli Township that day. The sheriff dispatched Anna Pancake who was looking into some spousal abuse near St. A de P, Cary and Anna pulling into the woods near the lake at the same time as Warden Debbie St. H, who was followed by State

Trooper Valerie Dooble who'd heard the whole thing on her radio. Trooper Dooble switched the videocam on in her car as she parked because it sounded like the sort of thing where drunkenness and unruly behavior might be involved. It is not rare in Maine that troopers are lured to remote spots with false reports of abductions, rape, or drug transactions, there to be humiliated by large groups of revelers sometimes happy, sometimes mean. Troopers can lose good portions of clothing, occasionally weapons. Sometimes they're beaten.

Pierre watched the arrivals and thought they seemed an odd, disconnected bunch. He wasn't sure he knew all of them. He'd expected maybe one cop, someone to take a report, to stare around meaningfully and conclude there was no risk of further gunfire.

"Sometimes they're just supposed to tell you what you already know," he told me. "That's how bad times end."

Cary Andersen he knew of, a strapping short *chienne*, a rough puppy by reputation and someone to be avoided— bruised knuckles and black hair as short as a banker's mustache.

"Dangerous," he had told Liam once, though it had only been a lunch conversation. "That provost thing is just whatever it wants to be. I have heard no good things about that Andersen woman."

"Noydland's girl?"

"Who?"

"Joyg Noydland," Liam said.

"I don't—"

"Township manager? He made the job. He put her in it. A little civics now and then, my friend."

"—get where you're going with this," Pierre added.

"Still—my opinion?"

"I'm listening."

"I think she's pretty, kind of thoughtful, too. A little deep."

"Or bitchy."

"But a cop," Liam said.

"Yes?"

"A pretty cop."

"Oh, man."

Liam walked over and shook hands with Debbie St. H from the warden's service, who was trying to be in charge of things. She was wearing a brown T-shirt and camouflage pants and was relacing a boot as Liam introduced himself. She'd been on the Pappadapsikeag most of the day. Liam noticed that her canoe, mounted on top of a Jeep, had a big hole in the bow. He also said her hair, blond and buggy, needed a good touch with one of those little hand vacuums. Her biceps, though—he noticed veins crossing over like something on a skinny man's neck. Debbie St. H asked Liam if he'd been shot.

"Not me," Liam said, but she'd already turned away and was talking to Anna Pancake, deputy sheriff.

Liam, disinterestedly received, turned away and noticed Trooper Dooble kneeling next to Igor. A first-aid kit was by her side and she was cutting away the electrical tape and Liam's nearly new hankie from Igor's hand.

"This is a lot of fuss for one man's hand pinky," he said, in English, to Valerie Dooble. She did not look away from the wound as she said:

"Did you shoot this man?"

"That's a powerful question to ask of friends," Liam replied. "Good friends, the three of us."

Valerie Dooble, finished with the wound, stood then. Liam noticed she was well taller than he. She had blue eyes, he said, though he never felt confident in judging eye color. The tiniest of rings was in one of her nostrils, the stone attached matching those eyes.

Impatience was part of Trooper Dooble's job, being friendly was less so. She stood close enough to Liam that he could see a loose eyelash under her eye. She did not flinch as Liam brushed it away.

"Not me," Liam finally said in French.

Liam noticed that Cary Andersen was talking to Pierre. "We have no firearms. We are drinking boys here to drink."

Trooper Dooble shrugged, said nothing.

"And camp," Liam continued. "Morning will find us clear-eyed, only slightly remunerative of gut." He felt obligated, in this close presence of the trooper, to feel guilty about something but they—the three of them—were on the forgiving side of all laws. Innocence, he told me, is not necessarily comfortable.

Cary Andersen saw the wounding as yet another symptom, and she'd been not at all private in sharing that view. Anyone who talked to Cary got a lecture on the collective fraying of our moral fiber, and it was not hard to find those people so that I could begin to build some kind of picture of just who this Cary Andersen was.

There was sickness in Quilli Township, Cary would say again and again, things that shouldn't be happening. Town was town and whether it was Quilli or St. A de P or Quiktupac, decay was evident and would not be stopped. The good churches were empty, the slatternly ones filled. Business at the Parental Guidance Clinic, where she had once worked, was booming, a consequence of "No" nearly always meaning "Yes." Sobriety, as far as she could tell, was increasingly viewed as a not at all desirable condition. And children, like dogs barking in the night, had lost all sense of direction and knew only fear.

Expected things. But in Quilli Township the earth was supposed to slap its face every morning and wake up fresh, rot and decay a function of biology and not moral depravity. Grandeur was supposed to be the least of all superlatives, the seasons alone ringing in majesty and delight like some grand, cosmic carillon. A thousand years of orderly propagation, of mountainous upheaval, and the surgical carving of iconic witchery by stream and river was meant to give people a grasp of their own mysteries and a sense of the joy at being the only creatures that could breathe the beauty deeply and then shudder in humility.

"It's all wicked skewed now," Cary said, her words bold and accurately quoted in the *Portland Press Herald.*

Expected things. The heinous was in her township now, the depraved. People were lost, the way back home filled with risk and agony. In the simplest way she could think it, there was order and there were people. It was conflict and it made sense. What also made sense to her, Joyg Noydland told me in one of the few chances I had to talk to him, was the mediator in this conflict, the touchstone of peace in Quilli Township. It was Cary Andersen.

"She liked to look at her job description," he said, the man cold and not at all likeable, "creatively."

Cary's official report says as much about her as it does about Ellen, and while Poison Gorelick has a lot to say about Cary, her own words in all of this are so scant it might be good to let her speak.

"I had a good idea what had happened. I knew Ellen DeLay. I knew the stories about Ellen, but didn't believe for a moment that Ellen was crazy. I'd have to admit, though, that for all the loose nesters up country, I'd never known anyone with as many stories swirling around her: that she was a retired intelligence operative; that she was an active intelligence operative, a million dollars in electronic gear squirreled into the scraps and bundles of trash she called home; that she was actually Colombian, a drug princess off on her own, slowly working a stranglehold onto civilization; that she was a cult figure, young people constantly in attendance, a relentless appetite carving out a hell of unredeemable sexual license; that she was a whore, treating her hunters to something more than a few pounds of packaged meat for a price; or just a drunk.

"A businesswoman is the most accurate label. I didn't doubt a certain core of it, that thought that arose in the hunter's mind, especially hunters of the sort increasingly stumbling through the woods in recent years: What do I do now? Few of them even know how to gut and field dress a kill, though they're well aware there are only so many miles you can drive with some piece of unemptied carrion draped over hood or trunk. Ellen was an answer to that problem and I accepted that, although it wasn't an answer to the question nobody ever bothered to ask: Why had Ellen thrown over a perfectly good marriage to go and live in a place where the sum total of civilization meant a single electrical wire and a single phone wire?"

QUILLIFARKEAG, MAINE
(Sexual Mores)

"Was you always faithful, Poison?" Bud asks.

"Faithful?" Poison says.

"To your wife. Like just her."

"I wasn't married a year, Bud. Beverly died. You know that."

"I see."

"You?"

"Me and Michelle?"

"You and Michelle. She was your wife."

"I tried it once. I don't know about Michelle."

"You tried it once. What does it mean that you tried it once?"

"Being faithful to someone else."

"And?"

"I didn't like it."

14

WILMA HAD READ Joe's letter because Ellen wanted her to. So when Ellen said during that bizarre, late-night call (that Wilma recounted for me on those tapes), "I did the letter again today," Wilma knew exactly what was happening. Ellen wanted to talk about love and Wilma didn't want her to talk about love. Ellen "on" love was Ellen walking a far galaxy, forsythia girding her waist, rhinestones studding her shoes; Ellen alluding to not only Rimbaud, but also Hobbes—maybe Joyce Brothers; Ellen (Wilma nearly angry) reciting from memory the entirety of her and Joe's wedding so long ago, even remembering the pastor's words. Wilma often said, *Go back to him.* Ellen wouldn't hear of it.

I have Joe's letter. He found it in Ellen's things and gave it to me because he thought I might find it useful. He also said he never wanted to see it again.

Joe wrote as though the conversation were still going on, wrote on wide-lined paper with three holes on the side. He wrote for three days, even putting off some jobs because it was tedious how his mind would race and his hand would go so slow.

"I suppose you would think that," was his first sentence.

Who wouldn't think that? A man all alone—so? This is a long time. He must have an awful need for sex, a crazed need. What a word, hey? A crazy need. He's beside himself because he's not beside anyone else. Ellen, dear, let me tell you about sex, about poor Joe and Joe's need for sex, and then you can throw this away because we are uncomfortable.

I was talking to Brenda the other day. Do you remember her? "Tight body" we used to say, something like that. Real hips, real waist, real boobs, and a butt that says hello in ways no one speaks anymore. (Do you remember "hubba, hubba, hubba"?) I know you seen me look at her before and I know you thought Joe is such a tomcat in his eyes, and even if you didn't believe it I'd still have to tell you there were things in her that just weren't me. I was not aroused. Like any man, if some woman don't seem to be bed-right, maybe she can be all right. How does that work? I liked her because she didn't stir me up? I honestly think a woman picks up on that damn quick, even if for nobody's fault there's kind of a putdown there. It must, still, be a good feeling that someone's not after you only for the bathroom parts, and it's not like she knew I cared only for her mind, as the joke goes. You don't have to talk to Brenda for long to know her mind is generally geared-up to handle only the next few minutes and "How are you?" and "That's pretty funny," and she's not a stupid person, only someone rising to the demands made of her and those aren't much. Like most of the world, if you're alive today then yesterday was a success and that's that.

But Brenda, I think this even if I will sound to you something crass, knew she could come up to me and say, "Hey, Joe, let's go somewheres and you can screw my brains into yogurt" (you know what I think of yogurt,

Ellen), and I would have said, meaning it, too, "Let's just talk, Brenda," and I don't think it's much for a woman to sense that you have some really old need for her and most of the available body holes can be left out of it.

So we talked and she told me her husband had left her. This is sad. She said he left her for a high school kid and he kept telling her the girl was an honors student and she made a joke about that. She said she was going to have a bumper sticker made at the print shop that said, My Husband's Trollop Is An Honors Student At St. Bleufard's. I had to look up "trollop," a hard job since in your mind you can spell it many ways.

What do I say to all the girls? You asked me that and you might have stuck a nail in my eye because it was a hard thing to say even though we were at the time being pretty good to each other. I think you meant it not the way you meant it, so this is why I'm here with this paper and all these words I guess to tell you how it is, Ellen, when a guy gets left, and where you are thinking me some happy guy with a plow for a dick (excuse me).

It's like I'm bleeding all over for you, Ellen, and hearing your painfulness and smelling your painfulness and living your painfulness and you won't let me have a part of it, and all of a sudden I'm doing the same thing for Brenda, whose husband left her for someone who puts rubbers on tampons just because at her age she thinks that has something to do with pregnancy. Well, anyway, so Brenda thinks me a prince because I listen to her a lot and I listen to a lot of people a lot, though maybe not you as much as you want because we have been together so long that everything around us, I mean everything, like our house and the towels in the kitchen and old chairs, rugs, lightbulbs; shoot, Ellen, food in the cupboard and something about wash coming out of the washer and pieces of dirt on a shovel you used to plant flowers with, and magazines with your name on them, now so old that new ones aren't coming anymore—all of that, the things around me, us, that was all a kind of listening because it was like we were a puzzle and as we got more and more of those pieces around there was more and more to us, too. So how could anyone say I didn't hear you when you started throwing all that stuff away after you got locked in the toolbox? I heard you. I *heard* you.

Anyway, it's the saddest thing to say to someone— you, Ellen—that the house isn't the same without you. It is not only a person missing but shadows and darknesses too, and there's light where you used to sit and that's all wrong, and in a way that's not my imagination I sometimes hear your voice, "Beans, Joe?" or "Have you seen my purse?" which is another way of saying my own mind has been getting a little bruised so the rest of this is probably all made up. I don't know for sure since my dreams these days seem to be more and more like things I'm living and the stuff I live is a whole lot like a big dream so who can tell these things?

Like one day I just flat out say to Brenda, "Brenda," I say, "let's go somewhere, maybe just down to Pizzle's Inn where you can take your clothes off and I'll look at your body and admire it because it's a nice body and I want to see it and tell you that." I'll even tell her that Ellen and I had always heard she had a tattoo somewhere and a thing or two pierced on her body, things you think of about women who paint their toenails bright red. What'd you used to say, Ellen? "Landing lights"? And maybe that'll be true, the holes and the pierced rings and things. Mutilation is always better than loneliness.

By this time I'm naked, too—if it happened, Ellen, if it was ever real—and Brenda, in whatever ways a woman does that, is prepared, reconciled—eager? But what I wanted, you see, from Brenda, was not a standard thing, and it's why I did take offense when you said there must be a lot of girls in my life. I got into bed with her, see, and we worked our arms and legs around in a way she wasn't expecting until we were face-to-face (they really are big boobs, kiddo, and they were resting on my chest) and we were breathing each other's breath and we were so close I could feel her waiting for something, but I just had a thought here so let me stop a second I want to write in a special way:

Isn't this something for a man to tell his wife?

and to get on with it. I could feel her eyelashes blink against my eyelashes. I could feel her body heat like a hard perfume rushing into me and mine into her, could feel a coolness, too, and that heat was nice, and way down somewhere our feet and toes were touching and there was something so personal about that, I smiled once against her lips and she could feel it. She smiled, too. Never has there been a kiss that went farther inside a man than that one and it wasn't even a kiss. I turned until she was almost on top of me and it seemed like for the first time in my life I could feel the *weight* of a woman, something a long time coming and it seemed important, like here was something being the way it was supposed to be, a bulk of hope that should have been you, Ellen, just the weight of both of us, love bulky, fat.

Eventually, there was wetness on my chest and on my face. There was wetness all over because Brenda was crying and I will tell you this maybe I was, too. I think I was. I didn't mind it.

I said to her, "I hurt real bad."

She said, "He's gone forever and I'm too young for that."

That had a horror full of meaning to her. It was like we were both turning into this awful glob of hurt of a selfish kind that had to be gotten away from, and yet still we each had to say, "well, here's where it's bad for me," and "here's where it's bad for you." These little confessions were like labels giving directions, telling of sites where interesting things were happening though you could sure as hell put off the visit. We could smell each other's sweat, and her smell made me feel like I'd been with her a long time, had gone through everything with her, her colds and her doubts and her bad days and the meals she ate, the soft happiness of a good old chair at the end of a day, and suddenly everything's gone. It's like everything's closed up, no one's doing business anymore so where do you go and how do you handle it?

The most of sex that it got was that she put a couple of fingers in my mouth. She didn't hurt me and I think her fingers were clean. But it was like my teeth and lips and like my jaw was some kind of ledge she couldn't get up on but she couldn't let go of either. So she just held on and she stopped crying and then she started again and it was the same with me, too. We held each other in the longest hug that wasn't sex at all or maybe it was, maybe it was only sex of a kind people don't think about anymore.

Ellen said she stopped reading for a while. She put the letter down and placed the vodka bottle on top of it. She got up—"drunk in the afternoon, buddy; doesn't happen often"—unsteadily, and walked into the stream. The ticks were gone, at least the ones she could reach. Careful as she'd been, there was still a light film of kerosene on her arms and legs and chest and stomach. A burning fuzzed around her stomach skin and she was pinking up. She thought she had some lotion from Don's Grocery, something Wilma had bought. That would help.

The stream was shallow and she wallowed around in the mud to wash off the kerosene. She moved upstream from the cloudy water then and rinsed the mud away. As clean as she needed to be, she lay back on the rocks of the stream bed. The water flowed over her and took some of the vodka smell away, the kerosene, too, so she wouldn't smell like an overworked stove on a frigid day.

"Am I boring you, Wilma?"

Wilma said she could talk about Joe all she wanted. She, Wilma, had seen him just that day. Did Ellen know he had one of those personal license plates on his truck now? No, Ellen said, and wanted to know what it was.

Miss U.

The ultimate sex act, one big fucking hug (excuse me). That's your sex-crazed, daring single guy, Ellen, and that's what he says to all the girls. Poor Brenda. She has that motherly smile that could start a car on a cold day. We walk a lot, see, often with our arms across each other's backs, hips touching. Mostly, though, we hold hands, another one of those things I think is, well, pretty genital. Hands have that kind of dirt-thing that's maybe behind what's put you out there in the emptiness. I don't know. I can understand that more in a man than in a woman, but I guess with so much that women are doing these days they ought to be able to go to ground, too, to sit in the woods and pull spiders from their belly buttons if it's time for them to do that.

Sometimes Brenda's hands are dirty and this gets to me even more, since just by holding hands I feel like I'm a part of all the things she has to do, a part of her *life* in its "here's today" part. I clean with her and hold and manage the messes and say "yes" in the way of saying be here, be now, be with me, which is what I want to say to you but you've decided that's not enough, that I'm okay (I know that) but I'm not enough. So I stretch myself thin atop dirty dreams, which of course aren't all that dirty even though they keep coming out, just hold me, feel me, love me, talk to me, be right here beside me when I wake and let's have coffee at three in the afternoon. I only wish I could say this really pretty because I think my thoughts right now are up there with the great people.

Maybe you just don't want to hear my words anymore, you're beyond words and that's dangerous, and you're beyond me, which is probably not hard to do, so all right, Ellen, all right I suppose. Maybe I'm not the jewel I could think I am. I am certainly not the success I always

wanted to be, and I even used to be better-looking, so I'm
not sure what compelling promise I could lay before you
other than saying there isn't anybody on the earth who
has been with you longer than this Joe here (me), who
truly knows you and knows all the things you're always
trying to break out of and why it's good that you try to
do that and I think that's something, honestly I do, something of value in a world gone cheap to where it seems
like every single thing that's done is planned and plotted
and scripted and a man's instincts and a woman's intu-
itions have been laughed away, a person, one link to
other links, to other times and good times, where it's the
people who are with you who carry you into tomorrow
and without them you hang and all the days are like all
the days. I think to myself I'm the fantasy, I'm the dream
and I can do it for you because there isn't anything else
I'm here for and you don't want it, Ellen, you don't want
me and you don't want tomorrow and today doesn't
seem all that wonderful and all of that's a sad thing, the
saddest thing I think I've ever seen.

15

IN A PLACE LIKE QUILLI, problems belong to those who find them in their hands. It is a corollary of autonomy, but there is also that of necessity about it, perhaps some practical wisdom, too. When things go wrong in a rugged place, it is a measure of worth that one solve one's own problems, a measure, too, of fitness for citizenship. There are also contained in such notions certain barriers to meddling, to judgment. If a solution cost an arm, a child, maybe a marriage, *you weren't there* comes quickly to the fore, followed by, *who in the hell are you to tell me?*

Those women up there, the officers, knew these things. Certainly Cary Andersen and Anna Pancake did. Valerie Dooble, early in the evening of that day, was actually thinking some of them, and Debbie St. H was incapable of seeing life in any other way, a consequence of her many small woodlands heroics (ironically, since it was most often she who came upon those for whom the call to self-help was ringing up a busy signal).

"You solve the problem," Val Dooble said one afternoon in Bud's. "You just do it. You get the job done." Anna and Debbie were also there, and they didn't so much nod in agreement with Val as they seemed to give a bored shrug of the shoulders over the self-evidence of what she was saying.

"Look, Mr. Doll," Val began. "We had a volatile situation

on our hands and it was up to us to calm it down—even if we didn't know what it was. Our job is like that—a lot."

It was getting late, however, and if they knew nothing else they did know one thing: a man had been shot. "That gets you up on your toes," Debbie St. H said, "real high."

Cary Andersen was standing near her Chevrolet, her service revolver, a shotgun, and a rifle on the car's trunk lid. She asked Deb if Deb was all right and Deb said she had the two .30-06s, one with a scope, and her grandfather's old Colt Peacemaker.

"A Peacemaker?" Val asked.

"It's a kind of reassurance for the old guys," Debbie said.

"Real old guys," Val said.

"A little show," Debbie said. "Sometimes that's all you need."

Val Dooble and Anna Pancake were similarly equipped, although when Val mentioned that she had tear gas in her car, both Debbie St. H and Cary said to leave it. Neither Debbie nor Cary had gas masks and besides, Cary said, it was woodsy and weedy up there, and it would be dark and murky enough and, anyway, wouldn't it be best just to get the woman out of the house and talking, sober her up if she was drunk? Get her talking—had she done any shooting today?—give her a little field sobriety work.

"Routine, troopers," Cary said, "keep it routine and then—"

Anna, Val, and Debbie looked at Cary.

"Then?" Val said.

"We shoot her."

"Jesus," Anna said, her voice a whisper.

"It's a joke," said Cary. "Lighten up."

"But you know her, right?" Val asked. "You said that ear-lier."

"On and off I have," Cary said. "She was a good woman down in Quilli but she stepped out of that. She might still be a good woman, but a lot think she's gone wicked creepy."

"So—" Anna started.

Cary interrupted her: "Could she shoot a man?"

Val Dooble had put her flak jacket on and was standing near Cary and sharing a cigarette with Debbie St. H. Val said quickly, "*Did* she shoot a man, Cary? I don't want to go look-ing for answers to the wrong question."

"What about the joker over there?" Cary asked.

Liam, Pierre, and Igor were sitting on some rocks near the water's edge, beer cans in hand. Pierre told me it was amusing to see the women sorting through all the assorted firepower. None of the men, when asked, said that they'd ac-tually heard a gunshot. Pierre said maybe, while Liam said he'd been staring at the pond, his thoughts not convenient. But Igor had been standing, Liam added, whole of person one in-stant, weighing just a bit less the next.

Val answered Cary: "It looked pretty consistent with gun-shot trauma. Of course there were no entry or exit wounds, but there was tearing, shattering—nice mess in a small place."

"Gentlemen?" Anna said. Liam got up and walked over to the deputy.

"Yes, ma'am?" he said.

"You fellas might want to go on home now. We're going to try to put this together and it's hard to know what might hap-

pen. Your friend, too. Trooper Dooble says the wound is sta-
ble but you need to get him to a doctor."

Pierre came up beside Liam and said, "Can't do it."

"Excuse me?" Anna said.

"We must stay," said Pierre. "There is recompense to be
sought from this shooting person."

"Um—boys? Not now. That can all be handled later."

"Ma'am?" Liam said.

"It was not a request, sir."

"I know that," Liam said.

"You have to leave."

"We can't."

"You can't?"

"No, ma'am."

"Why can't you?"

"We're drunk."

Anna looked at the beer cans in Liam's and Pierre's hands,
then over toward Igor who was sipping from a can in his good
hand. She thought there was something about the structure of
things as they were developing that was not as tight as she
would have liked.

Anna told me she didn't care just then if the three of them
got in their car and bobbed and weaved the roads all the way
back into Quilli, but, as she thought further about it, she decided she didn't want them back in town spreading the word
that something wild was happening up near St. A de P, something far better than the evening's television or a nap at nine
followed by bed at ten. There were other things at issue, too,
including a woman who lived less than a mile from where they
all were right then, a woman who, regardless of what the Andersen woman said, might not have even an inkling of what

was going on. A crowd of howlers could damage things, could escalate events before anyone even knew what the events were.

"Will you stay here?" she finally said.

"We will certainly do that, officer," said Liam.

"Just continue your party, okay? We'll be back later to tuck you in. This is really not a big deal."

"As you say," said Pierre.

Cary led the way up into the woods after showing the others that Ellen's road was not good and that it dead-ended and could put them all in a risky position if they took their vehicles up there.

"If it's nothing, it's nothing," she said. "We take a little walk back through the woods and we're gone—maybe a few beers with the boys, hey? But if it's something—protect your wheels; that's what I was taught."

Val Dooble said to me she was bothered by a certain flippancy in Cary's attitude. If this was all just a standard prank by some standard local prankster with whom Cary was well familiar, Val thought she should say so. As it was, they were carrying armaments and discussing strategies for a formal assault. Val was even being nagged by some statutory questions about Cary Andersen's position—township provost?—and exactly where she fit into enforcement, and who she was obligated to, questions that never came up until you were part of a situation developing and it was dark and you were even a bit hungry. For as much as they'd been on the scene for three or four hours now, Val wasn't sure that they'd talked the whole thing through enough, or that they'd really agreed on what they might be facing and how they ought to handle it.

• • •

It didn't seem that big a deal to her, Anna Pancake said. She kept trying to keep it small, to keep things in perspective. Hardly different from a quiet conversation in someone's dooryard, as had happened many times before—evidence of assault present in a puffy face; sure, you saw it all the time; the bruised arm of a young wife raised in affectionate affirmings of the goodness of her husband, talking about how all the time they had conversations that were spirited in nature, even argumentative, though now with the kids learning all about 911 right in school you never knew what they thought. *Well, obviously, officer, they thought something. One of them called that number? One of them really did?*

Or, Anna remembered, another time, an even gentler talking from an unbruised face, hair not even mussed, all grammatical bases covered, the woman educated, tolerant, amused that anyone would have thought anything so unkind—"My husband loves me. I love him. We get along well."—until: just a casual glance downward and it was, as Anna remembered, the ring finger broken all the way back and resting on the top of the hand, hidden for a time by gentility and soft speaking.

"Oh, that," the husband said when Anna pointed it out. She thought the woman must have been speaking through a lot of pain.

"Oh, that," the woman said.

Anna was the last of the four going up the hill. She felt sweaty and told herself she was thinking too much, distracting herself, more focus needed on the objective. She felt, too, her heart drop down to her boots as she heard the most distant of sharp, cracking noises behind her. She turned and, in what little remained of the evening's light, saw the three drunken men still down near the lake but slowly approaching the hill. She stopped for a moment, uncertain if they could see her, and waved them back. The gesture did as much good as she thought it would do. Looking up the hill, Anna saw that she was being left behind. Finally, deciding that the drunken men would most likely get themselves lost before they got themselves into trouble, she turned and ran to catch up.

They came to Ellen's road and stopped. A strategy seemed important, though they all agreed they had *disagreed* on exactly what to do. I told them I understood, that it must have been confusing.

"It wasn't exactly confusing," Val Dooble said. "It wasn't really that."

Debbie St. H said there was a stream nearby they could follow that would take them to a point not far from Ellen's front door. There was a spot where the banks were steep, she said, but the stream was shallow, an easy walk. Val suggested a walk directly up the road.

"We're almost there," she said. "Let's just do it."

Cary said, "The whole point is that we don't know where she is on the planet, the tilt of her head. She could be seeing us as snakes and dragons. She could also be waiting right in the middle of the road."

"Snakes and dragons, Cary?" Val asked. "What the hell are you getting us into here?"

"Don't be so harsh, Val," Debbie St. H said, "Cary's right. I've seen a lot of the shaggy willies out here and they invent things. They're not on anything. They don't hallucinate. They just have a world and you need to be damn careful how you enter it."

"There'll be a moon up soon," Anna said. "On the road we can be clearly seen—no dragons, no shaggies, whatever. If she's out and around, we're here to help. We tell her that."

"That sounds incredibly dangerous, Anna," Cary said.

Irritated, Anna replied, "I don't want to close off talk. We don't really know anything that happened here."

"We know a little," Cary said. "She's a risky person who's not afraid of blood. She's also—this is something I know and has nothing to do with the idiots back there—an extremely good shot with a rifle. She used to hunt with her husband all the time. She might still hunt."

Val finally said, "It's the road, isn't it? The only way."

"Why do you say that?" Debbie asked.

"We go into the brush, even follow the stream, that's nutty. We can get hurt, separated—probably end up shooting each other."

"Or lost," Anna said.

"A possibility," said Val.

"Through the woods," Cary said, her own view, though it seemed to be going nowhere. "I've had my say."

"I think the State needs to call this one," said Val. "Do you mind, Anna?"

"I'm fine with it, Val."

"Debbie? This isn't yours; I think you know that. In fact, you're not under any obligation to come with us."

"A shooter in the woods, Val? That's got the Service written all over it. But it's not my call. I don't have a problem with that."

"Let's deploy, then," Val said. "Keep it simple. Four abreast, firearms ready. Stay together. Cary, if we run into her, would you identify us? Nice and loud?"

"Yes, sir," Cary said.

"It's all right," said Val.

They had gone ten feet when they heard the first shots. Anna, twisting slightly as she dropped to her belly with the others, saw the three men down the road behind them. As quickly as the officers had, the men jumped jerkily for cover. One of the men fell, however. Anna, her breath now in short gasps, thought he'd been shot.

16

IT WAS EARLY DECEMBER and unusually warm the night Joe walked into Bud's wearing his Santa Claus outfit. I was taken aback until it occurred to me he must have been selling Christmas trees all day. So much was going on with me at the time that I hadn't thought much about the holidays. Grenada hadn't invited me out to the farm for Thanksgiving because she thought I was busy. I probably was. Joe was even wearing the knee-length beard.

Joe and Ellen had made a board-and-batten shack that held together with hinges and brackets. They could fold it flat, put it in the pickmeup, and take it down to the highway near the university where they sold the Christmas trees. They had an old woodstove inside and a little tape recorder with Christmas tapes so the whole scene was pretty cozy.

Ellen, Joe said, loved wearing the Santa outfit. She loved the kids when they came in with their parents. She had, Joe said, "this trick for the kids because one of them would always ask her if she was really, really Santa Claus—just the little ones, the real little ones. With a wink toward Mom or Dad, she'd take the child by the hand down one of the aisles of trees, and when they came back the child would be wide-eyed and covered with glitter dust. Before leaving for home with tree tied to roof of car, there would always be a secretive, and whispered, 'Thanks, Santa.'" Ellen said that sometimes it only took a small gesture to change the whole world.

Just behind Joe were Wilma and Poison. No one else in the

bar even seemed to notice this entrance, to notice Joe, and Bud only looked at them and said, "Folks?"

"Okay," I said softly as I felt hands on my arms and a gentle pressure that pushed me from the barstool and directed me toward the door.

We went outside and crossed the street to the bank of the Quilli Stream. A good breeze had begun putting a fringe of cold on the warm night, and the river was low enough that the various pockets and inlets of rocks, trash, jammed tree parts, and the unevenness of the river bottom caused a loud, gurgling clatter—maybe romantic if you were wearing a good sweater.

We walked down the street to the bridge—the one beneath which Poison had gotten broken up pretty bad—then crossed it maybe halfway.

"Sit, Pop," Wilma said. I looked down and there was an old bucket seat from a car leaning against the granite railing.

I sat and laughed because it was all quite funny. Through Wilma, I had said I needed to get her and Poison and Joe together, that I was up to my knuckles in things I didn't understand—things conveyed in quadruplicate on carbon forms, on computer printouts, in photographs, and even one old videotape.

Wilma sat down next to me on the sidewalk and held my hand. I couldn't remember the last time she'd done anything like that. Now and then a car would pass on the bridge, a moment's slowing down obvious. Joe, in that Santa outfit, just stood there, and as one car sped by you could hear a small voice saying, "Mommy?"

"I need to know how Ellen died," I said.

What they told me had, perhaps, nothing to do with the truth, but I began to think that in complicated things like this we will have our story. Often, we will have many of them, but in the end the only survivors are the facts we like anyway, "tempered by love," Wilma finally said.

Ellen ate that night, Wilma said, not at all hungry, but she'd been losing weight again so she ate three inches of rye bread from a round loaf, and drank more vodka from a fresh bottle. Her afternoon "with Joe" had depressed her, and she was determined to let work and exertion grind the roughness away.

Wilma stopped for a moment then and said to me, "There's a lot I didn't tell you about when I made those tapes, Pop. I kept thinking how I was Ellen's absolutely last connection to the world and it slowed me down; actually, it stopped me. It still might, but I'll do what I can."

"It's only time, Wilma," I said. "None of us have run out of it yet."

"Thanks, Pop."

On her cutting patio, Ellen dragged the headless moose onto the lifting canvas, hooked the canvas to the small overhead winch, and cranked the carcass up onto the cutting table. Purpose, however, kept nagging her as transient. She went into the kitchen and opened a can of tuna and ate that. She had another drink and some ice cream, her nerves propelling her around the house. In her tiny front room she sat on the couch for a minute, but that didn't feel right, then she went out onto the porch—things still unsettled.

• • •

Angled streaks, part cloud, part gravity, a rare orange, even red, slashed the horizon. A lot of people remembered that evening—brusque yet dreamy, the sky unfolding in a dramatic display of eternity fading to purple, an airborne waste of global frenzy.

"Red and purple," Wilma began, "reminded Ellen of churchly things from long ago. She said they reminded her of Joe, too, though she wasn't sure why."

Ellen said to Wilma this must be her day to think of Joe and she had done that, the thoughts always the same even after his letter had come because thoughts hardly ever changed. "A good reason to have a lot of them," she told Wilma.

Ellen heard sounds in the dusk, in the low woods that surrounded her small clearing, a brush and crinkle that seemed like sloppy drops spilling from the sunset. "Beauty leaks," she said to Wilma during their phone conversation. "It was a thought."

Ellen's place was smelly. Essences of dead meat permeated her ground down to the frost line, a richness of iron and copper. There was a moose, too, percolating on her cutting table, a moose that needed to be hacked into freezer parts before bedtime. Things came around sometimes, skunks in particular, now and then a fox. There should have been more, but Ellen would say, "They know. They really do."

Only the day before, though, on nearly the same walk as she'd taken today when she'd found the moose, she'd surprised a bear sitting in the middle of the road eating from a big branch of blackberries he'd ripped from a bush. The bear had seemed so calm Ellen had said, "Anything good on TV?" and calmly walked right around it.

Smells, though, the little signatures of documents still in process.

Wilma went on: " 'Joe needs a good hug,' Ellen told me. That's how she saw that long letter. She said she'd learned how to live apart from you, Joe, but it bothered her that she'd made you so lonely."

Joe had pulled up a flashing road barrier in front of me and was sitting on it, his feet on the curb.

"Ellen always knew where my life met my words," was all he said just then.

A night wind was coming on. Ellen liked working in the wind. The bugs couldn't hold on, and there was less smell. She would work, she decided, into the night to finish the moose. It was still dead-fresh, her depression even fresher but that could be handled. Joe was unresolved but then he always was. Living people were never finished. He wasn't. She wasn't. You stepped on the scale in the bathroom and the verdict was always provisional.

Wilma, she decided, maybe a call. She might want to get out. God knew, she'd want to talk. Wilma always wanted to talk and she loved to talk about Ellen. Ellen thought it would be nice to have someone right in front of her talking about her for a while, to hold her up to the house, the land, the business, even the courage of leaving Joe, and to say, "My, Ellen, you are a special person." We all need that, Ellen knew, usually often.

"It kept going on and on," Ellen said to Wilma, "*I really ought to call Wilma, I really should.* You've always said how much you like to watch me work, that it's like watching a surgeon or a really good plumber. Or we could talk about you, too, Wilma—maybe basketball?"

"She was bribing you, Wilma?" I asked.

"I think she was suggesting that everything didn't *always* have to be about her," Wilma said. "She'd come out of herself sometimes and really try to get with you. She didn't always make it, but she tried."

One night, both of them moody and drinking a blueberry wine that Ellen had made, tongues a slick cobalt, Wilma said, "Basketball, Ellen, my scholastic career, that is, was asskicking, never a dance. Your face in my face and don't call me pussy, pussy. I'd just hit someone, Ellen, and then run down the court humming, 'I enjoy being a girl' . . . well, sometimes."

"But grace, a certain grace, I think," Ellen replied, "motion, as in a theatrical script, a choreography of conquest."

"Oh, my," Wilma said.

With neither of them actually talking to the other, Wilma continued, "You have one thing to do, a simple thing. You want to go from this point over to that point. Then people get in your way. My coaches were always saying there was something about life in that."

"I don't see a lot of people getting in *your* way, Wilma."

Sitting that night on Ellen's couch, Wilma said, her legs stretched out, hightop boots on, baggy bermudas and a painty sweatshirt, she felt like she filled fully half the room.

"I was bruised all the time," Wilma had said to Ellen. Then she looked at me and said, "It was a good couch, Pop. A comfortable couch. Ellen died on that couch."

• • •

I risked breaking the mood for a moment, but I looked at Joe finally and said, "the Santa Claus suit?"

"Didn't feel like going home to change," he said. "It was such a favorite thing of Ellen's, the getup. I thought maybe you ought to see it. We had good times selling Christmas trees. Half the time I'd wear it, half the time she would. Once in a while, I'll wear it to sleep. It still smells like her. Isn't that something?"

"The beard?"

"I don't sleep in the beard."

Ellen kept hesitating on the call to Wilma. She had noises outside and she needed to look into that. "Perhaps moose mourners," she said to Wilma, "unschooled in grieving, as you can imagine. An ugly crowd."

She took her rifle and stepped off the cutting patio and walked slowly toward the front of the house. Anything on four legs could be scared away, especially at night. There were kids, however—not many anymore—who built into themselves her derangement, the savage frailty become the dared harassment. The mirth of choice was often eggs, sometimes a quick defecation on her porch. If she was awake, she would watch them. One time, one of the first times, she'd heard the noises near her porch and gone way out past the cutting patio, past the back outhouse and almost into the woods and fired a shot. A safe distance, but she had still heard the scurrying, heard the panic and the running. Moments later, from even farther, she'd heard the overgunned fury of a car scattering gravel and weeds.

The next morning Cary Andersen came out and she brought Joe, a patronizing gesture not lost on Ellen. She hadn't yet had a chance to clean the mess from the porch so they all stood around looking at it, Joe humble-faced, a blameworthy pity in his silence. Cary, however, lectured Ellen while Ellen stood silent, a whole line of civic argumentation running through her mind about paying taxes and disturbances of the peace. Just who was lecturing whom here, and who in the hell did Cary Andersen think she was?

That was never a good question to ask and Ellen hadn't asked it. Keeping the peace was Cary's job. Peace, however, was fragile and subtle: things that interrupted an old man's nap, a fist that got in the way of a young wife's face. Those kids, Ellen had known at the time, would hear from Cary, but Cary wouldn't give her, Ellen, the satisfaction of knowing that. "It's always," Cary said once, "the last beer that makes the world a changeable place. I am against change."

"I've never liked that woman," Ellen said to Wilma that night, "not a single bit."

Ellen fired one shot squarely into a maple tree, then three more. That was enough, more than enough. She went inside and put the rifle on the couch and got the bottle of vodka and finally called Wilma.

Wilma says she can still remember how the end of that conversation went. Ellen, she said, was sitting on the couch, phone in hand, and she'd decided to let the moose on the back table go to acid and stinky dissolution. She was, for the second time that day, flecked and speckled with its parts, and for as proud as she was of herself for everything she'd done, day by day, to pull sustained life from this nether neighborhood, for getting food and fire from land that didn't much want to give it anymore, her pride was a shaky match for a dress dotted with bits of beast, though she didn't think anyone much cared anymore if she was pretty. She thought she was, was reasonably sure of it, and she wished she didn't drink so much, and she wished she knew why she rejected Joe who only wanted to make her a part of his, well, you couldn't call it goodness, or maybe you could, but not some goodness learned in Indiana and exported here, not Joe, not always, the man had faults, wanted so little and got exactly that (Ellen felt revelation there as she said to Wilma, "I was everything to a man who wanted nothing."), was so laid-back he made the average corpse look manic, but his being, just the something of him in her life and the fact that there was no reason at all why he ever should have been—he just was, and now he wasn't and she had done that, had accomplished that, but more than all those things she wished she knew why trying didn't mean squat without luck, and why success didn't mean anything at all. No one she knew who'd had any had ever been at all happy with it. You were transported, they said, to a higher level of niggling and frustration and you lost sight of other things to pursue. Your light bill tended to increase, too.

She even wondered, weary as she was, why she couldn't seem to scare away whatever was out there. The noises hadn't stopped when she'd fired the rifle and fired it again and again, stubbornness, confusingly, not being a beastly trait. Some nether moose was in this nether neighborhood, or a nether deer or even a random, stray, skinny, and ugly coyote, all of which should have known they were dealing with derangement here, so it was said, and who could argue with whatever was said, with things unpredictable or, worse yet and deadlier, with disappointment?

Disappointment, she finally told Wilma—clearly drunk,

she said, on the whiny side of being totally bombed—is what I'm really good at.

"I went up there, Pop. I had to, though it was after midnight, because she sounded so—" Wilma stopped for a moment, then finally said, "The last time I saw her she was asleep on the couch, the rifle clutched across her chest like an old stuffed doll, maybe a teddy bear."

17

I HADN'T SEEN Ellen's life as all that grim.

She'd made friends in her business, and like any working woman had people in her life her husband didn't know at all. When Joe visited she would talk about them and Joe would smile and feel uneasy. Her stories were relaxed, even intimate, but Joe said it was like a stranger's words coming out of that perfectly recognizable mouth.

Joe found a collection of Christmas cards from Oregon, Florida, Nebraska, Belize, Okinawa, Anchorage, even places like Sleepy Eye, Hoopeston, Bullhead City, and Horse Cave. Many had warm notes citing her friendliness, her ability to make strangers feel at home in a strange place. Joe thought that was truly like Ellen, but he also told me he was beginning to feel more and more like a stranger and he wasn't feeling at all at home with her.

She had made, too, the painful progress from amateur to professional and she was good at something that needed to be done and that few people, even up here, would ever consider doing. The hunts were savage, she would tell people, weaponry against mindless instinct. The genetic parade that had brought this deer, that bear, this moose right here into being, was, for an instant, measured against the science of ballistic wizardry —and occasionally losing.

Ellen was especially gentle with first-timers. She'd seen boys of fifteen or sixteen trembling; slick and expensively outfitted executives mournful. Calmly, Ellen would tell them, "Let's get this all cleaned up."

There was no end of appreciation for that.

Grenada was the one to see Wilma come home that night, that morning—August 13—from Ellen's.

Not dawn at the time—hardly night. Ocean gray in a steep sky, more warmth in the air than was natural for a foggy time. For a while, the only sound was the whish of bats in the darkness.

Grenada had not slept well. A ping-pong slumber, she slept and woke, then slept again. In her nightgown she went downstairs and into the kitchen. Her night was gone so she flipped the switch on the coffeemaker and went outside. The moon ought to be all over the garden, she thought, the fog low to the ground, and she wanted to see it, to check, as she said once to me, "the naughtiness therein. Did you know tomatoes are terrified by a full moon? Their leaves curl inward, their sour pulp turns sweet. I talk to my garden, you know. It responds especially well to the reading of nursery rhymes."

Tomatoes, peppers, broccoli, beans; potatoes and cabbage and onions and peas—Grenada had, she always said, brought the commoners into *polis-assembled*. Adventure was for the agricultural conglomerates. She planted things you could eat because you were hungry, not because your soul was searching for some culinary amusement.

It's that core of amused wonder that has kept me, in spite of our divorces, from ever truly *leaving* her.

She has a scarecrow in the garden made from her old wedding gown—"worn three times in serious service. It needed new work," though I know the gown would still fit her. She cuts her hair in the garden, dark hair still of a carbon wash, here and there a sassy streak of white. With quick fascination she'll point to small clumps of it that have been appropriated by bugs she has no reason to kill. Occasionally, she'll spread like paint a bucket of blood Wilma has brought home from a visit to Ellen.

Grenada never met Ellen.

She heard geese that early morning, an unseen flight coming down from Madawaska, maybe over from the Allagash. Spidery honks, a draining, catch-me echo slipping under the moon like a summer tinsel. It was not cold, not even chilly. Grenada in her garden was like other people in church. There were things to be respected, along with liturgical smells and certain procedures. The broccoli appeared black, and she could feel the tingly acid of thirty tomato plants in her nose. Everything around her had a purpose.

Wilma was gone, which, as she told me, though she knew I knew it, was not unusual. Sometime that night Grenada had heard her voice, a dim dalliance on the cordless phone, things soft, things frantic. Whether she was in her twenties or thirties or even her forties, we never bothered to track Wilma's sexual habits.

Sometimes Grenada would say jokingly, "That girl will go anywhere to screw." But other times there could be a hurt behind it: stories heard, cranky hype over too much coffee in someone's kitchen. Sometimes you want to meet the gossips head on and just say, "It doesn't matter. Never has. Never will." Ignorance usually responds to that by saying, "Of course you're right. But I heard—"

As I mentioned earlier, there have been abortions and Wilma has never hid that from us, nor did she hide it that Bylaws had been born in an abortion clinic.

"Better than a log cabin," I told her once, "should he ever go into politics." That got me the wry eye until Wilma finally laughed.

Bylaws, Wilma told Grenada (I was living in town at the time) had exploded out of her at the beginning of the procedure, her uterus more starting block than nest. He was livid, she said, though nearly too small to live; hardly negotiable yet howling for a deal, a compromise, point after point being made with no one able to shut him up.

"I could not abscond with his victory," she told Grenada. "You're a grandmother now."

"That's not hard duty," Grenada said, "but you left here seeking convenience and you came home with obligation. Are you sure you know what you're doing?"

"If I knew what I was doing I'd be in the stock market," Wilma said. "He was nothing, though, and then he was something. He made contact. That was enough."

Bylaws, she thought, a good boy. Freshly born, he had almost been named Epididymis. Wilma loved the cachet of scholarship in such a name, a certain Greco-Roman boldness. Old things seemed always so good, but there was also a cuteness in it that made her smile even as she was leaving the clinic.

"No," Grenada told her. The smile crashed.

"Oh?"

"It's part of a man's testicles."

"I know that."

"You don't want to name your boy after his balls."

"It would make him spirited," Wilma said.

"It would also make him a prizefighter."

"Have you ever been wrong, mother?"

"Not in recent memory."

All the good names had been named then. Scratch Epididymis, even if it did mean losing something wonderful like an exclamatory, "Epididy Doll you get back here!"

"James?" Wilma said.

"Huh-uh."

"Robert?"

"What family you been living with?"

A name was everything, Wilma knew that: function, history, current posture. Bylaws was going to be tall, and it looked like he had a big brain. Wilma once said to Grenada, in a whisper, "I think he's going to be quite comprehensive."

So many things are different for Wilma that Grenada and I used to puzzle away long evenings just talking about her. She is more beautiful than most big women ever are, and there has never not been a man in her life since the time she fell in love with Poison Gorelick at around, I think, thirteen, Poison well older than she. There was Hubert Peterbuoy when he was just out of law school. Hubert got smote about as bad as any man I've ever seen, but she would not marry him. They still get together even though Hubert, older, has developed questionable ways and has endured numerous investigations as to his status before the bar.

Bylaws, she says, is the son of Quitno Blêd, a man in his seventies. Even today, she'll go over to his house and clean for him or chop firewood. She'll take the baby, too, and she says Quitno has already set some money aside so that someday By-laws can go to college.

"He asked me to marry him one time," Wilma told me, "but then he said he didn't think it was a good idea because he's pretty sure he's dying."

Wilma's easy to love, and she forgets no one who's been good to her.

Grenada said she might have noticed something sooner, "but I was annoyed by a preponderance of slugs beneath my feet."

Sometimes she salted the slugs, at other times left out saucers of beer or fruity wine. As often as not anymore she would step on them. Feet were washable, she said, almost everything is washable.

Something out there — she knew it. She saw color off to the woods, the unctuous dawn and low fog an easy pair of tricksters. Still, something where there should be only nothing, an imagined whiteness. Nonprimates did not stand out. It was in the design.

Grenada matched her hush to the hush around her, curious but safe. She twiddled a tomato sucker already in her hand and strangled it off the vine.

There was a sound, human easily. Primate gasps.

Another sound, a primate walking — a hip-twisting stagger it seemed to be. Something was happening on the edge of her senses, the most likely candidate a leftover from some night-long toot down on Ponus Pond.

Illumination was now a blend of moon and graying dawn.

Clothing was walking toward her, the walk unstudied on lumpy, grassy ground. Grenada didn't think she'd need a weapon, but her hand was now on a tomato stake. The walking was really not good. A leg gave out and the primate-shape did a hard flop to the ground. She could hear an intake of breath that had pain behind it.

Grenada had known longer than she wanted to admit that it was Wilma. She was crying, too. Grenada could see that now. Women of that age who cry, she told me, drag the centuries with them. They reach deep, and the current trauma emerges festooned with others' pain. Someone had once told Grenada no woman ever cries alone.

Grenada pulled her nightgown up to her waist and cinched it with a tuck and a tug. Dark enough for decency, she told herself. My daughter needs me.

Wilma was still a hundred feet off as Grenada stepped into the tall grass around the garden. Her legs were quickly wet and she could feel a slug squish out beneath one heel. She said softly, "Wilma?"—which was enough of a call. Grown daughters, she says, mothers themselves, can hear things in the night that others never can. "There's no gender metaphysics to that," she'll say, "merely an attunement to trouble, the lickety-split of risk abatement."

Grenada heard it, finally, two words: *Trop tôt.*

She said it again: "Wilma?"

The whiteness she had seen was the old denim jumper Wilma would wear for days and days if she wasn't leaving the farm, a frock the heft of old tissue, cream-colored, stone-washed, thin enough to rip in a context of catastrophe. "It was blotted now with circles and lines of blood."

"Whose blood?" Grenada asked. The jumper, delicate as it was, would be a chore to clean—perhaps burning was a better answer. Sex, Grenada assumed, kept getting Wilma in trouble. Now it was ruining her clothes.

"Wilma?" she said again, feeling like a landing beacon sending out hope to a troubled plane. With shaking hands, Grenada fumbled with her nightgown and let it fall back down over her legs.

Trop tôt, was once again the whisper, the sweetest dream, a throwback to childhood troubles. *Too soon? What's too soon, Wilma?*

Wilma told me one day that the phrase, in the coming weeks back then, would become a mantra for her, a small hook on which to hang her sanity when it threatened to blow away in the ghastly winds that beset her.

Grenada hoped there wasn't something here so foul, so demented, that Wilma couldn't talk about it, a deed of man or men you could only put down in a diary, and only then if you had agreed the diary would be destroyed.

Speak to me, daughter. Were you hurt? Were you badly touched? Do you want law and all of that?

Grenada had to remember to wash her feet before going back to bed, then recalled she'd already kissed that off. The coffee was ready. It was morning.

QUILLIFARKEAG, MAINE
(Tourism)

"Can I use your bathroom?" the young woman asks Bud down at Bud's Bar. She's wearing a backpack almost as long as she is tall.

Bud knows the type: a hike from the beginning to the end of the country, then the next ten years spent complaining how all the wrong people are running things. After that, mutual funds and pregnancies. Bud never backs away from sweeping thoughts.

Bud thinks she is about twenty. He says, "The police aren't done in there yet."

"The police?"

"There's a lot of blood and not much evidence."

"What happened?"

"The past, the future—all of it in a small place."

Bud watches her scan the bar, his afternoon customers finding a sudden, consuming interest in the Weather Channel.

"How about a nice rare burger?" Bud asks. "I make the best."

"I have to leave now," she says.

Somebody's daughter, Bud thinks.

18

I CAN IMAGINE BYLAWS standing in his crib that morning, looking out his window to the two tall women standing in the low mist. They would seem far away out in the garden, familiarity out of context. Perhaps his hand goes up because a wave seems the thing to do. Hunger could well be stirring him, or his hygienic needs. *Hey you,* does not yet spring out of that growing vocabulary, so he starts to laugh, something funny about being alone when there are things that need to be done. As any baby quickly learns, there is great humor in discomfort.

He watches them though they seem motionless, an odd state. Perhaps he wonders why one of them doesn't pick the other up and twirl her around. Dizziness is the greatest high of all. More than anything, I wonder how he will come to learn of these events, if, even, these words will ever be available to him. Life is better sometimes if the drunk uncle is simply left to sing alone out in the barn.

Wilma had gone to Ellen's after their phone call. She walked through the dark woods and around Ponus Pond, the path easy and familiar though it would have been a long walk. She came home the same way, her life no longer the same.

"Ellen needs nothing," Wilma said to her mother in that almost-dawn. "Ellen's dead. They shot her all over. I think she felt a lot of pain."

Grenada, the growing wind whipping at her ears, heard

none of that. She decided only that this, now, was not a time for conversation. She quickly finished her inventory of Wilma's obvious articles. She bent down and lifted Wilma's dress, touched her legs, looked at her, touched her shoulders, arms, stared at her with a squint-eyed scan that could diagnose but never mend. Grenada did not touch Wilma's hands, a crimson clenching going on there. With her forearms held away from her body and slightly forward, limp-wristed, it seemed clear that Wilma did not want to touch them either.

"Let's get you cleaned up," Grenada said. She turned toward the house, one hand on Wilma's buttocks. Mothers guide, she was thinking, they do not lead.

"No!" The word was harsh, not a shout.

Wilma's hair, tangled, sweaty, kept falling over her face, and Grenada kept trying to smooth it aside.

"Oh, damn," Wilma said.

So strong even the expletives are weak. A way to be, Grenada thought. She saw her daughter spiraling somewhere, sweet reason not an option but rage having too many faces. The angry child defied mastery in any parent.

"Damn's a start," Grenada answered, "not much of an ending. Honey?"

They were back near the garden. Wilma went to her knees in the tall grass, then back on her heels. A sigh escaped, a hacking cough.

"I can taste it," Wilma said. "This is something very ancient, even instructive."

"Wilma?" Grenada began. "What can I do? What's happened to you?"

"You think about legacies," Wilma said, her voice down to

a whisper. "Will anyone remember you? Is that even a good idea?"

"Ellen?" Grenada said.

"Yes."

"Something's happened to Ellen?"

"My nose was sniffing tragedy, Splotch," Grenada told me. We were having supper at the Mai Tai in Quilli one night, the flaming Poo-Poo Platter our favorite dish, and also a nice barrier between us. I wasn't averse to telling her I missed the sparkle in her eyes; however, that was not the time. "But Wilma's tragedies are always so—special, you never know."

Wilma said something about a shooting, her lower lip trembling, a child's confession. Grenada said, "What?"

Wilma was whispering now, herself both speaker and audience; a soprano with a slight virus, a tenor on the mend.

She asked did Grenada know that Bylaws's toes pointed outward, *sure sign of a sorcerer, Mom, another magician for the works.* She thought she might take a trip to Sydney on Cape Breton, maybe even take the ferry all the way up to Port aux Basques in Newfoundland, spend some time at sea. She said, "Yes, I think, that would be good, a place with no illusions that you're at the total mercy of anything that wants to happen, anything at all.

"Except the smell," she continued, "that's different at sea, a good smell and not this smell of taste and wretched bile, this taste, a certain taste of Ellen."

Something seemed to be working its way right into her heart and claiming a place there. Wilma didn't think she could abide that, didn't think so at all, and by this time Grenada was holding her and knew only that someone had been shot and it could be Ellen, whom she didn't know. Ellen DeLay, the blood lady—her garden's blood—the skinner.

Definitely, someone had bled and it wasn't Wilma. *Thanks could be given here. Put a note on the refrigerator: Find someone to thank.*

The note is still there.

Grenada knew these were unusual times and thought the coffee, on WARM, a whisper steam, would be getting stronger and stronger. She thought again that she knew no one in Wilma's life, not the men, which was a good thing since she didn't think Wilma knew the men very well, either, nor the women, but then she thought there was no reason why she should. Wilma had a world of her own where she worked from time to time, just worked and sometimes didn't, worked the way some people dieted, always keeping at it, success resting in the journey, not the destination. She had a language, products, dividends, and dreams within which she, Grenada, fit somehow as a gentle friend, the kind in front of whom you could walk naked or fart hard, but never did, or at least Grenada didn't.

My own presence in all of this was never doubted, but mothers have a hold on permanence in the eyes of their children that fathers seem never able to manage.

Friendship, in another sense, was being called to account. Grenada thought it really was like friends how they'd just gone on, working and living, always good food, clothing when it was needed, Wilma no more ambitious than she, but marking by her presence a way of saying, *I really think this is all just enough,* not a bad thing for a mother and daughter, and now that sweet little boy.

"*Trop tôt, maman.*"

"Of course it is."

"You were waiting for me?"

"I came out to tease the garden, Wilma. I thought it needed a joke, maybe a little slapstick. It was early. It's still early."

"I don't even know what day it is."

"Just a day, hon."

"Nor the time. Even the month is questionable."

"About five in the morning. It's August, Wilma."

"That's good. That's very good. Grenada?"

"Right here."

"I'm a mess."

"Yes, you are."

"But Ellen—"

"Very bad. I know it's very bad."

"What do I do now?"

Grenada sat with her daughter, seeing herself, seeing both of them as two exotic flowers that bloomed where blooming never happened, the tallness, the stiff beauty of lupine, Grenada holding on to Wilma, who was crying again and shaking. Grenada thought it had to be a coldness coming up with this wind, a windy day and it was hardly ever windy in Quilli, something clearly needing a good sweep and a gusty, blustery day would be just fine. Grenada felt sad for the sadness all around and hoped she would be enough of whatever Wilma needed. Your kids sometimes were never more than kids no matter what the age, trouble and craziness all over the place and you had no way to protect them from that, the world often like a bad virus with any cure unacceptable.

Still, it was enough just then simply to sit in the grass and be a mother. There were things to be smoothed and patted down, words that could be offered in solace, perhaps understanding. Events might be in control, but a mother could show up anytime she wanted and stop nearly anything with a quiet, *Now see here.* It didn't always work, but comfort was not an action, just a good presence.

It was not easy—friendship sometimes required the strength to overcome revulsion—but Grenada finally took one of Wilma's bloody hands in her own and leaned down and kissed it lightly.

19

CRIME SCENES ARE NOTORIOUS for confounding notions of time. For those not surviving the scene time might be found frozen on a wall or a wrist, might also be found in the way certain bodily processes slow down and cease. Witnesses can help, though no one is immune from the speeding up or slowing down of time during wrenching events.

Igor was shot late in the morning or early in the afternoon. Even after those boys discovered that he'd actually lost his pinky part they seemed remarkably unexcited about things.

"They were there to party," someone told me. "They'd bought beer, constructed various employer and spousal ruses. One of them said, 'we could not go back. We hadn't even eaten yet.'"

By late afternoon that call had been made and the officers began arriving. There, too, it took a while to realize that things might be serious. The afternoon was waning, darkness coming on. As far as I can tell, they started up to Ellen's no later than nine—about the time Wilma said she called Ellen. Thus, a discrepancy.

Wilma says they talked a long, long time, and the details she recounts on my tapes confirm that—maybe. She is certain that it was near midnight when they hung up and she decided to walk to Ellen's, and there is no doubt that she was right off the living room at Ellen's house when the officers opened fire.

Calmly, or in a panic—Wilma doesn't remember which— she ran from Ellen's and didn't stop running until she was at the lake. She stopped right there, she says, overcome. She might even have slept for a time on the shore before walking home.

Grenada says she was in her garden between four and five in the morning when Wilma came back. That's not unusual for Grenada. After talking for a time, she helped Wilma to bed where Wilma lay with Bylaws for maybe an hour—near daybreak—before she decided she had to go back to Ellen's, leaving for there just as Cary Andersen drove up to our (Grenada's) house. To do what? Who knows?

Maybe it works; maybe it doesn't. I do know it shouldn't have taken the officers three hours to go from the boys' camp up to Ellen's. In the end, it probably doesn't matter. Clarity anymore seems to be about as common as a credit card balance of zero.

"Over and over," Wilma began, "this one thought kept running through my mind, not a thought, actually, a sentence, as though that ugly night had forced me quickly, desperately, into theology, and just as fast forced me out again.

" 'There are some things I won't tell even God,' I kept repeating, 'and that's a problem.' "

It had come to her the first time that morning of August 13. She was lying on her bed, an elegant brass queen I'd refurbished for her long ago, Bylaws, wearing only a diaper, crawling all over her. He was at her toes and he had terrible gas, she said. Wilma wondered what Grenada had given him for breakfast.

"Revenge came to mind and then left, an old song beyond control. The music, as I thought about it, wasn't over. Nothing was over. God simply had no sense, another job bobbled again. Were you a supervisor, you'd want to put something in God's file, surely a fat file by now. Perhaps it was time for Human Resources to schedule a meeting. Options could be discussed; there were therapies. Oh, and for heaven's sakes, no one's talking about termination—not yet. Supremacy still has a lot to recommend it."

The doorknob squeaked and Grenada entered the room.

"Bad?" she asked. "Very bad?" It was a generic question. Grenada still did not know what had happened to Wilma. Her friend Ellen had had a difficulty. Had the difficulty been Wilma?

"Very bad," Wilma said.

"I can see that."

"I hope so."

Wilma hoped her feet were clean because her toe was entering a warm, wet place. All indicators pointed to Bylaws's mouth. She thought he was nursing on her big toe. That had to be comforting, a good baby-memory.

"There was a thing on the radio," Grenada told her. "Not much is known."

Sometimes too much is known, thought Wilma, and then there is no place to put it. She reached down and ran her hand over the baby's diaper. It was empty and dry.

For an hour she had been drifting, the feeling not at all unlike a minor cold coming on—the most delicate of fevers, a certain rawness. A thin buzz of thought, minimal care, had kept the baby on the bed. Wilma said to Bylaws, "Of all the mothers you might have chosen—think about it." Bylaws looked up at her. A long stream of drool ran out of his mouth and onto her foot.

• • •

Outside, a hesitant sun dabbled in the fog, while Grenada sat on the bed and rubbed one of Wilma's feet. Bylaws, thoroughly amused, continued to play with the toes of the other. In the dark, Wilma thought, a toe is as good as a nipple. A guy, she remembered, had said that to her one time. He had stayed just a guy.

"A lot of talk, very grim," Grenada said. "Did you shoot her?"

"Ellen."

"It's true?"

"They said that?"

"Hush. I don't know what they said. It was taillights and a hind end. I didn't hear a whole report."

Early, Wilma thought. Wasn't there always something about notifying next of kin? It's very early. But Joe was still that. Joe hadn't been there.

"I turned it off," Grenada continued, "but they said: 'Sn'A de P, a shooting, a killing.' That was it. I've always wished you could reread the radio. You have blood on you."

Still dazzled, Wilma told me, by images of Ellen, she wanted not to talk at all at that moment, not there in the bedroom, not to her mother; then she wanted to talk until she ran out of words. "That thing, Pop, she was a thing now— *chose'elle* (my word)—would still be there, a parcel—Ellen. All that was needed was a UPC sticker right there"—Wilma closed her eyes—"on her butt, the part still remaining, *gluteus detritus.*"

"I am evidence," Wilma said to Grenada.

"Do you want to wash?"

Trop tôt.

In the east that morning, the sun still not fully risen, the sky was red, a fit sign of travail, Grenada told me. She was alone with her tomatoes and beans, cukes and chard, wary witness to a master coyote not far away. Coyotes are common around Quilli, one reason why cats are not.

"It was depletion," Grenada told me, "purely that. Wilma had shrunk to the size of a flea. Can you see it, Splotch?"

"I can see it, dear."

"She was aiming for the fetal position but the baby kept her shifting around. It seemed good to leave her alone, so I went out back to the garden. In hardly a shake, she was with me, the baby back in his crib."

A perimeter of cutting surrounds the garden. Beyond that, a tall grass covers the old field leading up to the woods. The growing nor'easter whipped at the grass as Wilma left the house and walked to the garden. The wind sounded like a kettle coming to a boil, Grenada said, and Wilma's voice was hoarse and whispery.

"The baby's birthday is coming soon," Wilma said. "We'll have to do something about that."

"You don't want to leave that blood on you, on your skin like that. Did you know there's a handprint on the baby's diaper?"

Wilma went down to her knees and ran her hands through the dewy grass. "These things don't happen here," she said.

The wind was up and down and Grenada was hearing and not hearing Wilma. She heard that, though. She didn't know, then, what her daughter had done, only that something on the radio was real, was touching them. That was unusual and made a difference. There was always something sad when your child hurt a friend and age had nothing to do with it. Grenada stood with a handful of slugs and dumped them in the salt bucket.

"Things always happen here," was all she said.

Slowly, Wilma edged out to the line of tall grass, a destination set, the journey unclear. She thought she heard something down by the house, past the house.

Sometimes the wind could bring sounds all the way from Quilli. That was a nice thought, slightly communal. Standing right here, she had heard whole conversations: kitchen talk, people on the street in Quilli mustering up a structured acquaintance. For a moment, just the thought of shaking someone's hand felt wonderful. She had, however, heard raspy bedroom things, too, the moans of rue, here and there jealousy like a snippy cancer—one person on top of another person, a happening in the wind. The best sex was between two people who weren't feeling very good about themselves.

Wilma's dress flapped violently and her hair pulled hard toward Quebec and the west. Grenada was bending over, the hem of her own dress tickling her ears. In a quick glance up from her conflict with the slugs, Grenada could see Wilma looking toward the house, her arms not even trying to stop the fly-around dress, although she was in the big grass now up to her thighs. It was a whipped tease with no one to see it.

Wilma, arms folded on her chest, head down, walked toward the woods. She could hear the squawk, a screech, some sound coming at her, someone calling in two parts, the softer part simply Grenada calling her name, things mothers were required to do.

"There was another part, though, some sad scream of obligation that came from away like a wind-borne gravel, a familiar voice, but I decided I'd had enough to do with familiar voices. Why Cary Andersen had come to our house I didn't know, but I knew it was her. I knew we would have dealings, maybe harsh words. I also knew I wasn't ready."

She hadn't been home from Ellen's more than an hour, she said, maybe two, but the place called her back, that calling nearly theological, certainly ghostly. But she'd run from Ellen just as they'd killed Ellen, and no matter how much she might have been worried about her own safety, it had still seemed a shameful thing to do. Corrections could be made, however, and she would do that, would return to Ellen's and be there as a friend should be—a total mess (certainly), nerves shredded, her clothes, her *self,* dirty, but present—the imperative not hard to understand at all.

"No way would I let Cary stop me, Pop. Maybe I should have, but you'll find no regrets coming from me."

20

ANNA PANCAKE'S MOTHER works for Czy Czyczk in the lingerie shop, and since I live upstairs it was easy for me to meet Anna, Val, and Debbie in the shop one morning, easy and more appropriate than having them come up to my place. Appearances are important in a town like Quilli, and it just seemed better for us to be at least somewhat public in this meeting.

It wasn't lost on me, however, that I was tending that propriety surrounded by bras and girdles and all manner of sleepwear that had nothing to do with sleep. Nor did I fail to notice how nutty it was to see those three good-sized women in the middle of all that frilly matériel—the war between the sexes no match for those guns and badges and uniforms. Feeling unashamedly masculine, I feared we men had lost that war.

"We were busy, and the woman was dead," Val began.

The officers were all tired, she said—it was maybe two-thirty or three in the morning. They were angry, too, and procedure had not yet overcome thought. The numbing prospect of investigation rankled. That they had somehow messed up, that there could be recriminations—irritated. They had all been there; they were all responsible, yet no one really knew what had happened.

Other scenes went through my mind as they talked, things like Waco and the Philadelphia rowhouse bombings and the shootout with the Symbionese Liberation Army and the Chicago riots of '68—all times where procedure had not yet overcome thought, and the overriding thought had been, *We gotta get them sonsabitches.* I even narrowed my focus for a second and remembered the one time out in California and that Mr. King—Roger? Rodney?—all alone, really alone. *The policeman is your friend.* We need to believe that, but there in the lingerie store I was being pushed and pushed hard, and, for a moment, I felt sorry for those women. If we were a little more perfect, we might expect a little bit less of them.

State Trooper Val Dooble had Sheriff's Deputy Anna Pancake over by Ellen's stream. Val held Anna by her belt and leaned backward while Anna leaned forward, well over the stream.

An old maple stump was in front of the house, the centerpiece of Ellen's parking lot. Ellen was draped over it, shot- and bullet-pocked, marks that seemed at first glance as harmless as bug bites scratched too much.

Twice Cary Andersen approached it and kicked it: Ellen. Debbie St. H saw her do it and said nothing. It was no one's place to give advice just then. Cary, she supposed, might just be one of those people who apologized for some slight by punching you in the nose.

Cary kept walking in and out of the front door. The battered couch was smoking. A long strip, a keen ricochet, divided Ellen's small carpet perfectly in two. A framed photo of Joe was on the floor, the frame intact.

Cary told Debbie the whole thing could go up in flames and that would be just fine; the intact scene made her nervous. But there were things that needed collecting, items of the deceased that the state ought to be tending to. The state, however, was over by the stream helping the county settle down.

Debbie St. H came out of the kitchen and into the living room carrying the largest moose head Cary had ever seen. Its eyes were closed, the neck long. Severance had been close to the forequarters.

"Isn't that chargeable?" Cary asked.

"This time of year?"

"Yes."

"I suppose. What's the point?"

"She shot a man while illegally hunting? Write it up, warden," Cary said. Cary was not in charge. Val Dooble, in theory, was in charge, though liabilities were beginning to fly all over the place and authority was mixed. Cary knew that, but Cary was not one to leave authority lying around untended. Someone had to say something. Talk was necessary or else they'd all start building a structure that would look about like this hodgepodge they were wandering around right now.

"Unity is everything," she said to Debbie. "There can only be one story." Eventually, Debbie St. H took the moose head out the front door and sat it next to Ellen.

Cary bent over and picked up something shiny. It was a wedding ring.

They were not alone, of course, and it's always been thought that it was Liam who made that early call to the radio station in Bangor. The stories from those three young men as to what happened next don't differ all that much from those of the officers. They're just different kinds of people, is all, and we see things, as often as not, based on what we are.

"What is that?" Igor asked. The three men were lying behind a log topping the stream bank to the north of Ellen's parking lot. Igor, unable to hold on to the log firmly with only one hand, had both feet in the water.

They were not far from the house, but they were beyond the area Ellen had tended with flowers and the cutting of weeds. Heavy brush ran in patches in and out of the stream bed and on into the woods.

"What where, friend?" said Pierre.

"Where that cop is standing."

"A stump."

"And?"

"The head of a moose. Looks like a big one."

"Next to it, Pierre."

Pierre crept away from the log and then forward into the brush. Everything had been over for some time, but Igor said to Liam, "I hope they don't think Pierre's something and shoot him."

"Pierre thinks he's something," Liam said. "But they won't. He's barely moving."

"But they shoot. Great God, do they shoot."

"They are legal authorities," Liam said. "It's what they do."

Igor frowned, doubt like a hard candy in his throat. He had thought it a war scene, the night before, with all of them, including the legal authorities, falling to the ground at the first shooting, sounds that hadn't sounded all that close— more like the sounds of a hunt when a hunt is going on—sounds in the night of a high question. Then the police disappeared and Pierre had said, "Are we all here?"

They agreed they were.

"We might go home," Pierre said. "It would not be a matter of fault."

"I am a curious person," said Liam. "Have you ever seen anything like this?"

"I have not," said Pierre.

"Nor me," Igor added.

When the shooting began, they'd crawled on their bellies up the road for a distance, then decided that was a hard task and rose up to a low stoop. Beer was in them, but they all knew it wasn't the beer making them stop and pee frequently.

They agreed later it had been the fear, a good fear that had merit to it, a fear that experience revealed had been well-placed: an echoed expansion of violated air, a popping and thumping, an exploding that within seconds had a rhythm to it, eventually a smell. They knew they were close to it but they couldn't tell how close, each of them pressed flat against the ditch at the side of the road. Pierre said, his normal voice sufficient—a whisper would have been inaudible—"I believe they have uncovered a whole nest of rascals. This is a bad time."

"I hope they are not hurt."

"Do you have the cell phone?"

"Who would we call?"

"The police."

"They're here."

Sometime that night it ended. None of them could remember when.

• • •

Pierre slid backward through the brush until he was back behind the log.

"It's a body," he said.

"A body?"

"A human body."

"Only one?"

"Important enough—if you're the body."

"But captives. Shouldn't there be captives?"

"There seem to be no captives."

"One body?"

"I think it is a girl."

"Isn't this something?"

Cary left Ellen's house and noticed Val and Anna over by the stream. She asked Debbie what *that* was all about, though Debbie just shrugged her shoulders. Cary wondered for a moment if someone had taken a wound, as if they needed more complications. Everything normal was proving hard enough. Before long, she said, they needed to go down and get their vehicles. Each of them had reports to write and the forms were down by the lake, as were the evidence kits, and Val should have a bag in her trunk for the thing that Ellen was now.

"Or always had been," Cary said to Debbie. There was no point arguing degree of loss. Ellen DeLay was a decent-enough woman who should never have come out here. She'd gone to trash and that had started stories. She'd stepped outside, really outside.

Val said Cary was just "nutsy" on this Ellen DeLay. Cary said Ellen was wicked and she was phony. "Look around

this place," Cary said. You could see it in the way she lived
—boards and logs and a tar-paper roof; the intimacy of shit
rotting in a hole ("an outhouse, for chrissakes"), so little difference from a legacy of simian scrambling, of a million years
of desperation—humanity on the hoof. "Deny civilization,"
Cary told them, her eloquence so odd in those early hours that
Anna thought it was just panic, "whether Gutenberg or computers, deny that progress, that blood-sucking rise from stone
knife to laser beam, and your hand stamp no longer lets you
back into the dance."

Wicked, maybe, or simply nuts, Cary went on. Regardless, it had been a quick putting-down, not hard to imagine painless, though Cary did wonder—"As we all did, sir,"
Val said—how they'd all pushed the firepower like that, and
pushed it and pushed again, each of them consuming anywhere from thirty to forty rounds of ammunition, hardly a
major battle but a point would come when they'd have to account for all of it.

"Then Cary got this big-guy look about her," Val began,
"and said there was at least one point she would have to lie
about, that she would have to put in writing as a lie and answer truthfully in a lying way, and we had goddamn well better back her up whether it was the Township Council doing
the asking or the office of the attorney general, and that would
be that, *no, sir, there was no one else in the house. We didn't
know that of course, and in the scrambling madness of confrontation I would have to say there is a lot you don't know
because, really, sir, you're just working off your training, your
skills, you're not actually working from a plan, which might
be standard business practice. The objective, if there is one, is*

just a mighty STOP and you don't always know where you're directing that, but I would have to say that I did not see, nor was I aware of, any other person in that house, so any allegations to the contrary would exist in my mind as pure fiction."

"Ladies," I said, "I'm missing something here."

"She took a shot," Val said, "at Wilma, Mr. Doll. She shot at your daughter."

QUILLIFARKEAG, MAINE
(Social Classes)

Mrs. Sanderson Wruhreure comes to Bud's every Friday after-noon at four o'clock. A busty seventy-year-old with sexy legs, she comes to Bud's, she says, instead of the more upscale Le Père's, to smell the sweat of Quilli, to feel its grime on her fingers, to see how her investments are doing.

Aliana Wruhreure is extremely wealthy.

One afternoon, after her two Manhattans, she asks Bud a question she has never asked him before: "Do you have a pis-sitory, Mr. Crépiter?"

Pistelle Philomene takes her to the bathroom. When Mrs. Wruhreure says, "I've never used a facility in a place like this," Pissy offers to go in with her.

"How thoughtful," Mrs. Wruhreure says.

Later, Bud teases Pissy on her courtesy. He says, "So do the rich—?"

"She was prime gassy," Pissy says. "But she gave me this."

It is a check for five hundred dollars.

21

"WOMEN," WILMA BEGAN, "are so good with details." We were in the produce section of Don's Grocery, inspecting some Guatemalan sweet corn. I had invited Wilma down for supper at my place, Grenada, too, though Grenada declined as I expected she would. She's been sensing an increase in affection on both our parts lately and it makes her nervous. Sometimes it's hard to know whether our record together shows serial failures or serial successes.

It's been a long time since I've gotten together with my daughter where we haven't talked about death, but we're closer now than we've ever been so a goodness has arisen out of this bedraggled woe. What began that afternoon at Don's Grocery, however, and continued past supper, pushed me into places I rarely go.

Wilma ended that long phone call and took the long walk over to Ellen's in the dark, getting there sometime after one in the morning. Knowing nothing of what was about to happen—

"I was quiet, Pop," Wilma said. "Stealth was of the essence; Ellen had seemed so lost on the phone (okay: drunk, too), and I wasn't sure she really wanted me there."

—she stopped on the cutting patio. A sense, mostly nasal, of animal was like a curtain in front of Ellen's back door. The head of the moose, on the floor, shifted slightly as Wilma struck it with her foot. She reached down and at first thought it was a deer, then felt the rack and knew it wasn't. Better, however, than a bear. Ellen loved the bears, but Wilma could never see them as anything more than giant rodents, rats without a tail.

She'd been in the kitchen when the world exploded. She'd been right near the doorway to Ellen's small front room, a doorway filled with two lacy curtains from Ellen and Joe's bedroom in Quilli. At the first sound, which was not at all what she thought it would be when she later found out what it was, the curtains took a gentle puff toward Wilma, the air expansive and gusty, Ellen just beyond those curtains, asleep on the couch. The front door thundered open and to one side of Wilma a window disintegrated. A porcelain soup tureen on a shelf over Ellen's head exploded like a cherry bomb going off in the middle of a peony bush. Porcelain petals tinkled down into Ellen's wounds, which were hardly, as Wilma could begin to see even in the smoky dimness, wounds, since wounds suggested an element of healing, something to be learned from, perhaps, to brandish or show off proudly. Survival, Wilma had known right away, meant only that there had to be enough left of Ellen for burial.

In the middle of it all—that brisk death—someone had hit a light switch and activated a souvenir. Since Ellen tended more toward kerosene lighting unless she was working, the cutting patio always well lit, the bulb that went on in her living room was a moody four watts, the lamp a small ceramic cottage complete with lighthouse and an inch-long slope of lawn to a ceramic beach.

"So, yes, I could see her, Pop, could see everything including the rifle clutched across her chest like an old teddy bear.

"Eighty-seven shots fired," Wilma said, "a number I made up on the spot, most fired toward the overstuffed couch with the faded chrysanthemum print, the sort of print a man would choose thinking it's what his wife wants."

Joe had bought the couch for Ellen.

Wilma, there in Don's, sat down in a chair next to a table where a woman was frying up samples of a soy protein wrapped in soy bacon.

"Something ripped into the braided oval rug," she continued, "damaging the pumpkin pine floor. A collection of carnival glass was reduced to dangerous dust; a china set (Haviland, cheap, something Joe hadn't known and had always regarded as treasured crockery) become a sweepable cluster of china chunks. *In situ* wounding, Pop, nameable pieces. Removal of the *gluteus medius,* the *gluteus maximus,* and the *tensor fasciae latae* meant that a portion of Ellen's butt was shot away."

"An ass like an ache," Wilma said, repeating one of Joe's endearments. The woman frying up soy protein smiled at that. Such women know when to smile. I imagine it's in the training.

"As an example," Wilma continued, "serrating, tearing expenditures, gross, of the *pectoralis major, teres major and minor,* and *latissimus dorsi,* leaving the arm, the left one, secured by only the teeniest portions (that word is actually in there, in the account, 'teeniest') of *deltoid, triceps,* and *trapezius* muscles."

• • •

"I was thinking of chili," I said, picking up some packages of ground pork, "that and some corn." Wilma was on her feet and pushing the cart again. I kept putting my hand on top of one of her hands just to keep her aware that I was there.

She nodded her head toward the chili seasoning mixes, then turned to me and said, "I kept telling myself I could *think* my way through all of this, that I was prepared for change, flexible in the face of friends who come apart on you. I thought answers would come, and yet—here it is, don't ever ask me to repeat it—with a buckshot twink of the *scalenus medius, trapezius,* and the *sternocleidomastoid,* I was reminded of a movie I saw long ago—a movie, Pop!—where a man was hanged, a very famous man, I think, the scene daring and graphic, the man's head nearly parallel with his shoulders. That's how Ellen was for an instant there, a whole bunch of muscles and ligaments gone bad what with the excision of the *scalenus medius, trapezius,* and *sternocleidomastoid* along with 'other' damage to the neck, as they say, a crushing of the *levator scapulae* and a shredding of the filmy *platysma.* Ellen was no famous person, certainly not a movie star, but those ghastly wounds seemed to give her face, her demeanor, a look of infinite curiosity, a look that would have had some effect in a court of law had not Ellen's mind, which was a good mind, a kind mind—had not that mind and possibly lots of feeling escaped with the emanicipation of the left temporal lobe of the skull and the destruction of the *masseter* and *zygomaticus major,* the *orbicularis oris* and the hardly ever mentioned *buccinator* and *risorius* muscles.

"I studied Latin, Pop," Wilma said, pulling two cans of kidney beans from a high shelf. "It has made the world a more comprehensible place. My teachers said it would."

She had left Ellen's the night before when everything was over—which was a good way to put it, she said, certainly from Ellen's point of view—when the shooting was over and she, Wilma, was covered with blood because something had slapped into the big carcass she'd been standing next to.

"I went back through Ellen's woods and across the one road and down to the lake where the wind was coming on even through the starry night, a moon, too, somewhere up there. The chop on the lake was like a woodcut, scratchy and precise, a good place to stop. I believed, I suppose, that thought would come to my rescue, but that didn't happen. I screamed instead, Pop, a belly-rupturing cannonade like the last bits of sanity exploding from a madwoman: pure rage, pure hopelessness.

"It was sadness, stark and biblical."

She went to her knees, she said, then crawled some distance before going down on her side, before bringing her knees up to her chest and laying her head down onto the dirt of the shoreline, some sand, gravelly rock, her face hardly an inch away from the maximum inward creep of the restless lake.

Dawn was not yet inevitable and Wilma's skunk's-eye view of the lake was seductive, like some partnership to the glory of God. She imagined animals could see lake tides humans could not, could feel themselves lighter and more capable at certain times of the month.

"I was there for a long time," she said. "Perhaps I slept, perhaps not. Eventually, I got to my feet and made it home. It was still dark, but Grenada was in the garden as I came out of the woods and she helped me get to the house. 'Go to bed,' she kept saying, but I said, 'The baby. Where's the baby? I need him right now.' "

"The next thing I really remember was being back down on the lake and heading toward Ellen's. That should have been easy, but I had noticed Cary Andersen drive up to our house when I was nearly back in the woods, and then all of a sudden I realized she was running after me, chasing me."

Or it seemed to be a chase, Wilma told me, not being sure at the time that she was in it, that she shouldn't just stop and talk to Cary, the two of them reasonable people doing reasonable things.

"You know, Pop, I kept hearing you and Mom whispering, 'Just keep going, Wilma, keep walking, do what you have to do,' while at the same time I had this terrible need to stop and turn and let Cary Andersen come to me, to let her see that the ways of the law permitted excess in more than one fashion. I was upset, stark with lunacy, sleepless, too, and could see Cary Andersen again and again in Ellen's doorway, methodically emptying a pump shotgun into Ellen's walls and Ellen's curtains and Ellen's couch, and there must have been moments there when Ellen saw all of that, the destruction of her things, medial cadgings from her and Joe's life."

" 'Wilma Doll I'm telling you to stop!' That's what I heard eventually. You get yelled at by your peers, Pop—commanded—Jesus, it's an odd feeling."

"So much for gentle mediation. She was there, she was authority, and I think I was just tired of running—winded, a little pooped."

Wilma stopped then, she said, and turned to face Cary. Cary's face was bright red and, even in the morning chill, sweat blotched her uniform shirt. Her holstered gun had shifted around, too, and was hanging in front of her crotch.

"I am going to Ellen's house," Wilma said. "I suspect there are—have been—improprieties there. You look a mess."

Cary ignored Wilma's remark and said, "Everything at Ellen's is being taken care of. You have no need to go there."

"There are needs and there are needs, I suppose. I've been taking care of my own needs for a long time."

Cary, straightening her belt and holster and slowly catching her breath, said, "I guess we all know that."

"What you did up there," Wilma said. "I have to see Ellen. Memories, you know, things that need tending. It's how we remember friends."

Courtesy was everything. She could not, she knew, give Cary a reason to say one of her little police things, like "You're under arrest"—if that's what they said now, if the language hadn't changed since the last time she'd seen a movie—if only because that would complicate this painfully complicated morning.

"Cary was tough, Pop, looked like she worked out; the dark skin of the tanning booth, blue eyes, butchy hair. A reputation, too, with territory that had to be protected. I was wary; I'll tell you that. I wasn't afraid."

And she would see Ellen, she told me. She would su-
pervise some things because Ellen was not, now, a corpse
among friends, people who would read decency and good
looks into her, an acquaintance with poetry and a thousand
people and, for all that, loneliness, too—the tragedy of the
bear dresser. She was, now, with people who thought her stupid and cut off from things, risky, a disturbance; absent divine
intervention, a target. Judgments had been made.

"You are not to approach the DeLay residence," Cary said.

In a whisper, Wilma said, "Fuck you, Cary."

"I regretted the words because they were cheap and
trashy and, no doubt, they were words Cary, in her civic
sinecure, heard all the time to little impact anymore, but we
were at 'yes' and 'no' now, and it seemed right for a change
that Goliath do what Goliath ought to do—Goliath, after all,
had a following, while David only had dependents—and so I
rolled a soft uppercut beneath Cary's chin and watched her go
down, her face in the mud, but a breathing woman still,
alive—at temporary rest.

"I had not killed her, Pop. I knew that."

Trop tôt.

We had our supper —the chili powerful, the beer ice-
cold—and talked of oddly practical things: Bylaws needing an
ear drain; a valve cover on Wilma's van needing tightening.
Did I know, she asked at one point, that the doctor wanted
Grenada to have a new knee put in?

I did not know that.

We laughed at ourselves then, after spending a few minutes
talking about all the titanium and stainless steel litter—hips

and knees, maybe shoulders—buried in the cemeteries these days.

A few easy moments—why not? Around midnight, my papers and pencils and tapes at the ready, we started again, and in the space of a breath I felt once more like I was on a five-legged horse without a bridle.

22

A DOG WAS BARKING on the roof, Czy Czyczk's Lab-Doberman mix. Czy's lingerie store downstairs was burgled about a year ago. Everything he had in a size larger than twelve (I think; I know it was the larger sizes of some very small things) was taken, providing some interesting gossip around town for several weeks.

So Czy got a dog from the pound, and at night it has the run of the inside stairway, going from the main entrance to the store, up past my apartment, and then on to the roof. What Czy expects it to be guarding on the roof I don't know. When it's up there it has the run of every roof on the block, and more than one drunk (or sober) citizen has had his deepest thoughts rattled late at night by looking up to see this *hound* slobbering down on him.

Wilma looked tired, and for the first time I thought she looked—a little older. Her lips were pale, *wrinkled*, hair mussed. When she got up from the couch and stretched and walked to the bathroom she seemed stiff.

"Coffee?" she said.

"It'll only take a minute."

Wilma's return to Ellen's the next morning followed the same route as when she'd gone there in the middle of the night before—past the back outhouse and shed, onto the cutting patio.

"There are times when I think the world should be ribboned with yellow crime-scene tape," she said, "but I was surprised that Ellen's place was not. In spite of my set-to with Cary, I hadn't thought I'd even get close to Ellen's."

The second thing she noticed was that the moose head was no longer on the cutting patio.

"I entered the kitchen as I had the night before, and noticed dirty dishes in the sink: one plate, one fork, one knife, one glass, no serving dishes. I remembered telling myself once that if I ever lived alone I would always use serving dishes. Do you think I'll ever live alone, Pop?"

It was not a question she wanted an answer to.

"I thought those dishes should be washed, the kitchen cleaned up. That was not the time, though."

She stepped into Ellen's front room and wished she had not. "Ellen, as both presence and memory, was all over it, here and there in choices, selections, that ugly leather chair over there, that a man might love and only a woman who loved that man would permit in her house. Joe's chair? In Ellen's house? Greeting cards, hung carefully, squared up the walls, tasteful, even beautiful ones, all nicely matted and framed. There were plants, too, some still in pretty containers, others blown into the woodwork. Ellen's glasses sat—there, right over there, Pop, I can still see them—on a small Shaker table we'd found one day at Antonia's Antiques in Quilli."

Wilma noticed a long piece of dental floss on the floor in front of the couch. "That brought on the first of that day's tears, the string just so personal, intimate, something you'd never hear about on the news, and yet it said so much about her. I wondered if she'd had time to finish."

A foul litter was all about the room, and Wilma knew there

was much of Ellen mixed into the litter. A full clean up would have to come later and she would do that. She most definitely would do that. No discount cleaners, either—good sprays and soaps, rags purchased in a bag of twelve.

"What, though, had been the crime, Pop? That thought roared through me like a car stereo gone wild. Ellen a criminal? Sweet, reasonable Ellen? I couldn't help but think of all those times when someone is nailed for killing his wife or drowning the kids or just poisoning the neighbor's cat, and the next thing you hear are all these testimonies to how marvelous the person was—a person who could not do this terrible, terrible thing—how loving, giving, a good citizen, a churchgoer, and you want to say, *Yeah, well, so much for how you know your neighbors.* But Ellen? That *was* Ellen, Pop. It really *was* her.

"I began to think something needed to be straightened out. That was my word—prescriptive, dull—but it was a chilling thought, as primitive as can be."

Cary's voice was strident, Wilma went on, no nuance of negotiation to it: "Wilma Doll, get the fuck out here! My men are tired. We need to finish everything up."

Recovery from the sucker punch, Wilma thought, had apparently been quick.

"I think sometimes the leading edge of hysteria is a profound calm. Something was pulling me faster and faster and I thought I was actually going to swoon or start speaking in tongues. Hysteria is not to be feared, can even be welcomed. A hysterical witness has a certain credibility, a suggestion of tremendous things clearly seen that will come out once peace is restored. This reasoning, functioning persona, however, this calm thing, was far more threatening to Cary and whomever else might be out there. Complicity could be indicated, further action necessary. Someone out there might even be thinking that I, Wilma Doll, needed to be, as they say these days, 'taken out.' "

Someone had thought that of Ellen.

Someone, perhaps, hadn't thought at all, a schoolteacher's most withering charge.

"What now, Cary?" Wilma shouted toward Ellen's front door, truly frightened now, no longer sure that those whose job was to serve and protect knew which side of the ledger she was on, a question of how far things could go and still not be too far.

"Come out of there, Wilma Doll!"

"Where's Ellen?"

There was no response.

"Did they really want to shoot me, Pop? At the time, I had no explanation for what had gone on there the night before, and began to wonder if I'd just walked into something, if maybe Ellen had just walked into something—a wild drug bust gone crazy, some sex ring resisting closure, things that can happen in places where addresses are often approximate, where people are sometimes approximate, too."

She heard Cary once again. "On your hands and knees, Wilma Doll. Come out that way."

Big women don't crawl well, Wilma decided. Her belly, normally firm, hung down in that posture. Her breasts felt like something that should be tolling the hour to an anxious populace. She wondered how many men—males—Cary had out there. Some things you could do in front of a woman that you dare not do in front of a man. Squatting down, she grasped the bottom edge of the door and pulled it open perhaps an inch. She just wanted to peek—a womanly thing.

Terror made the sky a bit bluer. She felt her arms and legs begin to shake and then had an awful thought: *There is no one here on my behalf. Only me, and apparently they don't like me.* That would have been Ellen's perspective and Wilma was glad to share it. Terror seemed a quite lonely thing.

She was certain there would be no pain if Cary shot her. "But I thought about you, Pop, and Grenada; about Bylaws and what it would be like to grow up with such a heritage. All three of you—I couldn't bear the thought of your emptiness, nor could I bear the thought of your rage—and there would be rage, wouldn't there, Pop?"

Thankfully, she wanted no answer to that question, either. I remembered Val's comment about Cary shooting at Wilma and I wondered if Wilma knew. All I could think just then was, yes, Wilma, there would be rage. Let's not even begin to talk about it.

"What I couldn't fathom was this abeyance, this detention at the hands of someone I knew, someone with whom I'd grown up and with whom I'd shared a water table and air and the low angles of the sun and a supermarket and occasional concerns about joblessness or the health of crops or maybe a pending blizzard. This derelict *Get Wilma* was dreadful, the entire history of conversation going up in smoke.

"And then, Pop, about the time I wanted to say I'd have lawyers all over Cary like crunch on a drought—it got worse."

"Stay right there," Cary said. She kept a shotgun pointed at Wilma's head, and Wilma was close enough to see the tiny scratches on the barrel, the sheen of human oil on the stock. Police weapons, Wilma told me, always look so much deadlier than any gun anyone kept at home.

"You're way over the line, Cary," Wilma said.

"Just shut up!"

Cary took the bottom of Wilma's dress then and pulled the dress up over Wilma's back and shoulders and covered Wilma's head. Wilma on her hands and knees. Wilma with no one there on her behalf.

"Personally," she told Grenada later, "I am too old to be naked in front of anyone who isn't trying to reproduce himself."

Women crawling in public have an experience that's ineradicable. It would be written down nowhere, but everyone would know it had been. Humiliation never plays to an empty house.

"So I said to myself, Pop, 'Cary wins this one. No doubt about it.' But did you think your daughter would just let it go at that?"

"I wish you had," I said. I think my knuckles were clenched white with rage, but I said what a father is supposed to say. That's one of those things you learn.

23

WILMA WAS ON THE FLOOR looking at a photo album Grenada let me take the last time I left her. She was sitting cross-legged, a glass of milk at her side: Wilma in tie-dyed diapers; Wilma sitting on the loaf of bread we'd baked one time in an old wheelbarrow, three feet by two feet of monster gluten; Wilma and me with our feet on the running board of an old touring car, the pose Bonnie and Clyde—the Thompson submachine guns in our hands real, as are the cigars (Wilma is in her teens, the scene a carnival at Loring Air Force Base); Wilma and Grenada sitting in the green madness of a chard and zucchini bed in Grenada's garden—they are both naked and Wilma is about twenty, but the leafy greens bestow an innocence on everything but the imagination.

Wilma's sitting there and turning pages and talking a manic babble, my presence as audience understood, though not necessarily attended to. The pictures provide a gentle fundament as she tries to show me how wildly, how frantically she pursued reason and logic and all the tidy organizers in order to keep her soul (Wilma's word) intact.

Wilma had seen, in the dim light of Ellen's house, a body walk up and grab an arm of Ellen's corpse. The body moved easily and Ellen was on the floor like a pillow in a pillow fight, the alive body kicking the dead one with boot toes going into fresh wounds while laryngeal instincts, in Ellen, whooshed out fresh moans. There was a tumble of kicks and rolls over to the door until darkened hands grabbed the ankles—one, oddly, broken—and tossed the thing—Ellen—aloft, a slow-pitch arc out into the yard, the head hanging on like a loose-hinged shutter.

"I saw that," Wilma said, then decided no mind should be trusted in a crisis. That was something a friend of hers, the Quilli librarian, a wheezing grump with a sense of humor who'd been in Vietnam, and who'd fathered nothing within Wilma's ubiquitous fecundity, had said once.

"He'd been talking about war—that war, any war, all wars being totally identical—'a necessary exercise in creativity,' he said, 'in the need to take a significant part of any generation and pound it into mental chills and a willingness to take a job, any job.' I thought he was pretty clever.

"As explanation, though, for anything, let alone war, that had been lean, if not totally wrong, since he'd learned his sociology at a technical college from an adjunct high school teacher, except for one thing I've never been able to get out of my mind beyond the fact that he liked to spit in my mouth and I let him do it:

"'I was at My Lai, where two people were killed and that was it. It was all under accidental circumstances, an old man carrying a baby, his grandchild. They were run over by a Jeep, nothing more, the driver a young engineer from Terre Haute, new in 'Nam, confused, starting, stopping, backing up, going forward, trying to undo a whole bunch of life going bad and just running over them again and again because of conflicting imperatives, far and away not even in the same league as the bad stories about that place, but it was a bad day anyway and the two of them were buried and that was when the other story started, the one that went on too long. Any event that is important beyond forty-eight hours becomes an event unlike anything that really happened.

" 'I was there,' he'd concluded, 'which was exactly the same as not being there.' "

Astoundingly cynical, I thought, and if I'd been doing all of this work against Wilma's wishes instead of at her request, I might have thought she was trying to say how futile it all was—that the past fades, disappears, not only with each sunset, but practically with each passing hour. A point to argue, perhaps, or maybe it was just a weary Wilma forgetting that it wasn't she who had to put the puzzle together anymore. It was me—Pop—and I wasn't losing anything.

Still, with the tape recorder running, Wilma drank milk or coffee while I had a few beers. The Czyczk dog still barked, but it was somewhere over Gary's Appliances—seeing the things dogs see, unable to see, unlike myself, that Wilma was talking not history but revenge. Sometimes I wonder if there's any difference between the two.

Wilma kept talking.

"I saw—

". . . looking outside, through that narrow slit of door, an unrecognizable semblance of my friend, Ellen. Because her work required, in all decency, some nakedness, regardless of whether or not she was also trying to entertain, to do negotiable business, I knew her breasts, her navel, her hips, many of the checks and balances of her body. I had been there, at her home, as often as Ellen permitted and as often as I could stand because she was so intense. So I knew those things.

"We never had sex. Strange how you have to qualify friendships these days, as though something must of necessity have

been incomplete without it. Mostly, we just thought of ourselves as two old chicks who never lost the fire—just the firewood. Ellen, too, never got over Joe, who she'd left by choice,
left by cognizance and careful plan. Don't believe for a minute
that some hapless dead sheep was all there was to it. This was
a calculating lady, her education intact, though she always
complained she'd had too much of it. But she ordered books
and magazines and read them and we talked about them. Intellectual things, however, always seemed to make her sad.

"Regardless of what you might think of her strange business, her customers loved her, all the hunters from Downeast
and Rangeley and Saco, from Quincy and Garden City and
Aurora, Illinois, and Sleepy Eye, Minnesota. She was a story
for them, a small fantasy in a place where those hunters
weren't known and she knew that. It was for them she played
the part of either wetland hag or highly skilled whore. She
wore furs and leathers and now and then flashed for the hunting boys and hunting girls. She stank, usually, because they
wanted that, they wanted to see art rising out of dirt, to find
something unacceptable acceptable because of what it pro-
duced. Ellen was fundamental and she had class. She also had
a certain problem about being alive.

"I saw —
". . . on the cutting patio, though, a table holding a computer cash register and an old credit card roller. The small key-
board on the register was black from fingers that were rarely
clean."

"I saw —
". . . all of this, these events, were an interruption of a busi-

ness, a business problem, what one might even call a restraint of trade. Her last year, Ellen made over forty thousand dollars, which is a huge amount of butchery, and which was a barrier between her and Joe, something she couldn't tell him because it would have been so stark against his own gentle way of making a living, though it did lead one reporter into making a gaffish comment about the demerits of living by the sword and dying by the sword. Astounding. That led me to think you can't control the reporters any better than you can control the police, which is to say that I have strong doubts whether you can control anyone at all. We're all constrained by a moral structure with the strength of crêpe paper. Ellen and I even talked about that once, shortly after the time some guy tried to stiff her on eighty-seven pounds of venison, just stiff her by saying 'no' when she gave him the bill. He took his meat and walked out to his truck to leave and Ellen followed him with her rifle, the .30-06, and stuck it through his window and under his chin so his chin was resting on it, so she wasn't aiming at him, first of all, maybe a legal point on her mind. When he evinced the usual intelligence of the masses by saying 'Up yours,' Ellen fired, right under his chin and through the passenger window, which was open, so no damage was done. Later, as she told me the story, I asked what happened then and she smiled sweetly and said, 'He peed and paid.'"

"I saw —

". . . what must have been a thousand Canada geese flying overhead, honking, living things in a cloud, the fog wisping its way into a sunny morning. Much of her yard was packed dirt from where the cars and pickmeups drove in, a circular drive around an old tree stump. She had bordered the area with lupine and raspberry bushes. There was a narrow circle of marigolds and daffodils, too, petunias, pansies, dusty miller. 'Common growups,' she called them, 'the unassuming gardens of commerce.'"

"I saw myself—
"Not a few of them, the flowers, a bouquet, like a hastily gathered roadside weeping, had been tossed into what was now a canyon over the symphysis pubis, a bouquet I thought singularly appropriate—lupine, marigolds, petunias, daffodils, a sensitive theft from Ellen's own work. I vowed I would tell no one that I was seeing sorrow in the officers' faces.

"I saw myself telling stories —
". . . about how they'd sat her up against the stump and jammed the moose head down over her floppy head and tight against her shoulders, some manner of lessening what they had done. Oddly, really oddly, so odd I seemed to stare right through Cary, who wasn't ten feet from the door where I was on my hands and knees, the eyes of that moose, open and unglazed (yet), stared at me, its eyes now become Ellen's— rich, creepy eyes that seemed to say, 'I saw it coming and I didn't like it.'"

"and lying and lying and lying —
"It was a wondrous hat, that moose head on her shoulders, the goofy humor of Ellen right there in her own death. Cary, I think, could tell I was out of everything: out of time, out of oatmeal, out of gas, out to lunch, unmetaphored, unbuckled, and unsung because she let me stay there for the longest time.

Her pistol was in one hand and a shotgun in the other, but we both knew the violence, the retribution I was building went way beyond mechanicals. Now and then a cloud would lift and I could see, briefly, that small band of civil soldiers, the government forces of Andersen et alia, not a theorist in the bunch; yet, for tactics, they were nonpareil. Still, I had no room for conjecture anymore because Ellen was dead and already I was missing her, the kind of soreness that opens up and says, *My dear, how ever do you expect to go on?* I didn't know, but I was wishing Ellen would stop staring at me from out of that moose's head. She was looking as soft and cuddly as the best of friends often look, and it was in all of that that the memories were coming to be, sweet memories, dreams of things I'm not sure ever happened. As I think of all we did together I might be including the things we wanted to do together—maybe that's all, really, there ever was, but she was becoming my furry rascal: demure, sassy, refined, gross, nice feet and a big nose, my merry clown, and for as much as I might be forty-four years old I could still see my bed beginning to fill with a collection—*Bylaws, don't touch those!*—of puffed and foamed and furry moose, every one of them named Ellen, and for as much as my motive in telling it this way *(lying and lying and lying)* might seem rank viciousness—invention, after all, has always been the greatest destructive force on the human scene—there was nothing more to it than my needing to keep Ellen near me so that I could, at least once in a while, think that something mattered, that something counted.

"I told Cary the world would know about this, about all of it.

" 'No one will believe you,' Cary said. She was even reaching out her hand to help me to my feet, her revolver holstered now and the shotgun lying on the deacon's bench near Ellen's front door.

" 'Therein,' I answered, less a fool now, 'lies permanence.' "

"—until Cary broke."

24

POISON GORELICK HAS ALMOST given up on love, one of those things a man might say to himself or another man—but never to a woman. He has a woman friend, truly that. They talk easily, move slowly. Her name is Spicy Pelletier, a motel worker who, like so many people in Quilli, is never quite what she seems. A Bowdoin graduate, articulate, punctual, well-tended, she finds the little doors in Poison's soul and walks in and makes herself comfortable when Poison is so lonely he could cut off his thumb or challenge someone to a fight, something slap-ass physical.

Poison has always fought, his mode fisticuffs, his stance professional, a small man unpredictably dangerous. He's a small man, too, who rarely wins.

He recognizes in a fight something elemental, nearly academic, no partial truths allowed. His confrontation with Cary Andersen that one day—barely six months ago—had proven his point: she'd broken nearly everything in him she'd wanted to break before he much knew he was being broken.

But whether it's Spicy or, as it once was, Wilma, Poison calls it love in the same way that a salesman looks at a deal—success is worthy of heavenly trumpets, but success is repeatable. Love never is. Poison sees questions in that point of view, but he won't question it.

Wilma took him beyond success, but they lingered so long at friendship as to lose a certain intensity. Poison and Wilma liked each other long before they loved each other, and, as Poison sees it, loving holds a jiggly candle to liking every time. Poison hopes only that Wilma will live forever. That's as close as he comes to loving Wilma, but he thinks that's pretty close.

Like any plan, this one had flaws. That's hindsight. When I first heard about it I thought it was sheer idiocy.

"You were going to rumor Cary to death?" I asked both Poison and Wilma. I was looked at. I was stared at. I was found wanting, but there was hope.

"We were after her mind, Pop," Wilma said. "A little shaking, a little breaking—see where it all went. You know—let her run into things she didn't even know were there."

"The best offense, Splotchy," Poison began, "is the one the enemy doesn't know about. Isn't that right?"

"Or," Wilma began, leaning in close to me, "Cary created horror. She authored villainy."

"Villainy?"

"Yes, sir. It was her gift, and we wanted to give it to the world. It didn't matter how we did it."

"I'm lean on tactics and strategies," I said. "Why not just take it all to the courts? Talk never killed anyone." Somehow, I knew that was wrong the minute I said it.

"Joe's doing that," Wilma said.

"He is," said Poison.

"I know," I said. "That's my point."

"It isn't working," said Wilma.

"You didn't know that at the time, though, did you?"

"What I knew at the time, Pop, was that my best friend was dead, and I knew who had to answer for it."

"I'm not your accuser, people," I said. "Remember that?"

"We know."

Poison met Cary, that first time, in Bud's Bar.

"She was looking good," he said. "Nervous, though, but holding on to it. A tight blouse, I think—an announcement. She was wearing heels, too, her legs aren't so much shapely as muscular; and her arms, Jesus, I thought—forearm curls, twenty each. She bites her nails, though. I thought that a flaw. Her sleeves stopped at mid-biceps, on the sleeve hems the tiniest of ribbon bows, light blue, the biceps at rest still defined, a little twitch there, too. Lipstick—can you believe it?"

He got two bottles of beer from Bud and gave one to Cary.

"Down here?" he said. He pointed to the booth nearest the front door.

"As you wish," Cary said.

Poison thought that sounded a touch bureaucratic, and he wondered if he'd been an item on one of those sticky-notes somewhere.

"I don't want to get into anything legalistic here, Cary. Imagine you're tied up with a lot of things right now, lawyers and all—easy to compromise, screw things up."

"Poison?"

"Yes, ma'am?"

"No one controls me. I say what I want when I want to say it."

"Doesn't matter," Poison said. "I'm just talking the talk, the things I hear, what I'm thinking. It's not important to me that you lay out your personal position on freedom of speech. You got a reputation, babe—"

"Babe?"

"That's my freedom of speech, babe. You got a reputation, as I was saying, like a hound after its first hunt. There's people around be afraid to get a parking ticket from you."

"I don't do parking tickets, Poison. You know that."

"Maybe people don't know what you do, especially after what you did. Fear's fear, it doesn't break down into ideas."

Cary slipped her shoes off and tucked her legs under her. She looked down on Poison across the table.

"Nice move," he said, looking up at her.

"You weren't there," Cary said.

"Wasn't I? You don't know that. Most of the time I'm almost everywhere."

"The ubiquitous Poison."

"This isn't about sarcasm, hon. Your blood runs to the soil here and I know that; mine does, too. But you turn on your own, you go after your own people, and that changes things, changes them hard."

Cary took a sip of beer and put the bottle down hard enough to make Bud look over toward them. "If people think me crass and nasty, Poison, it is an earned reputation, but I'll tell you—and every short-order half-brain you talk to—this: Ellen DeLay was a volatile and dangerous woman, probably deranged, who almost killed a man."

"I wasn't talking about Ellen."

Control it, Poison told me. That's what he had to do. "She and me we go way back to where we were less than we are now, and we're both nothing now. Big neck veins, though. I bet you get her in bed you'd break something—not your heart, either."

"You weren't?" Cary said.

"Nope."

"You going to tell me?"

"Wilma. I'm talking about Wilma Doll."

Don't pull the pin, Poison thought. Not yet.

He was a kid, Poison said to Cary, with a kid's ways and a kid's cares, an only child as a result of his apparently grabbing at a souvenir as he left his mother. She, Luster Gorelick, healed, the prospect of no further children not an embittering one. Hard times were in the world, and the fates were dealing out far more heinous cards, occasionally to those who didn't even know they were playing a game.

"Sandy-haired, I remember that, my father with a pointy nose and wire-rimmed spectacles, tall, my mother was tall, too, someone pulling hard on a recessive gene in order to produce my height. My mother always had short hair, marcelled, red hair, everyone said, though I always thought it was blond, and she blushed a lot.

"It seems like my memories of her are from the night, in and out of shadows, creeping around during midnight storms, sometimes sitting at a window all night if it was snowing. She loved the snow."

Cary shifted, Poison said, glanced at her watch. Her tongue rubbed her lips so much her lipstick was fading. He'd worn a flannel shirt, his sleeves rolled up to reveal his long underwear; he wore suspenders, too, and hadn't shaved for two days.

• • •

"At a time, Cary, when I could barely talk, the world did not lack for talk, even our world up here, where the roads back then were nowhere what they are now, nor the telephones. 'We are fighting the Germans,' people said, 'and you, Lester Gorelick, you teach German.' So one day the police took him right out of the classroom and down to the county jail—actually, they took him twice, but it was all just one nightmare for my mother and me—suspected, they said, 'of being a spy for someone.' They held him without trial largely because they never charged him, they never even made him officially an inmate at the jail.

"So my mother lost the house when the bank said, 'this is not right' (we hadn't missed any payments, yet), and an apartment came along and, Jesus, a Polish landlord right here in Quilli, a man with only one foot who took the rent down a buck or two—"

He looked up at Cary then, looked her right in the eyes and thought they were drooping a bit—they were still on their second beer—boredom, he hoped, setting in, the grand crashing boredom of an oft-told tale repeated into inanity, thinking to himself, he told me, *it's coming, it's coming, but not yet*, as he said:

"—each time she'd let him screw her, which became more and more frequent because, for a while there, we had no money at all, at least not until she began taking in washing from some of the Indian women up near Quiktupac—Indian women!—the only ones who'd deal with subversive trash like us. She didn't care, of course. She was like an artist pulling together the disparate elements of survival, and she would have no truck with those who interfered with her vision—"

"Poison?" Cary said.

"What?"

"Wilma? You said you were talking about Wilma?"

"Did I? It's mostly been Ellen DeLay on my mind these last few minutes. Not being educated, I guess I lack a certain cognitive discipline."

Cary, livid, said softly, "You're hardly uneducated."

Don't be nice to me. Don't even try.

"—until finally I realized that her vision, her creation, was me. The mother makes the child; it is her reason for being alive. She said once, though, once when she was looking dreamy and uncentered as if drunk except we had no money for drink, when she was tired of being handled, insulted, even laughed at, that I was innocent and everything else in the whole world was guilty, guilty of everything. I wasn't sure about that. When my father came home I was mean but competent, a pissed-off little prick, but I was healthy and my mother was healthy and I hadn't killed anyone or robbed anyone and I sure as hell wasn't 'a spy for someone.' We were all right, my father told us, we were together and we'd made it and we were pretty small but we were a family. 'Your father greatly loves your mother and your mother greatly loves your father and you're a part of that, son, and a part of everything we have to do now.' Which was to leave the tiny apartment and move into an abandoned trailer not too far from St. A de P, money, as always, our nemesis. My father's teaching job had long since been filled, and even though he'd never been convicted of anything, the principal laughed him right out of the school the day he went in to inquire about it. My mother, too: We got her out of the rent problem, but the free trailer was too far from those Indian women so she lost the washing business."

"Stories," Poison said to Cary.

"There's always stories," Cary said.

"One of them—there are two—is that—"

"I know what you're going to say, Poison. It doesn't matter anymore."

Poison, pissed, pointed his beer bottle right at Cary and said, "Is there anything more repulsive that one person can say to another than, 'I know what you're going to say'?"

"I meant painful things," Cary said. "That you didn't have to repeat painful things."

Don't be nice to me. Don't even try.

"That he went up to Quiktupac and gave blow jobs to the Indians at five dollars a puff? Try hanging that washing out on your line to dry. That's what I grew up with and it was a hurtful thing with no way out. Can you see it? Can you go up there with him on it? He had no car; hell, most of the time none of us had shoes. So he's got long pants and an old denim jacket, a lunch—lunch, dig it?—from my mom, just your average, white, ex-not-quite-con hitching rides to Quiktupac up 161, a little "hi, boys" as he strolls into the government bar up there, a drink or two maybe, then a casual 'guess I'll go take a leak,' said not too loud but loud enough, and for as many times as I heard the story only one thing ever struck my mind as being worth thinking about. I just couldn't figure how or

where under those circumstances did you actually put yourself
aside somewhere and have lunch?"

"Anyway, Cary, it wasn't true. He didn't blow the Indians. He stole from them. Money. He was never caught."

Cary, suspicious, not wanting at all to trust anything
Poison was saying because she didn't know where it was go-
ing, finally asked, "The other story?"
"What other story?"
"You said there were two."
"I did?"
"You did."
Bingo.
"Oh. Sure. Wilma says you had sex with Ellen. With the
dead Ellen, after she died. That you had sex with a corpse. She
was there and she said you did that, had sex with Ellen's body.
Wilma Doll says that."
"You son of a bitch," Cary said.

25

POISON HAS OFTEN JOKED that he and Wilma are available for faith healing, water dowsing, or investment analysis. He is a bright man but, together, he and Wilma can sometimes seem almost spooky. That they would somehow weave and wrap and embroider themselves into the lowest, nearly unspoken, level of Quilli babble—working it to a profit—might seem the dopiest of gambits, but it goes, I suppose, down to roots, fundamental principles. The key to living well in a small town is to exist publicly within a very narrow band of conversation. No one ever forgets that knee surgery you had sixteen years ago, and if that's all you are, don't be too disappointed. It also means they don't have to remember anything else about you, either.

In other words, close the door on your life and no one cares if you write lyric poetry after work, distill booze from skunk livers, or wrap your spouse in barbed wire before sex. Let any of it get out, though, even the smallest thing, and suddenly people will start remembering you in ways you've never been—and there is no flattery in the process.

It was something like that—a little rural wisdom—that was beneath what Wilma and Poison were trying to do with Cary. There might have been more to it, too, even some doubts on Wilma's part that Cary was the one who'd really caused Ellen's death. "Shake her up," Wilma had said, although Poison told me one time he wished it had all been that easy.

"Cary has foam in her veins," Poison said, "lead pellets, diesel fuel."

Not a good day that one day, Poison told me. Rain thins the music, flattens the harmonies; a late winter, chilly, featureless, drenching rain. "March 4, 1995," he said. "Sticks in the mind like a day you got fired or had minor surgery."

The rain is hard and cleansing, a frolic for the Pappadapsikeag and the Quilli Stream. There is no flooding, although the sump pumps come on quickly in most people's houses. Much of Quilli pulls inward under barometric stress. At Bud's, the afternoon is busy. Outdoor workers are not good candidates for the soaps. Beer works.

Poison walks from his room above Gary's Appliance (on Main Street, across the alley and half a block up from Bud's Bar) toward St. Bleufard's High School. He is wearing a rain suit of blaze orange and a waterproof cap, and the suit warms him too much during the mile-long walk.

St. Bleufard's, formerly Quilli Regional High School, cattily referred to by the kids as St. Bullfart's, is not Poison's destination. He'll cross the highway just before he gets to the school, and walk down the short, sloping driveway to Pizzle's Inn and Stylish Rooms. In spite of the name, it is Quilli's only motel, home to the expected licentiousness to be found in rented solitude, but home, also, to university speakers, salespeople, business consultants, friends and relatives of various decedents, and faraway families of graduates.

Poison looks for the maid's cleaning cart under the long porch roof of Pizzle's and notes that it's where she said it would be, Room 12.

There is only one cart at Pizzle's, and one maid and one manager and one groundsperson and one handyman, and, with the exception of the cart, they are all one and the same: Spicy Pelletier, forty-six, olive-skinned, five-six and a hundred and fifty pounds. Her mottled mix of brown-blond hair is nearly always hidden by a head scarf, and she wears bulky work clothes: usually, high-top boots with insulated socks because her feet are always cold; khaki shorts; a denim shirt; and a sweatshirt. Spicy is always busy, presentable enough to handle a quick check-in at the desk, casual enough to mount the roof to check on a possible leak, or to grab the mower and trim the back lawn down to the small stream. She also painted and hung the three signs along the stream bank that read, NO SWIMMING OR DRINKING. POISONED WATER OF A SERIOUS TYPE.

"You put my name in print," Poison told her the year before, after she'd made the signs.

"That's past tense, Poison," Spicy said.

"I know that." He smiled and said, in an unusual show of self-deprecation, "It's how my friends regard me."

The signs are significant. The previous year, an itinerant evangelical pastor had checked in one night with three women. He rented two rooms, one to be shared by the three women. Nothing untoward, thus, seemed to be looming, although Spicy thought the women appeared a little dazed, one of them highly nervous. The pastor was a hefty man with an uneven potbelly (hernia, Spicy concluded), but each of the women was thin, skinny. Spicy, excited but uninquisitive, thought the pastor might be using Pizzle's as a way station on one of those underground railroads for abused women.

In the morning, just as Spicy was arriving for work, the pastor walked the women down to the stream. They were wearing dark terry robes they kept on as the pastor immersed them, a full-body cleansing of life and its iniquities, followed by an upbeat chatter, then girlish giggling, finally real laughter. Each of the women, naked under her robe, was covered by a mottled splotching as something in the water caused the dye in the terry cloth to bleed.

Early in the afternoon, however, the pastor came down to the office and told Spicy she needed to see something. Would she come with him?

"I won't go in there," the pastor said, as he led Spicy to the women's room. Spicy went in, the sight of three, nearly naked, women not the most bizarre thing she'd ever seen. Nor was the runny dye of much concern. Successive showers had brought the tint down to a light hue on the women, the two with the forest green robes looking slightly bruised, the one with the red robe seeming a bit sunburned.

"Can you believe it?" the red one said, not angry, not litigious, and quickly willing to drop her panties to her knees, an unnecessary move since Spicy had already noticed that the three of them, top to bottom, were as hairless as a bowling ball.

"Freedom's road," Spicy told Poison, "and toxic stops along the way."

As he reaches the roof overhang and walks down to Room 12, Poison pulls the top of his rain suit off. The chill air feels good. Even his arms are sweaty.

Poison and Spicy meet regularly for what they both call "unconventional sex." They are an odd match but a good one, neither of them wanting to risk love again, both of them generous—as friends only.

Poison, of course, has rarely released himself from the

bond that was Beverly, a celibacy that was initially necessary as a balm for grief, then evolving into a matter of honor and loyalty.

At fifteen, Poison impregnated the thirteen-year-old Beverly Hills. People said they were not surprised, since Beverly was the product of retarded parents (not true, Poison said), a child normal in all respects except for an aggressive bustline and an early ability to drink beer without getting drunk.

The young Fendamius—he was not "Poison" to Beverly—already going bald in a context of dark and wiry whiskers, couldn't believe that fortune's bounty, so long absent from anything to do with the Gorelicks, had brought him Beverly, frail and pale, but a quick wit beyond her years. Poison remembered she liked doilies, the silliest of things to a young man, and she had knitted little booties that slipped over the handles of their knives and forks and spoons. He still had those booties, Spicy the only person he'd ever shown them to.

During her seventh month of pregnancy Beverly developed what was then called rectal paresis. She became infected, as Poison occasionally says, "all over herself," and died. An attempt was made to save the baby, although it was quickly determined that the baby had been dead for a while.

"There had been no time for anything bad to have happened within our marriage, no time for annoying habits to unearth themselves, hardly enough time for either of us to assess the eating, bathroom, sexual, sleeping, or even family habits of the other. I was left with only bliss unbound, now cruelly packaged as if for storage."

Lester and Luster tried to be a comfort, themselves not

strangers to disappointment, but for as much as they might have spoken of first love and its power, and the way it digs a channel in the heart through which all subsequent love will flow, they also knew you were never actually supposed to *get* that first love—not permanently—so there wasn't a lot they were able to say. Lester, once, and uncharacteristically since he was an intellectual man, told Poison a story about a nineteen-year-old baseball wonder who'd pitched a no-hitter his first time on the mound. Where do you go after that? Is anything less than a no-hitter a failure? But neither of them liked sports, and when Lester was done the only thing Poison could think of to say was, "What's a no-hitter?"

There've been a number of times when Poison and I have been together during a confusing moment—maybe an odd piece of news coming out of the TV at Bud's, or a long point being made by someone in a conversation going nowhere —and invariably one of us will turn to the other and silently mouth, *What's a no-hitter?* It's a way men deal with pain sometimes.

The sex between Poison and Spicy is unconventional, Poison says, because he can call her Beverly if he wants to, a need that has lessened in recent years. Spicy, he finds it easy to imagine, looks like what Beverly might have looked like had she lived and grown older with him, Spicy, as she told him once, "a meandered soup of Icelandic and Gaelic genes." She'd been married—Poison lets her talk about this whenever she wants to; it causes him no pain—to "DamnJack Pelletier, a tall, nutty guitar-string of a fellow, a mathematician, and a lover of all things Mic Mac, mostly over at the Tobique Reserve in New Brunswick, and mostly female and in their teens."

Spicy and DamnJack never divorced and Spicy considers herself married and regularly celebrates their anniversaries.

Spicy loves to eat and loves to drink. She's never been fat but she has to work her weight all the time. Above all, she loves to talk. She talks to guests at the motel and she talks to herself when she's doing maid work or repair work. If she has time to sit at the front desk the telephone will be constantly at her ear. She's been known to put whole conversations on someone's answering machine when she called and no one was home.

Her talk, however, is more than the simple need for echoes, the noise of presence. She graduated in 1970 from Bowdoin College and feels comfortable with ideas and comfortable with the many different ways people work out their lives. She has seen much. Lives unfold quietly (usually) at a motel, but there is always litter.

Spicy and Poison like to lie on a bed in one of Spicy's rooms like an old married couple. It may be a time when they switch the names around—Fendamius (Poison), Mary Clare (Spicy), Beverly, DamnJack—or it may not. They talk about the weather, about impending storms and the angle of the sun at certain seasons. Food prices are always worth a good many minutes, coffee and meat especially since they are both meat eaters. Spicy's favorite is pork, but she'll tell anyone into her subject that pork in Maine is miserable—anemic and tasteless. On the other hand, about the only time a cup of coffee isn't in either of their hands or at least nearby is when a beer is. Dairy products get their attention, too, and it is not rare that Poison will show up with two half-gallons of ice cream, Spicy and Poison sitting cross-legged on the bed (the chairs in

Pizzle's rooms—Spicy has tried to work on this—are not good, not comfortable) and each eating a whole container. Poison always buys the same flavor for each of them—usually coffee, now and then butter pecan. Selfishness, he says, is not meant to be shared.

"Mrs. Pelletier?" Poison says at the closed door.

"Mr. Gorelick?" Spicy answers, then says, "Take your boots off, dear, I just ran the sweeper."

She is naked, Poison sees, and she notes his quick scowl as he says, "Not today."

Not wanting to embarrass her, though, he sits down on the bed next to her and presses his face into her neck just below her ear. She smells of work, her sweat familiar to him.

"You brought troubles," Spicy says.

"I brought answers," Poison tells her. He reaches over to the edge of the bed, grabs her T-shirt.

"Put it on," he says, sounding gruffer than he means to be, "I need your help."

After dressing, Spicy goes down to the motel office and comes back with a packet of motel stationery. A letter-head is important, the motel's perfect.

Pizzle's rooms have no desks, so Poison pulls a chair sideways up to the low dresser and writes:

Dear Ms. Andersen:
Tradition is like the old uncle you really want to shoot
but he looks so damn good napping on the front porch.
The Native ways, especially, deeds of the Mic Macs as in-
herited from the French—so hard to keep some of them

alive in the face of modern developments. That richness,
like old smoke caroming off a tanned hide, its preserva-
tion threatened. But you've done it, Ms. Andersen, so
we've heard. You trimmed her, the lithe and floppy Ellen
DeLay; i.e., you scalped her. That's what we understand.

Sincerely,
Boethius Pooty

Poison mailed the note to Cary at the township office. He
didn't think she'd have a secretary who'd open her mail.
He didn't care.

Pistelle Philomene walks down to the last booth in Bud's Bar and sits down opposite Michelle Monelle. Together they weigh over four hundred pounds, though Michelle carries the double-Franklin on that and sixty more.

"You look worried, little worker," Michelle says. One hand is resting on top of the phone Bud put in the booth for Michelle's taxi business. It has rung only twice today and it's nearly five o'clock.

"I need advice," Pissy, a journeyman carpenter, says. "Something about love."

"Clean underwear," Michelle says. It's what her mother always told her.

"I'm not wearing any underwear. Should I tell him that?"

"I was joking."

"I'm not."

Michelle smiles then and says, "Never tell a man you're not wearing underwear."

"Really?"

"Without mystery, Piss, we're just doctors and lawyers."

26

THERE IS MILEAGE to be gained from remorse. The child-killer, the family-slayer, the duper of the elderly, all can benefit if even a hint of regret follows verdict or confession. *If I had it to do over, I wouldn't have done it.* Even the pose counts for something, regardless of sincerity.

Naturally—what about Cary? Do I vilify her as faceless government butcher, or commend her for taking charge of a truly frightening situation and resolving it?

I had long talks with Poison because Cary hadn't been quite as silent as she appeared during their conversations. Meetings with Joyg Noydland, township manager, were scheduled repeatedly and repeatedly postponed, but I finally nailed him over drinks and mussels at Le Père's one afternoon, and for as much as he spoke the bureaucrat's language, I still managed to squeeze long moments of candor out of him. Perhaps it was the garlic.

Then there's Iona, Cary's daughter, whose memory can give you the eighty-ninth digit of pi, but whose speech permits it to emerge only indirectly. Iona is lovely and sad, and a devastating witness. She also has Cary's diary, the existence of which surprised me. I would hardly have imagined Cary as a reflective type. That's not being nasty. Some people simply never have a need to hit the rewind button to see where they've been.

Nearly everyone in the township office saw the letter Poison sent to Cary, I was told, and everyone freely talked about it. Office gossip never has a more fertile field than alleged wrongdoing.

Viola Fiona, on her own initiative, picked up the township mail at the post office every day, then sorted, opened, and distributed it before her regular duties began at eight o'clock. She also managed to read every piece of mail as well, and the first thing she did after reading the letter from "Mr. Boethius Pooty" was to make five copies of it.

Since three of the people Viola gave copies to made copies themselves, the atmosphere in the township office when Cary checked in at eleven was one of thoughtful smirking. Cary Andersen was not well liked.

On March 15, Joyg Noydland, Cary's lover until she dropped him following her confirmation as township provost, advanced bureaucratic sympathy by suspending her without pay until things could be looked at. As he later told Viola Fiona, who told it to everyone she knew, "You never know about atrocities. I rather enjoyed sticking it to her—excuse me, Viola—and only regretted there wasn't something more I could do."

At home, Iona refused to talk to Cary.

Cary made Iona's favorite supper the night after being suspended—fried Spam, au gratin potatoes, blueberry pie from the bakery at Don's Grocery—but when Iona came home from work she took one look at the meal and made herself a peanut butter sandwich, poured a glass of milk, and sat down at the table with Cary. Iona would have taken the sandwich to her room, but meals were always eaten at the table even if you weren't speaking to the other person there.

Rituals were important to Iona. Anything in her mind that

couldn't be connected to a time, a place, a pattern, or simple behavioral command tended to float away, valued but meaningless—a soap bubble. Permission was the linchpin in the process, defiance a matter of bold, even life-threatening assessment.

She heard the conversations in front of her all the time as she bagged groceries or sold cookies (the only clerkship she was allowed), heard them turn with circumspection and by innuendo to "those most awful recent events"—a girl's mother not usually talked about in front of her.

Iona was different, often called "slowsome" when she was younger—pale and winsome, the flower just barely blooming in everyone's garden. Her high cheekbones gave her elegance, her wide-set eyes suggested caution. She was admired for her dependability, pitied for her limited mind. Most people thought she didn't feel much, and few thought she could think at all.

Critics, some have said, are the ferrets of discussion. Even Wilma will admit that Cary was not well served by public opinion those years ago. She and Cary had worked together for a time back then, cleaning dorm rooms at the university. Shared work never made them close, but there was always shared talk—intimacy sometimes masquerading as work-weariness over coffee and a doughnut.

Those arbiters of town talk had not been snowbound with Cary in the trailer, as Cary told Wilma, no husband, no car, no telephone. She'd had all the firewood she would need for the blizzard, but it wasn't heat that would make Iona's fever go away. To make it a game, Cary had gotten them both naked and they'd gone outside to attack and enter the monster drifts surrounding the trailer, Cary eventually as blue from the cold as the child, Iona shuddering and pummeling the fever, working it, pushing at it, Cary just shuddering. The cold burned Cary's lungs, while the numbness, the lack of feeling, brought a whole breakfast up and out—from Cary, Iona hardly eating at all.

Cary screamed hard outside in the wind. She yelled and she sang and finally picked the child up with arms that couldn't feel her, and pressed her to a naked chest with no heat to share. She stumbled toward the door and tripped and watched as a perfectly painless cut opened on her knee, the flow of that cool blood, though, almost nonexistent.

"She still has that scar," Wilma said, interrupting herself. It was an interesting lapse. "I mean—"

The fever, however, would not leave when asked, would not leave when under assault, and seemed oblivious to the silent entreaties Cary made to a God she'd parted from long ago, the parting fair and friendly. For five days Cary watched as Iona glowed with a saintly vigor, her skin a blush peach, her eyes lit with a sparkle seen by parents only in the days before antibiotics. Iona kept reassuring Cary that she felt better, a little better, she was sure of it, and on each of those days Iona might as well have lost a foot, an arm, a kidney, a finger, an ear, so visibly did she diminish in spite of Cary's dosings and purgings and coverings with salts, vinegars, mustards, ices—anything she could remember from things she'd heard or things she'd read: Mic Mac nostrums, old wives' tales, hints from a small stack of supermarket magazines.

"In the end, though," she told Wilma, "it was like a long

and difficult plane trip where your luggage is missing when you land. There is a ritual, then procedures. You feel frustration, anger, resentment at being singled out; then, exhilaration and forgiveness when the luggage is found. Except it's ripped open and half empty. You just pick it up and move on."

Ashamed at one point, her mother's name so venomously skewered over fruits and vegetables and packages of meat; annoyed, too, that people seemed to assume she couldn't hear or that she somehow wasn't there, wasn't comprehending—Iona took her magnetic nametag and turned it upside down.

Cary tried explaining things to Iona, but they were both upset that nothing was getting through.

"I have to deal sometimes with unhappy people," Cary said. "That makes other people angry."

"I'm unhappy."

"I know you are."

"So I should leave."

"Why do you think you should leave?"

Iona was silent then. She'd laid down the prescription. It was inconceivable that other prescriptions might follow from that.

Joyg Noydland had said things to Cary, and Poison Gorelick had said things to Cary, and there were apparently things that Wilma Doll was saying to anyone who would listen, despicable things and foul fictions.

Cary had seen none of the others since the incident. Val and Debbie and Anna were rarely in town, and even more rarely in town when Cary was, at least up until now when Cary was in town all the time. Still, she didn't run into them and there seemed no point in actually seeking anyone out. They were on their own anyway, no one story agreed upon and things all the better for that. Investigations thrived on confusion, and just as vigorously ended up inconclusive.

Alone—the way of things. Cary had some savings so she and Iona would get by. Iona had always turned her checks over to Cary anyway, so they could do it. A clearing of her name would come eventually, one way or another. People forgot; they became bored. Yesterday's incident was no match for an increasingly flighty attention span.

Still, the constant assault on the facts was brutal, and those who knew Cary could see the bitterness growing—a tightness in the face, a clenching at a simple hello. She started smoking again to pass the time and, as I discovered, began keeping a diary—fat tablets where she writes cheerily about "a swell childhood," lovingly about Iona and Iona's troubles, and, throughout it all, dropped sometimes into the middle of a paragraph, even a sentence, a quick remembrance or some sad fact about "that skinner incident." Again and again she would grab my sympathy, but she would not call Ellen DeLay by name and so my response to Cary's words grew colder and colder.

She slept well, she writes, when she finally got home. The next day she drove up to a small cabin not far from Quiktupac where a young man—Tzolchefro Hugh-Drivet, usually called Lemon Boy by everyone—was said to be keeping his wife in a cage. It was clear, by the report, that the woman was not being *hurt,* just *kept.* What was known of Lemon Boy and his wife, Amelia, was that they had been trying since the beginning of their marriage to have a baby. While Amelia had been able to bring a good many of the children to term, she didn't seem able to bring them out capable of life.

Lemon Boy was at work when Cary showed up. Amelia gave her a glass of iced tea and together they walked to the tiny oak grove where Lemon Boy and Amelia had buried thirteen infants and four dogs.

"The cage," she said, "was my idea. We thought if maybe I could just be put away somewhere for a while that—well, it was a thing to think about."

Then Amelia added, "I was afraid, you know."

"What was the trouble?" Cary asked.

"Trouble?"

"Why were you afraid?"

"About you. Lemon Boy said you were coming. I was afraid about you."

"Mrs. Hugh-Drivet—" Cary began.

"It's just 'Amelia,'" Amelia said. "My husband would laugh if he heard you calling me 'Mrs. This' or 'Mrs. That.' It sounds oddly, too."

"Amelia—why would you be afraid of me? We've never even met."

"You know," Amelia said.

Cary waited, then finally said, "You've lost me."

"I even had to drag the cage over to the shed," she said, "and it's a heavy bugger. I didn't want you to see it."

"The cage?"

"It ain't made very good. Sometimes we screw things up. Me and Lemon Boy, I think, might be deciding we're too old to try anymore, but I was afraid you'd think maybe I was nuts with a big cage like that where Lemon Boy was going to hang it from the ceiling in the living room so I could watch TV while the baby was going on—"

Amelia told me she was shaking by then, the ice in her iced tea rattling, her shoulders trembling. Together, they looked down at the row of tiny graves, each marked with an identical oak board that read ARE BABY, and then the date. Four of the boards were marked FIDO, SPOT, FLUFFY, GENE.

" — and it is a piece of knowledge about the pretty famous Cary Andersen and the business of nuts, especially you know with Lemon Boy and me having ways that are not exactly expansive. Before he went to work Lemon Boy took me out to the oak tree, see, right over there, and said, 'She'll most likely tie your arms to the oak tree and generate some target practice like what happened over there at St. A de P the other night.' 'Well', I said, 'Lemon Boy, if it is your intention to petrify me you have, finally, for once in your life, been one hundred percent successful at something.' But then I got to thinking even if Lemon Boy was being mouthy and all, still, you just hear these things and you don't know what's true so I hope you don't take any offense by this. For most of us, all you hear is what you hear and if you hear something it must be true because there isn't always any way to hear anything different. I believe I have calmed down now. Thank you for the iced tea."

"Amelia?"

"Yes, dear?"

"It's your house, your iced tea."

"Whoops."

• • •

That visit ends much more cryptically in Cary's diary, some of which I've added below. I've had to be careful, since it's pretty clear that Iona can mimic Cary's handwriting quite well and that she's been in the diary—certainly not the first time on the planet that loyalty and history have clashed. Loyalty almost always seems to win.

Cary, shaken, pulled off the road onto a small bluff overlooking the St. John. Canada was right there, quiet and rational at midday, stark houses dotting the bare hills. Canadians had so little love of trees.

Clinically, she told herself, you can expect this reaction. The mind will find order in things. It will pick up and discard freely in order to do so. But it will have its way.

Cary is pretty famous. Cary might kill me cruelly.
Yes, I might.
If I hear it, it must be true since there's no way of hearing anything different.
As epistemologies go, limited.
—Provost Andersen, tell us exactly what happened that night at Ellen DeLay's.
—I don't know. I don't remember.
Prosecutors could make hash of me, no eggs, with statements like that.
—I really, really, really don't remember, but I think it must have been atrocious, ghastly, blasphemous, and perverse.
—Provost Andersen. Did you do it just because it was permitted, because it was included in your warrant, your job description?

—*Well I certainly wouldn't have done it if it hadn't been permitted.*

Starting her car finally, Cary looked into the rearview mirror and smiled at herself. Aloud, she said, "That's enough of that."

27

POISON AND WILMA HAD SET something in motion, but where it would go neither of them knew. As with instigators anywhere—catalysts, prime movers—their most common thought was that nothing was happening. Life was going on, Cary especially: buying groceries, paying bills, caring for her daughter. They assumed she laughed now and then, had a good meal, slept with resolution and contentment. She was still upright, though, still functioning—jobless or not—no matter how angry Poison made her.

Something would have to be done about that.

I'm a father bollixed, confused about a daughter, a grown daughter, though maybe it would be better to say that I'm a parent, perplexed at the direction of an offspring. Lots of friends there—every deviant, pervert, criminal, fruitcake, or irresponsible idiot is somebody's child. We don't know, we say. We can't imagine what went wrong. No man does wrong willingly, it has been said, so it must have been . . .

What? Wilma's healthy. She and Ellen used to jog the back roads, and even now she goes out and runs two or three times a week. She goes to the Ponus Health Fair at the hospital once a year and all her vital signs are sturdy. Although she still smokes, she rarely drinks, and if she and her mother ate any more grains they could both be baled.

She long ago opted out of the treadmill of stress and ambition. She graduated from a good university with honors—

both basketball and academic—but she also told me at the time that it was wonderful to see how really good she was at such a young age because now she didn't have to spend her life proving it.

She has seen Grenada and me enter and exit each other's lives, too, but she's never seen us as being anything but loving toward each other—or her. She's been to Boston, New York, and Chicago, but she will not leave Quilli because she finds life here manageable: difficult to find dementia in that.

As with anyone, she has holes in her life, pits and canyons that echo, but about Wilma, about all those women, you almost have to say, well, it must have been the weather, perhaps astral configurations. I've joked with Grenada already that there must be a women's satellite up there that periodically beams down an unhingement. I don't know. Ellen DeLay just tried to make her life better. Cary Andersen just did her job. And Wilma?

Wilma said one night when we were having supper at Blanche & Sophie's Supper Club, "The fact was, the true fact, Pop, I knew this, like seeing a tiny bump of skin cancer right there on your nose, that I was losing my mind. It was obvious to me, and felt a little like hearing bad news on a nice day."

"Skin cancer on my nose?"

"An example, Pop."

"Oh."

"I even said it aloud to Bylaws one time: 'Mommy's going nuts, baby.'"

"So how did it happen?" I asked. "This, whatever—final step?"

"You think all questions have answers, Pop. That's sweet. It must have made my childhood a comfortable place."

"You were comfortable—mostly," I said.

Days were just following days, she began. She hadn't seen Poison for a while, was even a little tired of him.

"Or maybe just tired. Bylaws was sick around that time. His muscles leaped and jumped on him in his crib and he smiled at the intrusions.

"Grenada said I was a little loose for mothering right then. I would have said I was doing all right if Bylaws had been a puppy or a hamster."

Grenada took the baby's temperature the one day, an anal poke up into knowledge, 105°. She was already wearing clinic clothes: a dress, a shawl, and low heels in preparation for a drive to the Hunellia Faulk Ponus Medical Center in Quilli. Grenada dressed in civilian clothes. Wilma told her she looked good.

Wilma had been in the bathtub for three days, with breaks. No disputing that fact, and Grenada hadn't tried. Grenada, especially, knew a woman's need to wash the tidal splash of past events from her skin. Wilma, though, decided that if she was losing her mind it was best to have it happen in the bathtub. Any parts floating away ought to be clearly visible.

Ellen may have been shot eighty-seven times, or that may have been the number of times she, Wilma, had conceived, her concepta terminated like some bold, but not strong enough, virus. She began to wonder if the life of a grown woman was, as she'd always believed, really more important than that of an unborn child. No one had thought Ellen's life that important. Wilma had heard the police had been at the house barely ten minutes before they began shooting. She, Wilma, had never had an abortion without preceding it by days and days of agonizing thought.

Death as a concept was sometimes not big enough to do all it had to do. Who really killed John Kennedy? Robert Kennedy? Indira Gandhi? Who caused the fire at the Happy Land Social Club in New York? Scampering rascals—Jesus! Police said if they didn't catch a murderer within twenty-four hours the chances of apprehension began to decrease geometrically. Geometry was good; there were angles to life and death that had to be watched. Wilma had always doubted that those odds, bad as they were, factored in easy air travel or proximity to the interstates. "Frankly," she said to Ellen one time, "if you don't catch someone right in the act of doing something, it's all just speculation."

This was not, Wilma admitted to me, a healthy direction to be going in. But it was a direction. She could only stay in the bathtub so long.

Life was memory, but memory was such a fickle ally. Within twenty-four hours things got forgot, that was all. Even killers got befuddled, confession the least reliable of all sources of belief. Who'd believe a killer?

"We're going now, Wilma," Grenada called up from downstairs. "Do you need anything in town?"

"No," Wilma said. "Do you have the prescription card? They'll probably want you to get something."

"I got it. Sure you don't need anything?"

"I'm okay."

"Don't forget to swim to shore once in a while."

Wilma had never thought about insanity before, though she had thought about cancer, hepatitis C, Ebola, AIDS, guinea worms, lice, herpes, and amyotrophic lateral sclerosis. Everything, it seemed, was being tied to a virus, the confetti celebrating major illnesses. Might not there be a viral link to this unstoppable chaos above her neck and behind her eyes? Could people themselves function as viruses, attaching themselves to you, replicating via conversational diversity, defending against the killing blow by turning over a new leaf?

I'll never do that again, baby, I promise.

Poison said he'd meet Wilma at midnight in the alley behind Bud's Bar because Wilma told him on the phone, "I'm going to kill Cary," and Poison said to her, "If you're going to kill Cary, you need to talk about it."

"I'm going to kill Cary," she said again.

Poison was sitting in the alley, his back against a Dumpster. Wilma was leaning against the wall of Czyczk's Lingerie, gradually sliding down until she was sitting not far from Poison.

"Ninety percent of the things you do are in your words, Wilma. Once you say things, you don't usually do them."

"It's the ten percent that's deadly, isn't it?"

"Cary's arrogant," Poison said.

"Yes, she is."

"Abrasive."

"True."

"Cocky."

"Are we listing *all* of her virtues?"

"Killing. Keep your eye on the ball."

"It's impossible," Wilma said. "I think I'm feeling the way

Ellen must have felt before she left Joe. Something absolutely must be done, but there's no way in the world I can do it."

"But she did it, didn't she?"

"Yes, she did."

"And people called her nuts and stupid and loose and foolish."

"And she called herself—"

"What, Wilma?"

"Happy."

"You'll manage. You're getting it."

"Are there mice out here?"

"It's a clean alley."

"Quilli's clean."

"People take pride in that."

"I know," Wilma said. "You've heard about it, haven't you?"

"The investigations? The hearings?"

"It's like it didn't happen, it all comes out so clean. Quilli clean. Wow."

"Why Cary, Wilma? Why would you kill her?"

"It wouldn't have happened without her."

"There were others, Wilma. They were armed to the nuts. Excuse me."

"It's all right."

"Three others, I think. Not a fair fight."

"Anna Pancake?" Wilma began. "Debbie St. H? They'll do anything someone tells them to but they won't do anything on their own. Even Val—her tendency would be to call in the National Guard or order an air strike out of Loring, but she wouldn't have just—"

"So it's Cary."

"Cary got to them. I don't know if she wanted to be a hero or if she's just an asshole or if there's really any difference between the two. But Cary has to go. Maybe she's just the lottery winner—or loser. Or maybe I'm sitting on something wildly primitive, something we think doesn't exist anymore—the ability to do something beautifully irrational in a perfectly rational way."

"Powerful, babe. You're on the edge."

"I don't care anymore."

"Zing."

"I rest my case," Wilma said.

"Resting is always good, Wilma."

"I have to eliminate her. I have to terminate her. I have to whack her. That's as current as I am on the terminology."

"How did it sound to you? How did it feel?"

"Pretty good—easier than I thought. Did I really say 'whack her'?"

"You did."

"Not very poetic, but I think the poetry exhausted itself up there at Ellen's."

"Just as well. Things like this, keep the poets out of it. So how you going to kill her?"

"Oh, yes."

"You need to think about it."

"How can I?" Wilma said. "How in the world can Mr. and Mrs. Doll's rapidly aging daughter even think about such a thing? This is not what normal people do."

"Normal?"

"Don't start. I've had my own doubts."

"You *should* have doubts. You lost a friend. Friends are what keeps your mind inside your skull. Trust me."

Quietly, Wilma said, "It didn't have to be the way it was. They just tore her apart—not exactly a trial by your peers, whatever the charges might have been."

"Everything has to be the way it is, Wilma. You can't step outside your life, and Ellen couldn't step outside of hers."

"You sound like Joe, Poison."

"He's not a stupid man."

"I know that. How are we doing?"

"Not there yet."

"I still want to kill her."

"So do it."

"How?"

"Start at the beginning."

"What?"

"You have to meet her, get together."

"True."

"Private. Real private."

"Out somewhere."

"One thing?"

"What, Poison?"

"Everyone—everyone will know you did it."

"They will?"

"Everyone. So concealing—that's not the point. You just need circumstances, maybe confusion."

"Confusion I have."

"Not your confusion. Confusion like what happened to Ellen. Confusion in the event, maybe many events."

"I was teasing, Poison."

"Maybe many events. Finally—"

"You're already an accessory, dear."

"I've always been your accessory, Wilma."

"Baby, baby. Finally?"

"I said that, didn't I?"

"You did."

"Last things. Finally—oh: no weapons."

"I have no weapons."

"You could get some, but don't."

"I whack her with words? Naughty thoughts?"

"We'll get there."

"I'm waiting."

"But no weapons. If someone thinks you found sanity in the dark pit of impulse, that's okay. But if you plan this out— equipment, you know—the gig will be you found sanity first and then you plunked her. That's not good."

"Plunked her?"

"Terminology. Better to make these things up as we go along."

"So—"

"You'll have to do it—"

"I don't know, Poison."

"—with your bare hands."

28

IT WAS IN AUGUST OF 1995 that Poison and Wilma stepped up the pace. Or, more properly, it was Poison who got things going again. I don't think you can separate the two of them in any of this, but Poison told me he took that midnight talk about homicide seriously. Since he and Wilma had backstopped each other again and again over the years it wasn't unusual for him to play this game however she wanted it played.

"But," he said, "she'd moved from loss and grief and sadness right into hate, whereas I was just looking more at a little social mischief. We all heal; it helps, though, to know you got a few licks in."

He arranged to meet Cary once again and, just as innocently as the first time, began talking about his family.

Like their son, Poison said to Cary, Lester and Luster had started out with all the right berries making the jelly: youth, passion, love, sass.

Lester was a tall man, early bald like his son would be (the bald part), fleshy and patriotic, who'd never had more than one testicle. This was more than enough (in a manner of speaking) to keep him out of the army and out of World War II, though it was something that couldn't exactly be broadcast to the neighbors, many of whom were lonely women and some of whom were fresh widows.

The first time Lester was put in the county jail he felt, as was his nature, almost good about it. There was risk afoot and the country was on alert. He cherished nothing about being a victim, but preparedness would have its natural flaws. He'd been sure he could talk correction into the mistake. They said it was "a matter of safety." No mention was made as to who was being made safe from whom.

The county jail was seventy miles from Quilli, and during that first incarceration Luster and Fendamius made the trip to visit Lester as often as the old Studebaker could make it. During the second jailing the car would have to be sold for food money, but there was initially an aura of adventure about the trip. Sometimes Luster sang to Fendamius as they drove along.

Lester told his wife and son he was very lonely and that there were strange people in the jail. A Japanese man was in the cell next to Lester's, an old man who'd been growing broccoli in the Quilli area since 1930. He was teaching Lester Japanese and Lester was teaching him French.

"Do you think that's a good idea?" Luster asked him.

"It's an opportunity, dearest. Strange place, but it's something."

"Maybe it would be better if you just stayed with English. Maybe that would be better."

Lester was released in October of that year. He went immediately to the school and found out they'd replaced him with a young woman who knew neither Russian nor German, but she was Quilli-French and could also teach typing.

He began to worry about money since neither he nor Lester had done anything long enough yet for there to be any savings. After losing their house during Lester's first jailing, Luster had rented an apartment in town, though she had to tell Lester

on his first night home that the rent hadn't been paid in three
months and she was really worried about it.

Cary, bored again, but familiar now with how Poison
was going to do this, interrupted him and said, "I thought you
said she was screwing him? That the rent was paid with the
world's oldest credit card?"

"I will tell my story?" Poison said.

"Yes, sir."

Lester offered to teach anyone in the landlord's family
some languages if the landlord would knock off a little rent for
it. The landlord said, "Are you nuts?"

He was a Polish man with beefy eyelids and one wooden
foot he would remove now and then to amuse Fendamius. At
the time Lester made his offer, the Polish man was in the
kitchen. As Lester talked, the landlord watched Luster wash
some clothes in the sink.

"She's a real redhead, that one," he said. "But your boy, he
don't pick it up."

"Doesn't look like it," Lester said.

"Gotta watch that, Pappa!" The landlord's laughter was a
spitty rumble. Lester let him have his joke unanswered.

"But you know," the landlord said, still wheezy, "you got
a nice family. You do got that."

"Thank you," Lester said.

"You got no money, though." He watched as Luster's dress
slipped around her hips and thighs as she scrubbed, then
added, "What are we going to do about that?"

"Things will change," Lester said.

• • •

Change they did. The second time Lester was jailed was on Christmas Eve of that year. This time they said he was a spy.

"It's all really mad," he told Luster. "They just use that one word, 'spy,' not 'espionage,' not 'treason'—all the big things—just 'spy.'"

Luster, who'd been badly bruised by a brass knuckle while fighting the police when they came to take Lester away, finally said, "Does it matter?"

"Does what matter?"

"The word. Does the word matter? You're here and we're way back in Quilli. Does the word matter?"

"Words always matter."

"To you, love. Only to you."

"Whose side are you on? They can charge you with theft or they can charge you with murder. The word matters. It really matters."

"Now it's murder? They're charging you with murder?" Tears were in Luster's eyes.

Lester, who'd been holding Fendamius on his lap, gently hugged the boy as he said, "Holy smokes. I didn't mean it like that. It was just an example."

"Not a good one."

"Maybe not."

"So are you?"

"Am I what?"

"A spy?"

Luster cut her hair because the Polish landlord told her to, cut it down to a quarter-inch.

In Quilli, not even the wife of a spy could be thrown out

onto the street. With her hair so short, however, Luster could go nowhere, nor could she see anyone. The Polish landlord brought them food, much of it old or stale, and the Mic Macs brought them laundry and a little cash.

"You both in prison now, I think," he told her, his laugh as usual, Poison thought, something you'd want to put in a bag and hide somewhere.

"I'd sit at the table and read comic books while he was there," Poison said. "I guess I could have made a bad thing out of it, but it all just seemed like business to me."

"Your mother being raped?"

"I don't know if it was that, if it was rape. The old man was ugly and he was fat, but he'd left his family and his foot in Poland so he might have seen my mom as just something nice for a change. I don't know anything about the dreams people had back then, particularly immigrant dreams. Might be interesting to know."

"And your mother's dreams?"

"Look, she was twenty-eight years old and a knockout. People were calling her an Indian lover and an old man's whore and the wife of a spy. She didn't have a goddamn dime, yet with all that, and even with the moldy bread and having to wear her husband's shoes, I think she saw the whole time as being just damned *interesting,* even the Mic Mac women having great fun telling the white woman how to do the shirts and pointing out stains on the underwear, sometimes paying her and sometimes not, but knowing they had her over a barrel anyway, had her out straight to where they'd make fun of her and she'd laugh right along. I think she saw the whole thing as one goddamn amusement."

Poison stopped then and went up to the bar to pick up a bowl of chips. When he returned Cary said, "Wilma?"

"You think this is a game?" Poison said.

"Are we getting there?"

"We are."

"I'm trying to hold on."

"I'm trying to be civil," Poison said. "Neither of us has an easy job."

One day, Poison said, he came back to their apartment after being out trying to learn a paper route. He was too young for it—about seven, he thought—and the newspaper man eventually gave up on him. The sun was barely up and Poison's mother, not at all shy about anything anymore, what with being the Polish man's whore and the Indians' washer-woman, was sitting naked on a kitchen chair, blood on her mouth, her chest, blood on her thighs. One eye was swollen, and she clutched a bloody bundle—a towel, something in it—between her waist and belly.

A shocking thing, Poison said, but not scary. It had not been scary because his mother said right away, "Taught the Polish man something, I think."

Poison got a washcloth from the bathroom and came back to her. He wiped her down and tried to take the bundle but she said no. He whispered to her that she could take a bath and he'd fry up some hash. When she said it all looked worse than it was, he said that was good and she could take a bath now, please, and then get dressed.

"Can you get up?"

"I have to—I don't know."

"Can you get up?"

He thought there might be money in the bloody towel, something from the landlord who was always making her do things that Poison knew were just the things adults did to get by, since his mother was always saying that, *We'll get by.*

"Can you get up?"

"It isn't anything," she said, "it really isn't anything."

"What, Mom?"

"This," she said, "this funny thing," which they both thought was interesting, exceptionally interesting, as she unwrapped the towel and showed Poison the landlord's wooden foot.

"She was quite a lady," Poison said.

Cary had tears in her eyes. Poison expected that, he told me. "She probably thought of herself as sensitive, too, a woman of deep feelings."

"No one talks about the heart these days," Poison said, "so we don't know the language of that anymore. She loved him hard and she loved him forever. She loved him in jail and she loved him when he became a thief. I guess as far as inheritances go that's about why I still love Beverly and I still love Wilma and I can't imagine Spicy not being in my life, though of course none of them are truly *in* my life, a man like me without a long list of accomplishments who can still say that, at least a couple of times, I opened up and said, *Okay, we'll just retire the defense right now and let what will happen happen.* It's been more than enough, even with Beverly dead, to make each day better than the last. The heart—what a bugger. Reminds me—"

"Don't, Poison," Cary said.

"Wilma says you ripped out Ellen's heart, that you did that, one big tug on the old heartstrings. What was it, babe? Trying to end the century the same way it began?"

Had to wind her up, Splotchy.

"Goddamn you, Fendamius."

29

"NOW MR. DOLL," Iona said to me, "I am entrusting these to you on your solemn promise that you will not lose them."

Thus, another small dollop of Cary's diary—two tablets. It was a cold day and Iona was wearing a heavy parka with a stuffed bear the size of a tennis ball pinned up near her shoulder. She smiled broadly as I filled out a receipt from a book of receipts I'd gotten at Netherland's Stationery. She put the receipt in a large and very old leather briefcase. As far as I could tell, the receipt was the only thing in there.

They met again, Poison and Cary, on June 2, 1996, not at Bud's this time but near it, across the street and along the Quilli Stream and the riprap, ducking under the bridge since it was raining off and on, Quilli slick, gray, damp, the old town buildings looking too old, worn, a downside time to all the times when the quaint ambiance of a tourist magnet had been the goal.

Cary didn't want to meet with Poison. "His smugness is irritating, uncomfortable," she wrote in the diary. She felt she already knew all she needed to know about how people were seeing her. The latest was always followed by the most recent, and it all got worse and worse until even Cary said she must have been a real caution up there, an adventurer in evil—no guide necessary.

• • •

But Poison was the connection, Cary herself the item. It was becoming nearly addictive to hear what she'd done and to wonder if she'd really done it. She was reminded of drunks seeking forgiveness by claiming blackouts. If you accept the premise, then anything goes. *I don't remember any of it, so I must have done all of it.*

Poison knew—and of course he teased: his whole goddamn life story. Cary knew about old Lester and Luster as much as Poison did. "Everyone knew back then that Lester Gorelick would steal the wow from the pow off those pathetic bastards up there around Quiktupac. He threatened to swindle, dupe, con, or bodily push whole families into an age darker than anything the anthropologists had ever unearthed. There was that, no matter how Poison dresses it up, and then there was the wife, agreed upon by nearly everyone back then to be a lazy, whiny, laconic, irresponsible slut who'd screw the grooves off a drill press for a loaf of bread if it would keep her from having to get a job, to work, as everyone had done, in the war effort (as they'd called it), Poison, the poor guy—it is not impossible to feel some sympathy for him—trying to build something away from all of that, to find something tolerable he can believe in because, after all, if one person can believe in something there will always be another. The only thing is, most of the old boys I've known, living still, most in their seventies and eighties, cut their sexual teeth on the blowsy Luster right there in her trailer while her old man was selling colic cures made of blackberries and garlic, selling them to Indian mothers who had more federal dollars than good sense, and where had Poison been in all of that? Had the man no memory? Had he no eyes as a kid?"

"I've been an outsider," Poison told me he said to Cary, "in my own town all my life. And even though I know everyone and everyone knows me, and nobody knows more about what goes on than I do, there are no—I'll just be blunt, okay, and a little squishy, too—there are no hearts that are open to me, souls as it were that seek my essence. There is no love and that's all right. You can live without love. You can live without anything except maybe a little food and water, and it has never been clear to me that those who have the love are all that better off than those who don't."

Poison, the outsider? I didn't question him on that. Even as he spoke, though, it was as much that he was saying it to me as it was that he was recounting what he'd told Cary. Kind of bizarre—Poison springing from the thin Quilli soil; Poison's parents ground down and then pilloried by the rougher edges of Quilli culture; Poison, who's worked every place there is to work and who knows nearly anyone it's possible to know; Poison and Beverly, Poison and Wilma, Poison and Pissy, Poison and Spicy: Poison, the outsider? How do you ever get "in," then, in a place like Quilli?

As the rain began again, Poison walked over and sat on a rock under the bridge. He pulled out a handkerchief and patted his forehead and his baldness dry, then reached into his pocket for a cigarette and lit it.

"People are kind of like shops in a mall, aren't they?" Poison said. "They're friendly enough, and they'll greet you and talk to you, but there comes a point when everyone says, 'Closing time!' and you're expected to be on your way."

Cary walked down the steep embankment, slipping out of her sandals as she stepped into the water. Maybe a trip somewhere, she thought, just mother and daughter even with all that that would mean. "I start with 'trip,' " she recounts in the diary, "easy enough. Here's what it is, Iona. From there I'll move on to doing things together, a notion not exactly unknown to Iona. Motels—places to stay. Where you are, dear, can vary but it's always all right. Home can change and it doesn't have to mean that you must change. We won't be gone long."

Cary moved farther in until the water was up to her ankles.

"Just a quick throwing of a mom's frilly and a daughter's frilly into a bag. Don't forget your slippers, your swimming suit. Tonight we'll eat in a real restaurant and you can order whatever you want, swordfish steak or three cheeseburgers and I'm sure they'll have plenty of ice cream.

"The breakwater—at this one place, maybe we'll go there —goes seven-eighths of a mile into the water, and there's a house on the end of it and the fishing boats come by and you can almost reach out and touch them. Sometimes they tell you to throw a quarter on the deck for good luck, which it is, I'm sure, at least for the fishermen.

"Or even just sitting there on a king-size bed, mother and daughter doing makeup things; at your age, I don't know, a little foundation, a blush of winter's cool and, look, over there, the cable television our neutral monitor, arbitrator through the silences.

"I'd be glad to talk about anything you want, nothing weighty, though. This is all just for fun. I don't think you've ever had a sauna bath, either, so we'll do that, you'll love it. After that, we'll go to the bar and listen to the band and have drinks and eat bar food, better than snacks at home.

"But one way or another," Cary concludes, "trip or no trip,

this has to end; the talking has to stop, and I need to get my job back, no reversing of directions permitted."

"Just a nibble out of your heart," Poison continued. "People are like that. Reminds me of how Wilma says, holy smokes, there was clear evidence, even preautopsy— the results of which, by the way, have been revealed to no one—of hepatic mastication upon the late Mrs. DeLay."

Cary, puzzled, the water on her feet and ankles the perfect temperature, the rushing, cleansing crispness of old snow still melting somewhere—looked back over her shoulder at Poison, his words understood, but not quite where they needed to be yet.

"Jesus Christ, Cary—you took a bite out of her liver?"

Cary didn't bother with her sandals, didn't even remember turning around in the water and reclimbing the bank to Poison, nor being careful to avoid sharp stones on her feet. She reached him where he was sitting and put her hand on his shirt and pulled him up and, with one solid, ringless fist, she punched him, the blow aimed directly at his mouth which made eighteen-hundred dollars worth of dentures into bonded plastic trivia, a sharp piece of which was driven into the roof of Poison's mouth, inspiring his usually cool analysis of things to conclude that medical attention would now be necessary. It would be an inconvenience. He also thought this was, certainly, proof that the plan was now working. Wilma would be pleased.

She hit him again just below his eye, breaking the cheekbone, then lifted him right off the steep embankment and threw him against the concrete bridge abutment. Poison knew his being thrown had cracked his skull—he could feel an uncertain wiggle up there—but he didn't lose consciousness until Cary reached down and grabbed him around his hips and, using his legs almost like a club, swung him again and again against the concrete, breaking his legs, as Poison later told Wilma, "in eighty-seven places." Wilma winked at him when he said that.

He faded, he said, he lapsed, the Muse of Nothingness paying him a call and not ringing the doorbell. The last thing he saw was a small crowd bursting through the door of Bud's Bar and running toward the bridge.

30

NO MATTER WHAT POISON SAID—the man had just been pummeled, after all—I have my doubts that he and Wilma ever moved from their talk behind Bud's Bar to an actual plan. The name of their game was revenge, and revenge never mixes too well with thought.

Wilma stops by my place occasionally and gives me something "that just occurred to me." She seems sometimes as if she's in a dream, her speech slow, deliberate, her pace set—the goal infinitely patient. Other times, she's as manic as a hummingbird. She'll say something like, "I've set nothing aside for retirement, Pop," and then, "I should go back and earn a master's, maybe in marine biology. You can trust fish to be fish."

Indeed you can, but be careful. Fish don't growl before they bite.

For a while she seemed to develop a new interest in Bylaws. She bought him new clothes and went over to the hospital to check his medical records—his shots. With her old van sputtering and lumbering, she'd take him out along the Pappa or up onto overlooks along the St. John. "Space," she would say, "I haven't done enough with him yet on this thing about grandeur."

A mother like that is to be cherished, although I'm not sure Wilma knows what Bylaws's favorite foods are. I asked her one time how much he weighed and she said, "I don't know, Pop."

He's a good walker, and she would take him downtown and they would walk the streets until he got tired. Usually, they would stop by my place to see if I was home, and if I was they'd come in and Wilma would sit at my table while Bylaws would hunker down on his favorite spot, two old sheepskins on the floor that are my only rugs.

We'd have coffee or beer and we'd talk about her later-life motherhood, about Grenada, about the Czyczks downstairs (a world of behavioral problems with their little boy), yesterday's rain, tomorrow's blizzard—normal things. Wilma was having no trouble with normal things.

Not then, but, months before, Wilma discovered that Ellen had not left her peacefully, had not left her at all. She had to work that out, she told me. "I clearly had to do it."

"What did you do?" I asked, the end already in sight, though I truly had no inkling of the details.

Nearly two years after the shooting, Wilma began visiting Ellen's place, her reasons vague if you pressed her, though on the surface she had no hesitation in saying, in various ways, "I honestly let her down, Pop." It was that "honestly" that kept puzzling me.

"I wanted to touch Ellen's things the way she had touched them, to hold a drinking glass the way she held it, to lie on her bed, maybe to open a can of her food and eat it. Facts are no good when you're remembering friends. I needed a ritual, Pop."

On her first visit, she spent two hours walking around the outside. She sat on the cutting patio, she sat on the front porch. Joe had repaired the windows and the front door, and had installed a timed yard light on the low gable peak. Wilma found a pair of Ellen's flip-flops under the deacon's bench on the porch, and picked them up and held them in both hands as she walked around.

"One day, maybe the second day, I went into the shed next to the cutting patio. It occurred to me that I'd never been in it, much in the same way that it might occur to someone that in a friend's house visited often in five years, ten years, there were still one or two rooms never seen, not at all."

The shed was filled with bones. There was a cold smell, the floor covered with the crunchy shells of some carrion-eater, bugs well fed and dead. Wilma tried to remember if Ellen had ever said anything about this, if some grinding company, some powdering company or feed company ever picked them up.

Looking around, Wilma felt the failure of all that old biology, the deftly clinging Latin that wouldn't leave her alone. These bones, animal bones, had no names. Order, a physiognomy, came from the board-and-batten walls, a structure in need of paint, things to be done. Any one piece was a piece of Ellen, long fingerlike things, great leg bones. In one corner, stacked like rifles at a military bivouac, spinal columns of diverse caliber. Not many skulls, though. People took their animal heads home, trophies not necessarily for book-lined studies or mantel hangings. As often as not, some poor skunk or fox, even a deer, a squirrel, maybe a moose would find its cranial center tacked to a wall in garage or basement. There were still women around the country with a "not in my house" attitude. Wilma thought that a good attitude.

Wilma was officiating, but at what she was not sure. Unordained, she had to make it all up: soft smiles and a low voice. "People leave secrets behind, bleak caches of pathos—rarely evil. Old people, strangely, don't always cleanse themselves of secrets before the end. Collections of ancient pornography, small illegalities, letters that should have been burned but weren't. It's almost like some postmortem sassiness—*I got away with it!*"

Ellen, though, Wilma thought, maybe Ellen hadn't had any secrets, or hadn't had enough secrets, maybe she should have had more. Like leaving Joe, leaving someone you loved like that, maybe that should have been a secret and not something she actually did.

Wilma spent several days in a row at Ellen's place. She sunned herself on the tiny porch, walked the places where Ellen walked, sorted through tools in the one building, and tidied up the cutting patio.

She gathered the courage, finally, to go and sit on the big stump in front, centerpiece of what Ellen had called her "parking complex."

The seasons had washed Ellen's blood from the stump, though there hadn't been much on it to begin with. Ellen, quick as anything, assisted by major vascular problems, had bled out good minutes before Cary and whoever had tossed her out across the parking area and up against the stump. The moose head, too—Ellen's last professional accomplishment— was gone. Wilma, pissed, couldn't imagine Cary and the girls taking it as evidence, and, anyway, evidence of what? What in the hell had been Ellen's crime?

"That accidental shooting?" she said one time. "In a state where a dozen hunters are shot every year, where only recently a woman was killed in her own backyard because someone thought her white mittens were the tail of a deer? No midnight attack there, was there?"

"I think the man did lose his job, though."

"Pop."

"I meant, there was disapproval."

She couldn't find the moose head and it began to seem totally necessary that she do so. She went into the woods for short distances, followed the stream up and down, checked the barn, the bone shed again. Nothing.

The house itself, for many days, beckoned her. She could not, yet, go back inside. The day would come, though. Wilma knew that. She still had to clean Ellen's house. There was duty in that, and duty is always stronger than fear.

A vigil, she began to think, though for what she didn't know. Ellen was not coming back and she knew that, but she still thought she was waiting for something; revelation, she decided once, good things clear and cleansing.

Maybe it's here, she would think, and go off into the back barn. Ellen hadn't needed the barn, nor had she kept animals. Animals tended not to come to her place live, nor did they leave whole.

She found one box that held a dozen flannel nightgowns, all of them old, worn, holes under the arms. *Things we cannot throw away,* Wilma thought. *She had even moved them out here from Quilli.*

She went farther out, no longer searching for the moose head, just searching. Crossing the stream, she walked into a stand of blackberries, a tight stand, stickers reaching out, scratching her. The berries were ripe and fat and she held her T-shirt out like a basket, putting in two, maybe three quarts, edging slowly away from the berries and into a small grove of wild plum.

"I started eating the berries and scooted around on the ground to get comfortable and kept arranging myself right into the wild plum needles, the berries as sweet as could be, a wonderful sweetness, the needles not leaving me alone, getting caught on my clothes, scratching me—all semblance of civility gone as I stuffed handful after handful into my mouth, my legs bleeding. But these were Ellen's berries, a very fine berry, something wild now being put into the service of something less wild. I kept holding my shirt and the berries and eating and trying to scooch away from the stickers, tears running down my face and dropping onto the berries.

"A sight, Pop. That's what I was. I finally grabbed one of those plum branches in my hand and squeezed it harder and harder until I could see my blood dripping down onto the berries—a real mess, sir. Jesus. But that pain finally felt so good, so wonderful, so much more adequate than that dull hum of grief that had been buzzing in my chest or scrambling my thoughts, my soul, for too long a time since Ellen had died.

"I remembered reading about the death rituals of primitive tribes where people would gouge out their own eyeballs or stab themselves with dull knives because when you lose someone close to you there has to be pain—the poor heart itself just not up to giving us a grief stronger than a mild indigestion. I wasn't nuts, Pop, just overloaded on forty-odd years of radio death and television death and movie death, all of which have been as real as they needed to be—they just don't hurt. I wanted to hurt for real and it hadn't happened yet.

"It snuck up on me, though; actually, two things did. That

grief-induced masochism, I kind of hit that and went beyond it before I knew I was even there. What did I think it was at the time? 'Variations on repentance,' something like that. There had to be at least as many ways to be saved as there were to be lost. That was where the churches ran so much to lean: sin in ten thousand ways and then sing a single song of sorry. I remembered how bad I felt when I nearly aborted By-laws. I spent six months helping Ans Pru clean St. Bleufard's Church—for free. That was repentance."

She'd worked on her knees, on her belly, on her back, up on tall ladders, had hung halfway over the choir loft with the good father holding her by the ankles and eyeballing her God knew where. Father Pru knew she was working something out and even asked her one time, "Would you like confession, Wilma?"

"I'm not Catholic, father," she'd said.

"Not necessary," he'd replied.

Nothing worse than the untrained penitent, Wilma had thought, though she'd only said to Father Pru, "I'm nearly redeemed. Don't change the music."

"The berries, though. Oh God, I was sad, I was funny, I was the child on the morning after Halloween and not a piece of candy in sight. Something was working hard inside, and it was working well."

Not yet ready just to squat where she was and relieve herself, she looked across the stream at the house, then noticed the front outhouse a few feet into the edge of the woods. The next step, she thought—Why not? Outhouse, bone shed, cutting patio. Perhaps she just wanted to do the scenes of innocence before she did the scene of the crime, though the crime itself still escaped her, some mercy in that maybe. She didn't want to know—really—the way or ways in which Ellen had been seen to be so awful that slaughtering her had been far and away the very best of answers.

31

IT ALL WASHES when the creek floods, don't it? Grenada said that one time, her backwash grammar intentional but not usual. Speaking of that good woman, whatever might be the fate of all these words I have put down, should she see them some day she will learn things about Wilma she does not yet know.

Fate swung itself onto the scene in a shirtload of berries. What a beautiful sentence. Wilma Doll, old lady-elect and somebody's daughter, stuffed herself into distress and sought relief.

It occurred to her that she could squat right there, in the stream, and take care of things, an unusual and exquisite sanitation, nature's bidet. Civilization, though, was creeping into her mind like some battered friend long discredited, the survivor that Ellen had not been. The outhouse seemed like the edge of a city, a beacon beckoning, and the need for a dark privacy was strong. This light privacy, this bright and early autumn splashing of mauves and hennas and vermilia and old greens, this dazzling dance with her own contribution of teary musing—time to move on from that. She needed to define and defend this progress where the inner house, to touch what was left of Ellen's things, to touch Ellen, was the goal.

As Wilma opened the door to the outhouse she looked straight on at the head of the moose, its long neck planted over the toilet hole.

Wilma said, instincts hardly ever trustworthy, "Oh, I'm sorry."

The reaction was natural, but there was, at the moment, no time for negotiation. Even grieving gave way to a colonic imperative.

Wilma closed the door and moved the moose head over. By turning it slightly, there was just enough room to clear the hole with one antler resting lightly against her shoulders.

"Excuse me," she said, as she sat down. She was glad to find it finally, surprised, though, that after all this time it wasn't simply a pile of dust—a moose bunny. There was no smell and it looked fine, not even its hide buggy. The vulnerable witness was composed, too, his eyes closed, a gentleman even in death.

Outside, the woods that Wilma could see through the gappy door—the birches on the other side of Ellen's parking area, Ellen's house, too, that shabby sad shack—seemed in motion as thick clouds rolled overhead and the sun popped in and out. Even the birds seemed tuned in to it, the chirpy babble stopping with the descending shadow, then starting up again as brightness returned.

When Wilma was a child, she would sometimes shut herself up in the bathroom for what seemed like hours. Grenada and I would hear her in there. Often she was singing, sometimes talking, almost always, when talking, maintaining a dialogue, the characters numerous.

"Who were you talking to?" we'd ask, serious, as though she'd just got off the phone.

"Hubert Humphrey," she said one time.

A man who tried hard.
"Elizabeth Taylor."
Okay.
"Carl Yastrzemski."
Hm.
"Philo Farnsworth."
Philo Farnsworth?

A conversation with a moose then, in the outhouse of a friend. Some things never change no matter how much the wrinkles multiply or how gray the hair becomes. Her only caution, as she gave me what I'm about to put down, was to say that it tended to change whenever she remembered it.

"It's shorter," she said once, and I had to laugh, "in restaurants."

"The moose," she said, "seemed prepared to listen and that was good. At the time, I was prepared to impale myself on a dead pine so any restraint was welcome.

"Call it, Pop, if you want, Ellen's eulogy, those things we say when it's no longer possible to say what we should have been saying all along. I tried to tell myself for a long time that I didn't really love her, that I wasn't even much of a friend. That was, of course, a child's way of facing the hurt. In truth, I was there during many times of need. I listened. I touched. We laughed. God, how we laughed. Friendship needn't be devouring, needn't be anything more demanding than a snowflake falling on clasped hands. What Ellen and I had was never meant to be eternal. We existed in time, right here, and then time ran out.

"Listen, Pop. There are some people who will fight anything, who will tangle with the wind if they don't like its content, its direction. The whispered petulance of old lady stock-holders has been known to bring whole industries down, and whispers gather speed and torque geometrically. Even gentle Joe is fighting because they've said no one was at fault and he's pretty sure someone was. What they mean of course is that the whole damn thing is so frightening they'll never know what happened for absolute sure—so there. Certainty can be found in epidemics, never in singular deaths.

"A singular death—I told it to the moose, Pop. I said, 'I see you nodding, Mr. Moose. You've been there and it didn't amount to much, I bet. No little moose communities lowered their flags for you, no to-do list of bothersome chores was left incomplete. "What a waste," we always say, to which the only real response is, "Of what?"

" 'This rich, this famous world finds its highest virtue in randomness and disorder. But it's us, Mr. Moose, even you guys, who put the puzzle together. I've seen you out there, a half ton of suet standing on a cliff and looking out over the horizon and toward the faraway ocean. By that very act you stop things, you make from the speeding flux a moment. We, on the other hand, we *Hominidae,* we scream sometimes, we shout, we do all our human things like laughing and arguing and questioning and occasionally shaking in terror, and by so doing we become more colorful than any dawn, more dazzling than the fastest comet speeding unchecked for a million years. We're something, all right. We're done with work and heading home. It's like here—' "

"I had to stop talking to the moose just then, Pop. Motion was presenting itself outside, disorderly conduct in the weeds. 'Oh,' I told myself, 'it's only Cary Andersen.' Not a good reason yet to abandon the needs of my moose—Cary was walking slowly up Ellen's road—which needs had mostly to do with understanding and the short history of explanations."

" '—like here, Mr. Moose, where the last frontier is simply will against will, it is in our nature to kill every living thing we see unless someone stops us from doing it. I can be miserable when I say that, because I don't like the truth of it, and I can wax with the best of them on all our arts and our great cities and civilizations, on the accomplishments of our businesses which, as they have risen and fallen, have brought a music to life beyond that of the sound of fingernails clawing in the dirt seeking worms and seeds. But, I don't know, none of it ever seems to be much more than prelude to a massacre. The sweet pastors and the sweet philosophers and all the sweet people will take issue with that. They will argue against me from the velvet couches in the moody boardrooms of towering buildings, and they will argue against me from the lecterns of chrome-plated pulpits in glass cathedrals, but they are easily ignored, more easily shut up, because it is fact that dooms the dreamers every time, the fact that it's all struggle, the good child and the bad child, the good child barefoot and the bad child wearing leather shoes. The bad child has a knife and cuts the toes off the good child while the preachers smile over the good child's restraint, her poise and humanity. The preachers see only light of a crystal translucence, the light of piety and serenity and decency, the light of all mankind pouring forth. This is glory, but I don't see it that way. This is magnificence, but I'm having trouble. The light seems to miss me as I look closer. If there is music I've lost it to the sound of ripping flesh, the cracking of bone. In that I hear humanity—the sound travels far. In the end, the good child is headless. It is a superbly ghastly sight—the sight of justice. Can I say it in a more complicated fashion? With much, much more poetry? Can I say it all in Latin? Assuredly, I could do some of that, but you seem an audience, friend, of limited patience.

" 'Ellen was a normal person who made another normal person angry. Such people become targets because that's the way it is. We give our police guns and tell them they can kill people. Why wouldn't they? Could there be any greater kick? Cary's life and the lives of those other women are richer now—dare I say more human?—because Ellen gave them that. They have unspeakable memories that would make them superb poets if they ever tried to untangle them. Years from now, they will be sought after for information and they will make of what happened something totally unlike anything that happened. In the end, it's all just a story, isn't it?' "

Wilma turned to me then, her face dead serious, and said, "At the risk of sounding repetitious, let me say that I was never *not* aware that I was all alone in an outhouse and that I was saying all of these things to a dead moose. In a way, Pop, maybe that part of it was the real eulogy—the real howler with Ellen bowled over in laughter somewhere as I went on and on."

Wilma told me she began to worry about the approach of Cary, that it looked like she was carrying something, laboring with it. She was hoping that it was just a coincidence that the two of them would be at Ellen's house on the same day— June 3, 1996. She didn't think, though, that it really was.

"'A need to hurry, then, Mr. Moose. I see your attention span beginning to wane so let me make a final point. This whole thing never caught the attention of the national press and that has perplexed me, even though there was some good in that. Mostly, I think the reporters and the editors and the managers all thought it was just another nut gunned down and that's really what we think we should do with all the nuts. Maybe so. Of course some of them have started gunning back so as either theory or tactic there might be some holes to fill.

"'But me, Mooseboy, what do I think? I think Ellen was just someone's fun, and don't you dare think me hard and mean for saying that. It only took one shot for all the rest of them to start shooting, and I know Cary took that first shot. I think she wanted to hear Ellen scream, to see her twist and writhe in pain because we've lost so much of our humanity this century that we have to push ourselves, or anyone handy, right into agony just to see if we're real. Perhaps cops just lose it faster. I hear it's an occupational hazard—another reason to keep an eye on them.

"'Anyway, let's talk about you, Mr. Moose, the guy with the bony fedora, you and me. The woman out there is Cary Andersen, something of a police officer but highly local. She can't write you a speeding ticket but she can kill you, which is itself one of the more amusing verities of small-town life in America. She has this feeling that forces are gathering against her and she's trying to clean some things up that are blowing around behind her; hence, that gasoline can. This is a natural thing—can you see it now? After all I've said? In our species, the most common currency is change, but no one wants to be behind the cash register, no one wants to handle the loot. She's destroying evidence because Ellen's husband, Joe, has brought everything into court and Cary's worried about how she might support herself and her daughter, Iona, a beautiful daughter with many needs. Why didn't she think of that before all this? Because she didn't. Consequences don't exist until things are done.' "

Wilma, finished with her hygienic needs and inwardly soothed, kept watching Cary through the slatted door. Her one hand was stroking the moose's muzzle.

"I thought Cary was being pretty sloppy, Pop: a splash of gasoline here and there, neither system nor plan, no measurement of wind over here with estimates of flame flight over there. Splash and burn."

Wilma told me she felt relieved she wouldn't have to go into Ellen's house now. Since that very first day she'd been finding nostalgia in the weedy garden and heartbreak on the tiny front porch, and even a certain shared (with Ellen) commercial triumph by standing in the parking area and remembering how every now and then there might be half a dozen cars here, people with money and corpses and a livelihood for Ellen.

"But going inside kept confronting me as a stern ultimatum, as though there would be something critical to learn in there. Learning is everything. It's what we do, isn't it, Pop? Tell me that. Tell me that learning is the most important thing there is so that I don't have to believe that the whole goddamn planet is just tumbling off into an orgy of force and farce.

"Mostly, I wondered if blood spots would mold, or if there would be fuzzy things lying about that I wouldn't know whether to throw away or bury. So I kept putting the entry off and instead had prowled, nothing more, scratched, a little dirty, a woozy sentinel, distracted by an old moose in the early stages of needing to find a landfill. As sentinel, too, lax, since things were about to go up in smoke."

She said she felt a push against the outhouse door as the gas ignited with a thumping whoosh. "Now Ellen's house was on its way," she went on, "ashes to ashes. Overall, it didn't seem a bad thing. I just wished it hadn't been Cary doing it."

Cary staggered against the explosion—a little too close, Wilma said, caution being another kind of oft-ignored sentiment—but did not fall. Wilma saw her not fall, then saw her glance over toward the outhouse. Instinctively, Wilma put her arm across the back of the moose's neck and pulled it closer.

" 'Thought is going on,' I said to the moose. 'Cary is musing. She is pondering. "Waste the outhouse, ice the country phone booth." ' "

Behind her, the house was burning hard and Wilma began to feel the heat and began to feel Cary's decision firming up. Cary knew where they'd put the remains of the moose, and, an innocent moose or not, she'd want it gone.

"Strange, Pop, how guilt and innocence all became the same thing in this whole horrid business with Ellen. In a few minutes—time was of the essence—the smoke would be high enough to bring the volunteers out from St. A de P and Quilli. Those were good people. You had to admire the risk in saving a dead woman's house, ignore the lack of same in saving the dead woman."

Wilma dropped off the bench to the floor of the outhouse. With the moose head held tightly, she pushed the door open and stepped outside. Cary, startled, stood with her hands on her hips, her mouth open, one hand near her gun, a private gun now with Cary unemployed, but a gun.

"*Maintenant, Papa?*" Wilma said to me.

"*Trop tôt?*" I said.

"Not anymore."

As Wilma said later to investigators, her thoughts well-collected, her words prideful and succinct, "It was all over then. Cary was putting the torch to her pain while mine went on and on because Cary was my pain. I knew my pain would end if Cary would end so I picked up the moose, both of us calm though I still had functioning eyes, and walked over to Cary and Cary laughed at me."

There is a curious aside, however, in one of the records. A question must have been asked though it was not recorded. Wilma's answer, however, is clear: "Excuse me, sir? Oh—no. No, I didn't know about Poison at that time, about the beating he'd taken at Cary's hands, though it would have made no difference. A redundancy of motives, that's all it would have been."

"Cary told me to look at myself, Pop, to see how stupid I looked, about as stupid as Ellen looked all torn apart. Cary kept ragging me on the stupidity and I was taken aback. I kept thinking that in all of this there has never been anything stupid—fiendish, maybe; unforgiving, devastating—but never stupid. It all fit somehow, the logic of agony, a thing grotesque and painful, things that should never have happened. But it wasn't stupid nor was I stupid nor Ellen, neither Grenada nor you, Pop (she slammed you both pretty hard)—your bulbs never burn dim—which Cary kept repeating until finally I put

my hand on her throat and I thought, yessirree, when the government, laid-off or not, comes after you, you just squeeze
hard until you can feel the Constitution receding back into
shape. Cary struggled in that small space, the moose not helpful (they never are), but his simple presence cutting down on
Cary's leverage, and how she could or could not move as she
realized that I was damned serious about strangling the life
right out of her.

"Which is why I did it, Pop."

QUILLIFARKEAG, MAINE
(Local Government)

*In 1948 Chastamian "Pop" Hobadopp married Ann Mass-
abeesec in Bar Harbor, Ann with twelve brothers in a fishing
family. Ann and Pop had one daughter, Livvy, and Ann was
pregnant with another child when her father and three brothers went out lobstering one morning, taking Ann for one last
time since Pop, Livvy, and Ann were moving to Lumpilliwog
where Pop had just gotten a job as a fifth-grade teacher. Father,
brothers, and Ann were never seen again and there were
rumors—it had been a calm day on the sea—that the group
had been kidnapped by a Russian fishing trawler, a factory
ship, that they had been processed into little cans called—in
the Soviet Union—Eisenhowers.*

*Despairing and miserable, Pop left the coastal emptiness
with its infinity of useless answers and took the new job. He
was fired in a month for reading the palms of fifth graders and
for telling the other teachers that he and his daughter had supper with his wife every night, even producing "womanly" ar-
tifacts that he said he washed and mended for her.*

*After that, he and Livvy joined a commune near Wytopit-
lock where they stayed until 1964 when the commune was
devastated by an outbreak of hepatitis. Fearing for Livvy's
health (and his own), he fled to Quillifarkeag in the far north
where he opened an auto repair/palm reading shop.*

*Pop Hobadopp has been mayor of Quilli for twenty-seven
years.*

32

IT IS ALMOST AS THOUGH there are two films on Wilma now, each running concurrently with the other. One has her in the recent past, the other has her in the present, not quite with me. For myself, I am cluttered with a mélange of things I'd like to say, but they would be fatherly things, of greatest use when I'm shaving or when I'm walking downtown and I stop and stare at myself in a store window—the impulse being to say, "Well, look at *that.*"

In the first of those faux films, she has become a function of her government, a task to be performed. She has, in the person of her most salient characteristics, been sketched out and logged onto multicopy forms, data on the forms to be eventually entered into computers. There are no nefarious purposes here, simply efficiency. People are paid to do a job and they do it.

Wilma has walked the clean, long hallways of the new courthouse many times. The water fountains are always spotless— no lumps of chewing gum clumping up near the drains—and the bathrooms bright and nice-smelling. All three phones in the public phone bank near the front door work, and there are phone books, untorn, hanging from the metal holder under each phone. Government, she thinks, is working well. It's what you would expect of the government in a town like Quilli.

She has met with investigators from various agencies and they have all treated her with kindness and respect. When she has had to go to the bathroom that has never been a problem, and she has been amused by how many of them are inveterate coffee drinkers, always willing to include her in the next round. Wilma drinks her coffee black. She has always drunk between eight and ten cups a day, so the courtesies of the men and women looking into things have been appreciated.

Grenada, of course, warned her about her upcoming dealings with "those people." She is not a cynic about government, but she told her they'd speak a language she wouldn't begin to understand and to watch her butt. It's not the first time, Wilma and I agreed, that her mother has been wrong.

Wilma has found everyone quite tactful and quite human. She's seen them loosen their ties and slip off their shoes, watched them blow their noses and tend carefully coiffed hair battered by an afternoon's quick nor'easter. They've shared homemade sandwiches with her, brown bags pulled out of well-used briefcases. As to language, nothing could have been more easily understood. The record speaks, its permanence precluding any need for hyperbole:

"You were upset over the death of your friend, Miss Doll?"

"I was upset."

"You believed Miss Andersen to be responsible?"

"I did believe that."

"You were certain there was no other recourse, that she would, say, be brought to justice—in your opinion—through normal channels?"

"The investigation was leaning toward commendations for the four officers. Do you want to repeat the question?"

"We see."

The government was musing over the whole thing, the series of incidents, but the government did not know what to do.

There was no doubt in anyone's mind that Wilma had murdered Cary on June 3, 1996. Life always happened on the record, and it was life that had driven Wilma and Cary into their consequential meeting that day. But there were no witnesses and Cary's charred body would yield no forensic markers.

There was no doubt in anyone's mind that Wilma had murdered Cary because there was no hesitation on Wilma's part in saying so.

"As she struggled, I held firm. It was the thing to do."

Very well.

"Justice was in the forearm, though I think she bumped her head hard on the jawbone of a moose."

All right.

"I would have thought my strength spent. But with one arm I tossed her, right onto Ellen's cinders."

We need you, then, to sign a confession.

"No."

The investigators, over lunch with Wilma, declared her unstable, explained the query was at an impasse. Then they said, Wilma thought, the oddest thing, a young woman with red hair and gray eyes doing the talking—*Quilli will reclaim you now. It will adjudicate and seek redress, find placement and balance. You will become lore, even legend, and there may be shame. Some will find in your actions a laudatory cachet. Some will not walk in the same mud you have stepped in on a rainy day. It is ever thus, this loyalty to a friend.*

The other film is simpler and more prosaic and begins on familiar ground.

Wilma was sitting near the mailbox when Joe came over shortly after the decision had been made not to file charges against her. She heard his truck as it topped the hill, then watched as it made the downward dip and the upward climb to our (Grenada's) lane, the end of the road.

She hadn't talked to him for a long time, she told me. Once, in the courthouse, they'd passed in the hall and he'd stopped and given her a long hug, a tightful thing, no words, and they'd both walked on. Another time, she watched him on television down at Bud's. The sound didn't come out on his tape until he was almost done, so she didn't know what was important about him at that moment, but he'd looked good, his eyes clear and kind, his great silver mustache still looking—as she'd joked with him that one time—like two pigeons sitting on his lip.

"I have told what I remember," Wilma said to him. Joe had parked his truck near the mailbox and they were both sitting on the tailgate. "There was outrageousness, that's all I know. I have to pick my way through that."

"We both do," Joe said.

Wilma wanted to tell him something different, something good, to give each of them a story and a memory that had something besides "wretched" written all over it, to tell him, *It was only a heart attack, mere atrial dissent. Ellen had been dressed in a frothy blue peignoir and snowy mules. She was at peace with civility and seated at her tiny Shaker writing table.*

"She was writing of love, Joe," Wilma would say, *"not an easy thing to write about these days."*

"I know," Joe would answer. *"She wrote often."*

"She was tired of living alone and she wanted you. She wanted to care for you, wanted to fix your meals because you were you, to iron your shirts, your overalls."

"Simple things."

"Felled with pen in hand, Joe, freshly bathed. A love letter her final act," Wilma would say.

Then Joe said, "My lawyer doesn't think you're telling the truth."

"Hubert Peterbuoy?"

"Yes."

"He's very perceptive."

"What's going on, Wilma?"

Wilma looked over at Joe and took one of his hands and held it in both of hers. Joe looked down the road.

"They ripped out her heart, Joe."

"That's been documented. It can be explained."

It can be explained? *You can explain that?*

"Wilma?"

"Yes, Joe."

"I need you to answer me a question. It's just me—Joe— Wilma. Just answer it for me."

"Can I answer it?"

"I don't know."

"I'll try."

"Did I let her down, Wilma?"

His mustache quivered, and Wilma thought this one of the

most profound questions one person can ask of another. Love can be anywhere at any time. It can be effusive, diffuse, illusory. But help, support—*I need you. You have me.*—was like a knife that either stuck, and it stuck right here and right now, or it didn't.

Wilma was ready, as always, she told me, to debate such a question, to lie in bed and think about it, to talk to Bylaws about it, always her foil when she could get him away from Grenada. The boy might grow up thinking his mother had a mouth only drowning could quiet, but he would never think of her as a shadow figure, an unknowable puppeteer weaving strings through his parts and his moods, pounding nails through the dark boards of his silences. Not Bylaws. Not Wilma.

"Yes," she said. "Of course you did." That was cruel; then she added, "So did I."

"How? I mean—you? Me? What did we do?"

"Did you ever worry about her? Out there all alone, strange men coming over with this big—stuff, bloody stuff, all those dead things? 'Look at this five-hundred-pound thing I just killed, little girl. Look at it.'?"

Joe moved off the tailgate of the truck then. He walked a few steps from Wilma and said, his back to her, "It wasn't anyone like that who killed her."

"Did you worry?"

"Of course I did, Wilma. Those kinds of people, though, that was business. I mean, licensed hunters, people on record. I worried more about some nut—you know, with his sex more in his head than his crotch—finding out about her and going out there, something to do on a lonely night."

Wilma said, quietly, "It wasn't anyone like that who killed her, Joe."

"I know."

Wilma could see Joe's shoulders shaking and she wondered if this was the first time he'd cried over Ellen's death. It seemed so long ago, she told me, but grief honors no timetables.

At the funeral—I remembered this—he'd been mannerly, almost professional in an odd way, a help to the news people and Ellen's customers, some of whom had driven a far distance to get to Quilli—money spent always a foundation for sadness. Cool and efficient, suited up, shoes shined, Joe had been cordially grim. Now he was a reappearing name on a court docket and no one was listening.

She slid off the truck and walked over to him.

"Joe?"

Joe's lips were tight, a line of restraint he tried to smile through. Tears ran in shaky streaks down his face.

"They just wanted to kill somebody, Wilma. That's all there was to it. They wanted to do what they were told they could do. It's authority, Wilma. It's like a sickness. Ellen was the cure."

Joe was searching, but Wilma had flown from witness to avenger with no stopovers for explanation.

Joe finally reached out. He put his hands on Wilma's shoulders, though he looked away from her, well past her.

"I was only the witness, Joe. Maybe I'm not the one to explain it."

"Of course not."

He was holding her now in both of his arms and Wilma

could see Grenada up the road, Bylaws on her shoulders. Sometimes, when he was carried that way, the baby would reach his hands down into Grenada's mouth and grab handfuls of lip and cheek. The distortion in her mother's face when that happened was hilarious, and Wilma and Grenada and even the baby would approach hysteria laughing. A certain facial flaccidity, however, followed the release of the baby's grip, causing Grenada to drool for hours afterward. "Premonitory," she would say, "but premature. I'm not there yet."

"Grenada, Pop — you keep letting her get away but you never lose her. There has to be some luck in that, big-time luck, or maybe you just know a secret no one else knows yet. Seems like there's a lot of secrets in the world, not the least of which is the one we both know that Grenada — Mom — does not, that her daughter strangled a woman with her bare hands, that she violated commandments and principles and even common sense in order to bring a certain order back into the world. Tough cure, isn't it? I could tell her all of it, and then she could hold it in trust for Bylaws so that Bylaws could know it, too, could face the awkward silences that will follow him all his life whenever his mother is talked about. But I don't know that he should have that, all of that truth, nor Grenada, either. Some of the best gifts you can give to those you love are the ones they never know about. Truth changes all the time. The silences, however, never go away, and love is always in the silences, isn't it?"